**<u>TIME MAGAZINE</u> RAVES ABOUT
THE BLACKING FACTORY &
PENNSYLVANIA GOTHIC . . .**

The Blacking Factory—"Sheed's tale is more than an ironic pathology of the right-wing mind; more, even, than a wry diagnosis of a severely fractured nationality. It also captures the comic anguish of a youth who begins to understand himself just at the moment when he loses the sense of who he is."

Pennsylvania Gothic—"Even this grisly story is lightened by comic touches. As a companion piece to *Factory*, the story sharply emphasizes Sheed's overall theme: the harmful consequences of clutching at visions of the past, whether they are mythical but life-sustaining visions like Jimmy's or real but death-dealing ones like Charley's."

"Sheed constructs a bright, cutting prose from the dross of everyday slang. He wields that prose with a subtle ear for speech rhythms and a sardonic eye for the telltale gesture . . . he is justly rated as one of the nation's most gifted writers."

About the Author

Wilfrid Sheed was a leading nominee for the National Book Award for 1966 for his last novel, *Office Politics*. His new book, *The Blacking Factory & Pennsylvania Gothic*, is comprised of a short novel and a long story closely related in theme and dealing with that time of crisis in the lives of teenage boys that perhaps shapes the course of their lives.

Wilfred Sheed is now well into his next novel, a long and major work, and has won a Rockefeller Foundation grant which should allow him to complete the book before the end of 1969.

His other novels are *A Middle Class Education, The Hack, Square's Progress,* and *Office Politics*. He is also film critic of *Esquire*, a book review editor of *Commonweal*, and a frequent critic of contemporary fiction for *The New York Times Book Review, The Atlantic*, and other magazines.

The Blacking Factory
and Pennsylvania Gothic
Wilfrid Sheed

A short novel and a long story

Ballantine Books   •   New York

Copyright © 1958, 1968 by Wilfrid Sheed

Library of Congress Catalog Card Number: 68-13009

A small portion of *The Blacking Factory* appeared,
in a very different form, as a story entitled
"The Happiness of Pursuit" in *Vogue*

This edition published by arrangement with
Farrar, Straus and Giroux

First Edition: November, 1969

Cover design by Gervasio Gallardo

Printed in the United States of America

Ballantine Books, Inc.
101 Fifth Avenue, New York, N.Y. 10003

author's note

When Charles Dickens was twelve years old, he was abruptly removed from school and put to work in a blacking factory. The effect of this episode was such that he mentioned it to no one for twenty years and only broke down when somebody recognized him from those days and somebody else (his biographer, John Forster) asked him about it. In his subsequent account, Dickens wrote: "I have no idea how long it lasted; whether for a year or much more or less." In fact, it lasted for less than six months.

contents

Pennsylvania Gothic

As he looked back on it, Charles Trimble could see that the Freddy Walton fight had been a bad scene in at least three respects. Respect no. 1: It had previously been understood that twelve-year-old Charlie could beat up eleven-year-old Freddy any time he wanted to—Freddy more than conceded the point, was willing to eat grass if necessary and bleat like a sheep—and now it was suddenly understood that he could not. In spite of a 15-pound weight advantage, and a big edge in morale, Charlie had blown it. Freddy clawed his way out of a hammerlock and began to jab, first tentatively, then triumphantly, until

Charlie, plodding after him in the thick heat, was obliged to admit defeat.

And first there was the "say uncle" ritual to be gone through. Freddy insisted on it: Freddy unbearable with victory in sight, smirking and jiggling, with enough breath left to talk. He reminded Charlie that he hadn't wanted to fight, had been a miracle of patience in fact; true. Charlie, bored to death with the garden and the summer, had punched and chivied his friend to the brink: "I bet I can beat you up." "I bet you can too." "You want me to prove it?" "No, I believe you." Why, why hadn't Charlie let it go at that?

Freddy bobbed and weaved and snaked out a last left. Charlie's nose spread flat, broken for sure. He lunged forward and missed by two good feet. Freddy, small and unattainable, with fists like bees. So, uncle it was—and always would be.

As Freddy swaggered off, jaunty and thin-shanked, the second bad condition came into effect. There was no one else to play with. Freddy was the only contemporary in five miles. There were no young families left in Tewksbury. It was an awkward place to live, just the wrong distance from everywhere. The trains to Philadelphia had dwindled to two a day. Charles' parents had moved here a couple of months ago for their own mysterious reasons, into this big old house and absolutely jerky garden, and left Charlie to his own devices.

The Walton debacle started off a chain of feeling lousy that lasted through the rest of the long day. Charlie had lived up to now in Philadelphia, and didn't know what the country was *for*. Beyond the garden there were more gardens—that much he knew: the one to the left was presided over by a witch named Miss Skinner; the one to the right was untenanted, adding three acres of weeds to his kingdom. Several times as he paced out the estate, Charlie had a strange dizzy feeling, not sure for a moment where he was—the garden tilting as it had when Freddy pecked at his nose.

The heat smothered him in hot cushions; he lay down, stood up, took off his shirt, and then quickly got tired of carrying it and put it back on; thought of joining the Canadian Air Force in six years' time and abandoned the scheme—by then the United States would be in and out of the war. His father left no doubt on the point. Then he couldn't think of anything to think about at all, and he sat down under a tree and everything went completely black in the heat. Even the memory of Freddy had a blacked-out face like a photograph negative. The compressed air seemed to smash at his face like a boxing glove, and sure enough, when he investigated, there was blood crawling down his upper lip and over his fist. His nose had opened up again. Three o'clock in the afternoon. His mother off shelling peas some place. Oh boy.

At supper, he found himself lying about the fight, claiming victory, which seemed to be what his parents wanted. Here too the assumption was that he could beat up Freddy any time he wanted to, that anyone could beat up old Freddy: thus, to avoid imputations of bullying, he went so far as to suggest that it was Freddy who had needled him. He didn't say it outright, but Mr. Trimble's questions led him, almost anxiously, in that direction; and that was the way it came out. (Mrs. Trimble thought it was dreadful, whoever won—but she seemed vaguely relieved that it was Charles all the same.)

Charlie went to bed quite spent, and found right

off that he couldn't sleep. The final, official version of the fight bore no resemblance whatever to the real one. Oh well. Tomorrow he would either have to make peace with Freddy, on intolerable terms, or spend the whole day by himself, starting with breakfast. His mother napping, working in the kitchen; Miss Skinner conferring with her gardener; maybe a rabbit watching him, Charlie. Meanwhile, no sleep for now.

He tried reciting the Catechism, which used to take him out fast, once upon a time.

"Who made you God made you" ho-hum. "Why did God make you he made you to know him, love him and serve him—slow down now, Trimble, this isn't a race—in—this—world—so—as—to—be—happy—with—him—forever—in—the—next." Forever and ever and ever. Ever is a word meaning a long time plus another long time plus another long time, and then you would be getting near the end, right? No, of course not. The middle? No, it wasn't like that at all.

This train of thought had never bothered him before but the afternoon had been so long, and it was only one afternoon. He rolled his head around the pillow, scorching the surface evenly. Yes, imagine day after day after day after day after day, just like this one, one after another, torn off a calendar that never got smaller, everyone moving very slowly under a hot blue sky because what other kind of weather would they have up there? In a big, still garden. He agitated his wet legs, stirring the sweat in. Couldn't God stop it? Or did He have to go on every day with the others? Charlie tried making a joke of it—God mopping his brow and fanning his whiskers. God is a spirit, Charles, *you* know that . . .

Did hair grow on a resurrected body? How about

teeth? He had never thought about that. Could you stop things from growing for a while? Or did they keep churning up dismally, hair and teeth and grass, forever and ever? And if so, was there any way of getting out of this, for him personally? No, Father Devlin, their pastor in Philadelphia, allowed no exceptions. Everybody was in it, forever, either up or down. It didn't have any outside. Father Devlin had told the congregation (and it had stuck in Charlie's mind) that, even if you didn't believe in God, you were still stuck with the mystery of space: that even if you went out walking forever, or driving, or flying, you would never get to the outside of the universe. Charles lay down again, sinking, half-swooning, into the soggy cotton.

Felt the hot earth turning and turning under him. There must be some piece of machinery that would stop it. A master button you could press. He thought of the silver knives downstairs. He didn't think *about* them at first, only that they were there, sitting in their velvet box on the sideboard, glistening away, like people smiling to themselves. Cold Steel. Somehow outside of this growing, moving business. There was, King of the silver-box, a carving knife with a big, sweeping handle like a scimitar: touch it and it opened a gash inches deep. He knew. His father's finger had trailed blood all the way across the dining-room carpet and up the stairs. You had only to touch it.

Rest here for a while. Cool as water and very handsomely mounted in red velvet, downstairs in the dining room. Well, there was no harm in thinking about them—slash, across the stomach, the way the Japanese did it. Ah so. What a mess . . . would it put you out of eternity, Father? No, of course not. You'd go to hell, which was even worse than heaven. Forever and ever and ever and ever

If you're going to stay here with us knives you have to play it our way. The big carving knife sat apart from the others, gleaming on a royal, satiny cushion. That would be the one. Japanese man goes over, picks it up and weighs it, kneels down, swish across bright yellow robes. Folds over knife and urges it in through belly button. Ah so.

"No!" Charlie said sharply. There was no other sound except for a distant clatter of crickets somewhere in back of the house. He was used to the night noises of the city. If only he could hear a bus or a trolley, everything would still be all right. Meanwhile, knife, knives, knife: cool and silver, cold cold water. Slithering in, like an ice-cold snake and releasing the hot blood. They used to cure people that way. Then you went to hell, where it was plenty hot enough for you, but perhaps he had no choice now. He didn't very well know how he was going to stop himself. He knew for a fact, and without having even moved, that he was quite out of control. His body would take him downstairs in a moment and do what had to be done. It wasn't up to him any more. "Oh, no"—he couldn't believe this crazy turn of events, and tried to force his mind into the old channels. But it wouldn't go. Not now.

He stood up, and resorted to cunning, to making plans. The big thing was to get miles away from his boiling, bursting head. "Mother," he started to call, but checked it. Hands crossed over the white bones of her chest, confusion. His father saying, What do you mean, forever? What do you mean, knives? Everything would be worse. He could only find his winter pajamas to put on, crisp and smelling of camphor.

How to get downstairs without passing the silver cabinet? It would have to be a death or glory run, swoop down the stairs in four jumps, and one more extra-big jump onto his knees and out through the front door without looking around. He planned as he went. It was a crazy thing to be doing, he hoped he would never have to explain it to anybody, but he had to get out of the house before it was too late. The old woman waiting on the landing with a rope around her neck bothered him less than usual. He understood fully that she was a lampstand.

He wooshed through the screen door, and allowed it to bang behind him, the Trimbles were heavy sleepers, he supposed—anyway, they were quiet now —and out over the wooden slats on the porch. He flung himself straight down on the front lawn and clutched at the grass and got some of it in his mouth. He could see from about five feet away a fat little boy rolling on the lawn in the middle of the night in his pajamas. But the grass didn't taste right, the ground didn't feel right.

He lay on his back, puffing, feeling worse than before: hotter, and now silly too. The homemade exorcism hadn't worked worth a darn. He had done some thing crazy, and it hadn't worked. Maybe it would be the knives next. And then, what would his parents think in the morning? He couldn't go on thinking like this tomorrow, and the next day, and the day after that . . . the leaves on the trees dripped black overhead: the grass prickled cruelly. The garden was just as bad as the house.

He writhed round onto his stomach, just to keep moving, and saw the light glimmering in the next house. Miss Skinner, the witch, was still up—a pale light like a gas jet in one of the upstairs rooms. A witch might be just the thing.

He had watched Miss Skinner over the hedge a few times. Not a real witch maybe, but a very frosty old woman, abnormally dignified, with a face that said Don't. His father said that everything in her house was fragile: priceless old china, withered things in glass cabinets, dusty figurines. Even the toilet bowl had you worried. Nevertheless, there she was, he wouldn't be waking her or anything and the thought of her was itself curiously cooling. Don't touch those knives, young man, she might say: and he just possibly wouldn't.

He ran through the hole in the hedge between the houses. Her front door was open and he plunged in, and helter-skelter up a fresh set of dark stairs.

She sat in a front room, enshrined in bric-a-brac, looking out over the lawn, over his lawn too. The granite face was set pleasantly, as if she had been expecting him ever since the sculptors put her there. The gas shot kindly wedges of shadow up her cheeks.

"Hello, Charles," she said, her voice deep as a well. "You must be having trouble sleeping too."

"Yes, Miss Skinner. It's awfully hot."

"Isn't it, though? I can't remember *when* it's been so hot around here. And I've lived here an *aw*fully long time." She was fanning herself with a musty, yellow fan, but she looked as if she didn't need to. She could have been made of marble. "It looks to me as if you've been in a fight, young man. Let me take a look at that nose of yours." He brought it over obediently, and she touched it gently. "My, but that *is* a nose, isn't it? It's as big as two. I don't know when I've *seen* such a nose." Miss Skinner's talk was carefully arranged around the stressed syllables. His own scratchy tempo gradually slackened and with it the tendency to blurt.

"Who were you fighting, Charles?" she asked. "I didn't know there *was* anybody around here to fight. We're all very old in Tewksbury, you know."

"I was fighting Freddy Walton," he said.

"Oh, yes, Freddy Walton. Well, if you had to fight someone I suppose it might as well be Freddy Walton."

"Why, don't you like him?"

"Well, between ourselves, and I suppose I shouldn't be saying this, but he's given you a black eye, so you might as well know, I don't care for Freddy as much as I might. I think he's rather a slimy little boy. Now you mustn't go repeating that."

"I won't, Miss Skinner." All the same, it was good to hear. She didn't ask him how the fight went. Just having fought slimy Freddy was enough.

"The Waltons came here only a few years ago and bought that big, white house over on Carter Street, and what they do with it nobody knows. There are only four Waltons all told, and the house is simply enormous . . ."

Charlie was afraid that she was going to stop. He didn't usually go for this kind of thing, but tonight it was just fine. He listened now with utmost concentration. She didn't like any part of the Waltons it seemed, never had and never would. This was important to know.

"I don't know what they see in a town like Tewksbury either. They're fashionable young Philadelphia people with a lot of new, funny-money, and we're all so *very* old out here, and dwindling. Gracious, there never *were* such old people as we are."

"Perhaps the Waltons are on the run from the law."

She laughed, "Ah-ha!" and threw back her head and said, "Perhaps that's it. I hadn't thought of that," as though he had said something funny and interesting. And if she thought so, perhaps he had. "That big house would make an excellent place to hide. The man who built it was very eccentric, Horace W. Fisher, you know, and they say he used to sleep in a different room every night . . ."

Miss Skinner's woolly footnotes grew more footnotes, and the clock beat a tattoo, and slowly the knives went back in their box, the hasp fastened, and Charlie found himself getting blessedly bored. Still, he mustn't give up quite yet. The Fletchers and the Pennyfeathers, he asked about them all. He wasn't quite ready to go home. "Whose brother did you say Herbert was?" It was good, at this point, to have *facts*.

Charlie was never asked to explain why he was there. Miss Skinner behaved as though it was really the middle of the afternoon anyway, and she went on chatting, half to herself, until the sun came up. When Charlie rose to go, in the safety of daylight, she signaled him over and gave him a kiss, like old feathers, under his purple right eye and said, "Gracious, it's getting late." It left no trace; it was like a kiss in a dream.

The next few days were like a slow convalescence. He could not believe he had seriously wanted to kill himself. He wasn't the type. Nevertheless he felt he had better go carefully. His mother said "Good morning" at twelve o'clock as if nothing had happened, and talked about the heat (where had it gone?) and he went out to examine the frowzy flowers at the bottom of the garden. It was all quite strange. He was glad to be alive, very glad, but sensed that it was on sufferance. The leaves riffled the front window, but you couldn't be sure about leaves any more: they might be concealing some kind of poison. He would have to come to terms with them slowly, and with the scorched, patchy grass on the front lawn. Nothing could be taken for granted.

He mooned about the garden once more, nursing himself back to health, avoiding this thought and that, and building up a small core of dependable outposts: the hedge between the two houses was absolutely all right, the birdbath halfway down the garden, some of the back lawn, but not all of it; Miss Skinner's wistaria? No, that was too gaudy and sinister, the splash of color and the sinuous vine. He would add to the list later, but now he must stick to the absolutely trustworthy. The important thing was that he *had not* killed himself. He had not touched the knives. He had taken steps.

Freddy did not show up at all that day or next, which suited Charles fine. Boredom was not the problem but survival. He knew for a fact that he must not go near the knives: he rerouted his downstairs life to avoid the dining room. Cautiously and voluptuously, he inched through those days; and then the nights as well, sitting up and reading a baseball novel by John Tunis and enjoying the cool wind that puffed steadily through. The nights were nothing like as bad as he expected. He didn't need Miss Skinner at all.

The second day was better than the first, and the day after that better again, and then the whole thing was gone. His mind was mended, and he couldn't imagine how anyone could feel the way he apparently had. Afraid of leaves, grass? Couldn't remember it. The garden was empty and spiritless. September was rolling up and he would soon be on his way to Brookshire Academy, his father's old school, to start seventh grade. Freddy Walton was, he learned, summering in Cape May, New Jersey. Charlie was famous for his cheerfulness, and he returned to that now, making his mother laugh and occasionally his father too.

With the fever gone down, he found Miss Skinner just as dead and flat as the leaves and grass. She invited him to tea a couple of times before he left for school, and the second time he felt he'd better say yes, as did Mrs. Trimble (although Mrs. Trimble didn't feel up to going herself). He was fidgety about seeing Miss Skinner again; it seemed like an unnecessary episode, like visiting the doctor when you were quite well. A doctor might always find fresh trouble.

But over he went and they sat together over tea in the living room, which was musty as the basement of a museum and hard to keep awake in. It was here that her rubbish collection (as Mr. Trimble called it) really flowered and ran over. First, the two glass cases by the door, packed tight with Civil War surplus: rusted swords and caps and uniforms, covered by a fine dust which seemed to hold them intact; next, a full-length mirror repeating the whole clutter, between flaking gold curlicues; after that, the marble table with the green statuettes and fancy paperweights and the canary cage; and so on round the room, with no inch of floor or wall left to chance. Above the jumble hung Miss Skinner's ancestors, mouths drawn, noses thin as pencils: a dozen women in black dresses, and two or three old men in side whiskers. And in the middle of it all, Miss Skinner herself, cool as a corpse, older than Charlie could imagine, pouring tea for him and talking to the cat.

"*Don't* you keep looking at that poor bird. You've already had your dinner." Charlie knew nothing of cats. The insane green eyes glared steadily at him from beside of the mossy sofa: the canary chirped with fright, trapped in the crowded room.

"Nobody has tea any more," she said, "and I think it's a great pity. It was a *civilized* custom, and there are so few of them left."

Why did she bother to say that? Charlie felt nervous and overtrained. The gossip about the Pendletons was brittle as chalk.

"Boys generally like pink cake," she said. "I haven't the faintest idea why. My brother Henry practically lived on it for years."

How soon can I get out of here? Miss Skinner had been dead for at least ten years, these were the things she had chosen to be buried with. If he hit her, she would crack like a vase. He wanted to hit her and see.

"Charity O'Brien is a cousin of mine, in a roundabout sort of way. Her grandfather married my cousin Prudence Skinner, oh, years and years ago. She was the rebel of the family, insofar as the family had a rebel. Marrying an O'Brien seemed like the height of daring in those days. How times have changed. But I don't suppose you want to hear about that."

No, emphatically not. The conversation along with the pink cake was making him slightly sick. She smiled at him, for the first time, quite coquettishly, flashing stone gums, and just as suddenly fell asleep. Her mouth flapped open all the way and commenced an energetic rasping sound. This seemed to solve his problem. He stood up quietly. She wouldn't expect him to wait, would she?

He took a step backwards, and the cat finally made

its move: a tense, hissing leap for the sofa. The bird screamed in fear, and Charlie jumped backwards, banging against a marble-top table.

Miss Skinner laughed in her sleep. "Don't be frightened," she said.

He didn't bother to pick up the green statuette that had fallen at his feet, its green head severed: but hurried out, leaving the old lady to her own devices. He wouldn't go back there if he could help it. The place gave him the creeps.

By Christmas of 1941, Tewksbury had begun to gird itself for war. The train service went into further decline (you could sometimes flag down the Philadelphia express, otherwise forget it). Two handymen and Jim Pennyfeather marched off to war. Nobody else was anywhere near the right age for fighting. The Anglophiles were exhilarated and acted twenty years younger, the America-firsters shook their heads but prepared to take an interest; the servant problem became acute. There was excitement in the air, but not much of it got out of the houses: the streets were as quiet as ever, as Charlie Trimble made his way home from the railway station, on his first vacation from Brookshire.

The widow Pritchard watched him from her wintry garden on Carter Street. She wandered about in the snow like an old rag picker. "Home already?" she said vaguely. Peace talks at Appomattox concluded successfully. In the window Mrs. Pritchard's aunt sat waiting to hear about it: he could see her frosty, winter's nose through the glass. Mrs. Cornwall and Miss Cavendish sat on their closed-in porch. Miss Fothergill's house seemed to be empty. He had learned the names from Miss Skinner, and remembered them all.

He could see the back of his own house now, from between the trees at the bottom of his garden. A gaunt box stuck in the snow.

Mr. Trimble was sitting on the porch, cleaning his glasses. As soon as he made out Charlie looming along the drive, he jumped up and greeted him warmly, not as a mere son but as a fellow Brookshire man, and took his briefcase, which was the only luggage Charlie hadn't sent by railway express. Charlie put his little felt hat on the hat rack in the hall. What do you do here in the winter, he thought, if there's nothing to do in the summer?

The talk at dinner was entirely about the old school. How was the debating team these days? And football—how was the football? And what about old Mr. Fuchs, was he still there? And was he or was he not a character? Mr. Trimble glowed and burgeoned. Charlie attempted to rise to it.

"The debating team is as good as ever. We walloped Pomfret."

"Good, good."

"And we massacred St. Cosmas."

"Excellent. We scored an amazing victory over St. Cosmas the year I was captain . . ." Mr. Trimble clutched his lapels for a moment and deepened his voice: "'I apologize to my learned friend for comparing him with a pig. There is really no comparison.' A very good night."

Charlie laughed, but felt that there was some terrible misunderstanding involved. Mr. Trimble's memory must have enlarged the importance of the debating team. At any rate, it wasn't of much consequence now.

The house was quite spooky in the winter. The dining-room walls were high and bare—a stripped-down version of Miss Skinner's, in fact. They made his father's jokes seem awfully dry and hollow. Charlie felt suddenly tense and exhausted: he was making too much of the debating team, of Brookshire altogether. His father was urging it out of him somehow. It was a bad thing to be doing.

The hanging lady on the landing bothered him slightly on the way out. Also he wasn't mad about going up to the third floor to take his bath. (You expected spiders to crawl out of the faucets.) He missed the lights and noise of Brookshire, the radio blaring in the recreation room and the swill of root beer. Not a bad place, although, repeat, nothing special.

The talk after supper ran to world affairs. The folly of Roosevelt, the uselessness of trying to save Europe from itself; all that was magically gone, swept away during the last term at school; now it was the valor of the English and the fine qualities of Mr. Churchill. Mr. Trimble was just as firm on that side as he had been on the other. Charlie, too, was excited about the English war effort. Who wasn't? But again he found himself overdoing it slightly. It was a funny feverish thing.

He was surprised, as he lay in bed later, to pick up a mumble of voices from his parents' room. Had the walls become thinner in his absence, or had his parents never talked at night before? There was a note of excitement in the male voice that the female seemed to be trying to douse. They were still at it when Charlie dropped off.

He slept late the next morning to pass the time. His father had plowed off through the snow to get to work. His mother chatted over breakfast, though there wasn't much to chat about out here. By the

way, though, she said—Miss Skinner next door had
been rather upset over a glass figurine that Charlie
had apparently broken. The thing was, he hadn't
apologized. The Trimbles had offered to pay, but that
wasn't the thing.

Crumby old woman. Charlie felt absolutely disgusted with her. He went out in the snow and threw
snowballs at the back of her house. The ground was
flat, so there wasn't much point in sledding. Freddy
Walton? Have to face him some time. The memory of
Freddy's fist on his nose was still fresh, though. He
could also imagine trying to catch Freddy in the snow
—a hopeless task.

He felt really sick and bitter about Miss Skinner,
betrayed and embarrassed. She was his personal
friend, if she was anything, and she should not have
brought his mother into it. However, this did not
keep her from inviting him to tea, or him from ac-
cepting, because the neighborhood was bare of ex-
cuses.

When he got over there he found Mrs. Pritchard
and Miss Cavendish in attendance, two of the Carter
Street Brahmins. They looked at him critically, making him feel too young, too fat, and from a hopeless
family, all in one go. He shook hands with Miss Skinner and perched a sliver of backside on one of her an-
tique chairs. I'm sorry I broke your statue, he almost
said despite himself.

Miss Cavendish was a gaudy old lady with pink
feathers around her neck and unidentified pink drip-
pings down the front of her dress. A fine museum-
piece for Miss Skinner's sitting room, stuffed and
mounted like a tropical bird on the sofa next to the
canary cage. Mrs. Pritchard across the way was

dressed in black, with a black felt hat over her eyes, the fashion of a few years back. He had assumed she was crazy, but saw that this was not necessarily so. She had fat legs. Miss Cavendish had thin ones. Charlie wondered when they would be leaving.

The decline of Philadelphia society seemed to be the text: Miss Cavendish seemed especially angry about it. "The people you meet at the Junior League these days, they're all new faces to me. This Euphemia Van Buren, for instance, a New Yorker, I believe . . ."

"Yes," said Mrs. Pritchard, "although the Webbers tell she was never quite accepted, even there. A 'Van' gets you almost anywhere in New York, but there are limits. Even there."

"I suppose she's come to Philadelphia to see if she can do better," said Miss Cavendish. "I must say, that shows excellent judgment. Anybody can be accepted in Philadelphia these days."

Charlie looked at Miss Skinner, expecting her to be annoyed or amused: she had been pretty satirical about the local snobs that first night. But she seemed like a different person in their actual presence.

"I don't believe that young people care very much about society these days," she said, "except as a means of getting ahead in the world. It's a pity, in many ways. I think they're missing a great deal."

"Miss Van Buren cares about society," said Mrs. Pritchard, missing the point grandly. "She seems to be into everything these days."

"That, of course," said Miss Cavendish, "is how you can tell. They *always* try too hard, don't they?"

"Absolutely," said Mrs. Pritchard.

Charlie thought this one over. Was *he* trying too hard. How could you tell? Was he casual enough for, say, the Junior League. And if so, what was the Junior League? Miss Cavendish didn't seem casual, as she bit into Miss Van Buren. But she did manage to imply that it didn't really matter to *her*—it was just a pity in a general kind of way. So maybe that was it.

"If everybody can become a debutante," she summed up, "then there's no point in becoming a debutante at all, is there?"

The other two nodded. "Absolutely not," said Mrs. Pritchard.

"And if anyone can get into the Social Register, then it becomes just another address book."

A fresh shower of worries: Why was she saying all this in front of him? Were the Trimbles in the Social Register? From the look of Miss Cavendish they certainly weren't. Not even in its present debased form. "I don't mind so much for myself," she said, actually glancing his way. "I'm rather too old for these affairs. But it doesn't look well for the future."

The future certainly meant him. Charles Trimble, climbing, straining up the ladder. In their deep yellowy shade, her eyes might in fact have been anywhere, on him or across the room. But he knew where they were. He slipped silently from his chair onto the floor.

"Are you all right, Charles?"

"Yes, Miss Skinner."

The chair had a shiny, slanted top. He had almost brought down a table of valuables as well. Just what they were talking about, of course—the kind of boy that Philadelphia turns out these days. Can't even hold his seat. He hitched himself up in wet confusion.

"Those chairs aren't really meant for sitting," said Miss Skinner, a little stiffly. She didn't like clumsiness, he knew that. Mrs. Pritchard's fat legs were pillars of scorn. The chair seemed suddenly like a greased slide; he began to concentrate on it like mad, and the voices sounded farther away, like chant from a choir loft: land taxes, fixed income, maids—everything playing into the hands of the upstarts. Meaning Charles Trimble. Escrows, trust fund, second cousins by marriage. *Not* meaning Charles Trimble. Most adults dropped this stuff now and again, to ask after his school or whether boys still wanted to be engine drivers. But this seemed to be a sterner generation. Miss Skinner paid him no more mind than the others: until, at the stroke of five, Miss Cavendish rose, and like a good acolyte, Mrs. Pritchard rose too, churning herself upright.

Charlie stood up too, but Miss Skinner motioned him to stay. He would have had trouble anyhow, inserting himself in their leave-taking: the hip-grinding huddle around Miss Skinner would have crushed him for sure. (Powdery kisses, so nice—and then Miss Cavendish sailing out like an ocean liner, and Miss Pritchard sailing out like another one.)

"Well, Charles." Now Miss Skinner attended to him all too closely. "I haven't seen you in a *long* time. How was school?"

"O.K. I'm sorry I broke that thing."

"What thing? Oh, my little Apollo. Well, that's all right. I was afraid the cat had done it." She spoke lightly, but he could suddenly imagine her flaring up viciously; hissing like the cat and darting at his throat, if he broke one more thing. He thought of hitting her first, chopping at her neck and stretching her wax body on the carpet. Like the bones of a beached whale. He froze on his chair; Miss Skinner connected in his mind with disaster.

"Did you have enough to eat?" she said. "I'm afraid

I haven't paid you much attention. I don't see a great deal of Miss Cavendish, you know—it's rather like a parish visit, every six months or so, to see if I'm still alive. So I have to make an effort for her."

She bent forward slightly, looking almost roguish.

"You know, Charles, I shouldn't be telling you this, I suppose, but I'm the only one old enough to know it, and someday you'll go away and forget us all for the old ghosts that we are. But," and she leaned forward with an evil old grin, "*Miss Cavendish hasn't always been in the Social Register herself.*"

Charlie couldn't wait to get out of there. Her face seemed flushed and disorganized like the painting of a clown. He feared she might have a stroke like his Aunt Clara last year. Then he would have to drag her body onto the sofa or out in the hall, and she would weigh 500 pounds, like a drowning man. Her voice trilled, though, like a girl's.

"She forgets that I know; she tries to im*press* me."

Charlie got out as soon as he could, leaving her chuckling to herself over this insane piece of good news.

Mr. Trimble was more subdued that night. He brought up Brookshire once or twice, and Mrs. Trimble said, "Charles is on vacation, he doesn't want to talk about that." Which was true enough in a way—because they would wind up doing college cheers together, and Charlie would feel, what was all that about? Instead, Mr. Trimble described some case of maritime law he was working on, a longshoreman struck by falling cargo *after* working hours, and calm was preserved. Afterwards, they listened quietly as Gabriel Heatter warned of dreaded pyorrhea, which only your dentist can cure, and gingivitis, a lesser ill.

Again, he could hear the voices mumbling in their

room, half the night or ten minutes or however long he lay awake. Miss Skinner's light was on behind the winter branches, in case anything should go wrong over here; the man's voice rose, the woman's voice poured ice water over it. His mother seemed to be alarmed by any enthusiasm at all. There was a feeling of fragility in the house; he half expected a thin beautiful scream from a madwoman. The old owner. The new ones.

It wasn't a romantic house. He looked at it the next day, wedged in the snow, tall and graceless, from behind and then in front and finally round at the side. His parents, he gathered, had scooped it up from among Aunt Clara's effects, because nobody else wanted it. Aunt Clara's effects—the phrase suggested old red cats and shawls and wigs, nobody could possibly want any of them. And this gawky-looking house. Mr. Trimble had done time here as a boy, fishing and boating on the Delaware, and had made a big thing of returning. Now they were stuck here.

Miss Skinner might have sensed that the last visit hadn't panned out too well. At any rate there were no more tea invitations. Luckily the winter vacation was short. He took two trips to Pranksville with his mother, once to the movies and the other time just a trip, and after that he went back to Brookshire: where he had a modest reputation, which he was sincerely ashamed of, for bullying the smaller boys.

Winter at Brookshire: a dream of gymnasiums. Also, learning to ice skate on George Washington's birthday. Hold those ankles steady.

When he got back to Tewksbury in the spring, he felt he was a lot older and smarter. Thirteen years old. He saw things as they *really* were for the first time. The house was not ugly and useless, but a quaint piece of nineteenth-century architecture. So was Miss Skinner. So was Mrs. Pritchard. His father was a maritime lawyer in Philadelphia, distinguished-looking, quite successful, nothing to be ashamed of at all. His mother was the socially acceptable Lydia Prescott—her family was wedged deep in the Social Register, Mr. Trimble's only slightly less so. All that worry had been in vain. Miss Cavendish had not disapproved of him when she frowned like that; she was setting high standards for him.

That was how it all looked from the outside. He had never seen it from the outside before, never seen the edges and shapes of things. Now, talking it over with his friends, he knew that his set-up looked all right; from where they sat, his father's profession was entirely suitable. And then, chatting aimlessly with old Mr. Fuchs, he saw that in the larger picture, it was no bad thing to be Charles Trimble of Philadelphia. "Of course family isn't everything," said Mr. Fuchs (who was a "character" about most things, but deadly serious about this), "but it helps enormously."

He approached the house in a signorial spirit. Already the garden looked smaller as it did for actual grown-ups. His own strides were longer and springier, bouncing him across the spring scrub and the damp, sweet-smelling earth. He wasn't so fat any more. The upstairs bathroom wouldn't bother him. Miss Skinner's living room could be handled. In spring of 1942 the war was revving up, and the excitement of it made you grow up a little faster.

The house folded its bat wings around him. His father hadn't come home yet. The stoop of his mother's back in the kitchen offended him on sight—what was she doing out here all the time? They didn't eat that much. He could overlook the fact that the Trimbles didn't have servants, with the war and all, but his mother's life was unforgivably cramped.

He just thought he'd mention this to her: but then suddenly found himself almost too angry to speak. He wanted to pick up something and hit her bent back with it, drive her out of the kitchen, drive her into wearing a nice socially prominent dress. He had been back for no more than five minutes and he was already terribly restless. There was nothing to do here; he had been in this kitchen all his life and there was *nothing to do*. He caught his mother's eye. She was watching him closely, almost clinically. He dropped his bag and ran outside.

He went right over to Miss Skinner's, not sure exactly why, but anyway, Lily the maid said that Miss Skinner was sick with the bronchitis and couldn't see anybody. Lily had a red, cooking-sherry face which there was no arguing with. So he decided to walk by the river for a while and calm down and start again. What gave with his mother anyway? He didn't understand her at all. The Delaware, when he got to it, was dark and sluggish. He half expected to see buzzards skimming the oily surface, snapping up spiders. He threw a pebble and the industrial gook from Camden seemed to buoy it through five long skips.

On a distant jetty, he saw what looked like an old man fishing, legs dangling like a boy's. But when he got closer, he saw that the man had no fishing tackle and was just staring out at the dirty water. And when he got closer still, he saw that it was his father with a briefcase on his lap and a handful of stones.

Mr. Trimble seemed to be angry about something, the way Charlie had been angry a few minutes ago. A funny coincidence. Maybe it was just his face, which Charlie had never exactly noticed before, and which appeared to be drawn and vexed. Mr. Trimble had sandy hair and rimless glasses, and a bright red band under his eyes. He did not see his son coming, but gazed at the water venomously and dropped a stone in it.

"Hi, Father."

Mr. Trimble stared blankly for a moment and then jumped up and shook Charlie's hand. He seemed uncertain what to say first. Was everything all right at Brookshire? The debating team O.K.? "I like to walk home this way," he explained, "although they've ruined the river. You won't believe it but we used to swim in this mess once upon a time." He shook his head. He had apparently been sitting here raging at the river—no, that was unlikely.

"Can't something be done about it?" Charlie asked politely.

"Well, we're trying one or two measures." They started to walk back and Mr. Trimble outlined the various schemes. He was, Charlie realized, still seething—it couldn't just be the Delaware. Was anything wrong at home? "Philadelphia is ruined, of course, beyond repair, but I never thought they could ruin Tewksbury too. That's rivers for you, though, isn't it. They can carry corruption, like bad blood, anywhere in the system. Just *look* at that water."

It isn't that important. Don't take it so hard, Father. It's only a river. Charlie looked sideways at his father and caught his mood for a moment. He found himself getting angry at the river too.

Mr. Trimble must have realized finally that this was a funny way to greet his son after two and a bit months' absence, and he dropped the subject. They walked in silence until they reached the end of the short strand, where they had to turn in; and Charlie thought to himself, "I shouldn't have gone up to him right then, he wanted to be left alone with his thoughts"—anyway, Charlie, don't go by this. Peter Samson, one of his friends at Brookshire, had a taxidermist for a father—now that was something *really* peculiar. Mr. Trimble was a lawyer, which was perfectly all right.

"What do you suppose you'll want to be when you grow up?" Mr. Trimble asked suddenly, urgently, as if they must settle this question before they entered the house.

"I don't know." Charlie had one foot on the porch already and didn't know whether to proceed with the other one. He had been resting this subject for a spell, and for a moment he couldn't even name any professions, let alone choose one. "A lawyer, I guess, like you. Maybe you could get me into Dunphy and Brocklehurst some day."

Mr. Trimble stared at him a moment, and then nodded solemnly, and they went on into the house. Charlie had gotten the exact same foot on the stairs when his father called out again, "I suppose you'll be going to Penn first, will you?"

Charlie nodded, helplessly. Yes. Why not?

"I had a pretty good time there," said Mr. Trimble.

The meaning of all this was to become a little clearer a couple of months from now. Meanwhile, he made his way through the spring vacation somehow, by ignoring practically everything, working on a special war scrapbook all day and being snotty with his parents in the evening (he was to regret this).

He tried Miss Skinner again and she received him

with a croaky voice. His present position about her was that she was better than nothing. At least she remembered things about the First World War, and showed him pictures of her brother in a National Guard hat. He got a feeling toward the end of the visit that she didn't like him as much as she used to. Her talk was crisp, so far as her foggy throat permitted, and impatient. But it was hard to tell with Miss Skinner.

He was getting slightly bothered about this kind of thing. "Trimble talks a good game . . . Trimble is stuck on himself." His cronies at Brookshire had given him this pinch of self-knowledge in the last few months. "Trimble the show-off, Trimble the boy wonder." Mild criticism, no worse than anyone else got, and it hadn't struck deep; but now in this echo chamber, under the eye of this fierce, ugly old lady, it came back with a roar. He could hear himself showing off, see himself being some kind of brat.

There was nothing he could do about it. Because when he tried to be self-effacing, it came out smarmy. And when he tried just being himself, the way he used to, he couldn't remember how that worked. And Miss Skinner didn't like any of it, he could tell. He felt, briefly, crushed and disgusted with himself, and thought, suppose I tell her that? Would it save the day?

No, she would just tell him to pull himself together.

By paying no attention at all to his parents, he found that life at home could be somehow suspended. When he resumed school, it would be as if nothing had happened. His mother's kitchen vigils no longer bothered him, because he never went near the kitchen. He didn't feel he had to go in and see if she was all right. And when his father smashed the coffee table over some Gabriel Heatter item, his own gorge rose only part way in sympathy. He was simply thinking about something else—and praying devoutly that the vacation would end and he could leave this house.

Just before that, the Spirit of Tewksbury came calling, in the persons of Miss Cavendish and Mrs. Pritchard. It was a Sunday afternoon, so Mr. Trimble was home for once, doing a little city man's gardening in his waistcoat. Charles saw him standing hands on hips, contemplating the wistaria at the side of the house, as the two women came surging along the drive: Miss Cavendish in her spring print, Mrs. Pritchard in black for the late Mr. Pritchard, ten years dead, bringing up the rear in every sense. Charlie began to giggle about this phrase, so he had to keep his distance.

He was actually returning from a walk of his own, and he stopped at the other end of the crescent driveway and watched them shake hands, Mr. Trimble dropping the brambles he had pulled out of the vine and removing his gardening gloves, Miss Cavendish removing hers, and then everyone going in the house. Mr. Trimble looked a little nervous, with his shoulders bunched up in back.

Charlie did not wish to spend another afternoon with those two monsters. On the other hand, he was curious to know how his father would tackle them. He considered how to manage this. Straight eavesdropping was not very practical: they eventually heard you creaking around outside and asked what you were doing. And sent you miles away. So he settled at first for trips up and down the hall, as though on various errands, to fetch his gloves, to find his hat, etc. You could keep this up for hours, or so he hoped; anyhow, let's give it a whirl.

The conversation was cut into sections by the living-room wall. He could hear swatches of talk through the two doors, with a mumble in the middle, like the space between radio stations. If things got interesting, he could possibly bivouac in the hall closet, rooting among the galoshes. It was a workable system, at least in theory.

Mr. Trimble was talking now. What was it? war, yes—a touch of war. A pinch of rationing. Miss Cavendish wouldn't mind so much if . . . Mrs. Pritchard agreed, wouldn't mind either, if . . . red tape, bureaucracy and hoarding, those were the trouble. One even had to hoard a little oneself, in self-defense. Charles had completed one lap already and saw no occasion to pause at the closet this time. He started back. The whole country badly run but most especially Philadelphia. The wall. Mrs. Pritchard: Democrats. Mr. Trimble: quite. Miss Cavendish: and of course, after the war, they'll expect the same thing. The wall again. You don't suppose taxes will ever go down again, do you? Don't be silly. Quite. Taxes never go down. Naïve, silly, quite.

Charlie was back at the front door. This was an absolutely terrible system, and the conversation was hardly worth the trouble. He scratched his head as if he had just thought of something else to look for and started off again.

"The decline in manners . . . the other day a taxi driver . . . the age of the common man indeed." This would have to be his last journey. He stopped at the closet and tried to decide what to do next: whether to give up and go to his room, or to try the garden or the river. They were talking, inevitably—Miss Cavendish drifting toward it like a juggernaut—about the disappearance of style.

Charlie did want to hear his father on this. Mr. Trimble had referred a few times to the snobs around here. He had mentioned Miss Cavendish by name a few nights ago. Mr. Trimble remembered her from his boyhood: an ill-favored young woman whom nobody was game to marry, retreating into social superiority, a silly, idle woman—now let's hear him go get her.

Miss Cavendish heightened the suspense by stretching her essay on style to great length. Examples of bad manners littered the place like salesman's samples. Strangers using her first name in vain, nephews bringing bold girls to tea unannounced. Charlie picked up a pink rubber belonging to his mother, looked at it, put it down. "Style" reminded him of boots and shoes, high buttons, dancing pumps, rancid galoshes.

Mr. Trimble spoke at last in a voice that Charlie didn't recognize for a moment. The dryness and mockery that he had grown up under were all gone; in their place was something liquid, gentle. A woman's voice, that's what it was. And he was agreeing with them. Charlie left the closet and started for the stairs, just in time to hear his father linking it up with the pollution of the Delaware. "You remember, Isabel, how it used to be": there was some awful tenderness in his voice. "When we were young here" . . . Charlie stomped on up the stairs and yanked out his war album.

After they'd gone, Mr. Trimble was just as funny about them as Miss Skinner had been on the day of *her* sell-out. "Poor old things, worrying about charity balls while the world goes up in smoke. Fussing about this year's debutantes."

Mrs. Trimble had been out shopping when they called, and said, "I'm sorry, I try to keep them away as much as I can. I tell them you're busy, that you're in town a lot."

"That's all right, I enjoy it once in a while." Mr. Trimble was expansive. "I gave them a few *real* things to worry about, the spoliation of nature and so on, but of course it won't make any difference. 'Society is disintegrating, my dear. Mrs. Drexel has cancelled all her appointments.'" Charlie had never heard his father do an imitation before, and it was a startling experience. It was a voice Charlie had never heard before, not Miss Cavendish's or Mrs. Pritchard's, but a real voice all the same. Some dead old lady inside his father. It was the same voice his father had used, in earnest, earlier this afternoon.

Charlie felt some of the old fears of the house that night. This was very annoying, with the end of the vacation in sight. He gazed at Miss Skinner's light and tried to tune out the voices in the next room, the excited man and the cold, wet, calm woman, and he thought, well, they're strong enough to overpower me, that's one thing; and Miss Skinner could get through the hedge like a whippet, if called upon finally. He was too crafty to explain exactly what he meant by this, too crafty and, thank heavens, too sleepy. He got off lightly with a couple of bad dreams and two days later was back safe and sound at Brookshire.

Fat Jack Sample, the school comedian, rapped out "shave and a haircut, six bits" on his door and came in without waiting for an answer. Charlie was by himself, this being a Saturday, and his roommates being off playing ball some place. Fat Jack wasn't that funny, but he was awfully big, so he got a gratifying response on his gags.

"Hey, Trimble."

"Yes?"

Jack just stood there grinning hungrily. Hungry for humor, for the stuff of laughs. He might or might not have something on his mind, time would tell. Jack liked to string things out. "Hey, Trimble, I didn't know you had a sister." This referred to a small glass elephant that Charlie kept on the mantelpiece for luck—pretty ornate for Brookshire. "I didn't know you went in for the larger game. Where d'you bag this fella?"

Charlie went on reading. This stuff didn't bother him, quite the contrary. He relished it, like Jack, wanted it to last forever.

"By jove, he's a big one—the bearers had legged it back to Johannesburg, by then, I daresay, leaving you to cope with the maddened animal." Sample just kept going like this until he came to something funny, a humor of attrition. Jack was sixteen, but preferred a younger audience; Charlie was a special favorite, because he was bright enough to lean with an older man's jokes.

"Trimble, they tell me you made a big hit with some girl at the roller rink. Any truth in that, Trimble?"

"Oh sure. I'm always doing things like that."

"No, seriously. They say she couldn't stop talking about you. A cute little blond number. Remember her by any chance?"

"No."

"Well, she remembers you all right. In fact, they

say she has a regular case of the hots for you. Warm for your form, Trimble. Ask anybody."

"You're kidding. I don't remember any blond girl."

"Sure you do. Blue dress, nice little butt. You went round with her one time, and I don't know what you said to her but you racked her up good."

Charlie did remember something that might have been what Sample had in mind. The Brookshire boys went skating every Saturday and there was one dance number thing where you rolled vaguely alongside any girl you could keep step with. Could that have been it? *A blond* girl? Amid the pounding roar of the skates —he struggled to remember, his groin suddenly aflame.

"You *do* believe me, Trimble. Promise me you believe me. And make me the happiest of mortals."

Oh, for heaven's sake. Charlie shook his head feebly. "No."

"Attaboy, Trimble. You're learning. Three months ago you would have been halfway down to the rink by now." He slammed his fist onto Charlie's bicep, into a cluster of his own purple marks. "I didn't come to see you about that, I came to see you about something else. Mr. Fuchs said he was looking for you. In his office, any time. You know what I mean?" He twitched his eyebrows and hips. Fat Jack couldn't tell anything straight.

Mr. Fuchs' office was on the other side of the school. Charlie had to cross a lawn, and he remembered afterward that it felt parched and flaky, like a summer lawn. He had only been back a few days, but spring had already dried out. Or at least on this one particular lawn.

Mr. Fuchs got to the point right away. Undue

crispness, his face half turned to the window. Bad
news, swallow quickly. Charlie's father had died during the night. So—that's over, thought Charlie. Can I
go now? Fuchs, with his aureole of white hair, with his
face distorted by years of pedagogue's whimsey, was
not being a character today, but very serious; which
made him truly, for the first time, comic. "Your father
was a fine boy," he said, clown's eyes glistening.

"Did he, you know, do it himself?" asked Charlie,
hardly pausing to think.

Fuchs was taken off-guard. "They're not sure."

"Did he do it with a knife? Or was it something
else? The river or something?" Crazy questions for
anyone else, but Charlie was at home in this territory.

"They're not sure," said Fuchs, desolately.

Arrangements were made to get Charlie back to
Tewksbury right away for the funeral. He found a
small hassle in progress over the choice of graveyard.
Mr. Trimble was technically a Catholic but had broken with the Church by killing himself. (By drowning, Charlie was relieved to hear.) Father Devlin
came out from Philadelphia to explain the difficulties
to Mrs. Trimble and she passed them on, in watered
form, to Charlie. Devlin was willing to make every
concession to reasonable doubt. Mr. Trimble could
have written the note and then changed his mind
and fallen in by mistake; or changed his mind
later, as the current ripped at his legs. But it seemed
that Mr. Trimble had actually given up on the
Church at about the time the family left Philadelphia.
He had argued all of one night with Father Devlin
over certain unnamed points of doctrine and had
stomped out forever. Mrs. Trimble was necessarily
vague—she was not a Catholic herself but had stood
by while Charlie was first raised as one and then sud-

denly not raised as one any more—and could only accept Father Devlin's word for it that there was no reason to suppose that her husband even wanted a Catholic burial.

. . . so that was what had happened to Sunday school, thought Charlie. He had imagined that the whole thing was dropped because the Catholic church in Tewksbury was all the way to Pranksville, three miles distant, a long ride for the spavined Chevy that served as town taxi. But now he had this picture of Mr. Trimble arguing it out with the implacable Father Devlin, raging and pleading and beating his fists on the black starch, begging for an exception to be made in his case, and stalking out, angry and frightened. Certain points of doctrine indeed! The cruel last word of the Church.

The Episcopalians would take him, though, bloated by dirty water and industrial waste, so the funeral was held at All Saints on Carter Street. Charlie was a big help with flower arrangements and invitations. He sensed on the day itself that everyone was watching him, waiting for him to crack. But he was good and calm. This was his turf. Miss Skinner didn't come because, he now realized, she never left her house for anything. But she sent twenty dollars' worth of flowers, by Charlie's estimate, and a nice note.

A spring funeral was like a spring planting. Charlie underwent flashes of pure joy as the box slid into the fresh earth. Everything was quite clear. I'm still here, I'll have no trouble now. Mr. Trimble had done it, so he didn't have to It was that simple. It was all he could do to keep looking serious.

The limousine they rode home in was huge and furry and quiet as a cathedral. Mrs. Trimble was composed, with a small rug around her knees. She wasn't happy, like him, but relieved and tired. When they got home, she made some tea and, with a sincere apology, took it upstairs to her room, with a couple of women's magazines hitched under her arm. He heard her slippers flapping overhead as she plumped the pillows and turned down the spread. And then silence.

The house began to empty slowly, as if real moving men were here. Charlie washed his tea cup and dried it, and the china handle came off in his hand. He frowned. Everyone left you alone after a funeral, to grieve. He didn't want to grieve. He thought of telephoning someone, arranging a party of some kind. A wild dance on the grave would be a nice thing, until you collapsed or were carted off. He suddenly realized that he was getting excited, like you know who: tried quickly to calm himself, but you had to be like a cat to head these things off.

It would help to run upstairs to talk things out quickly with his mother, but she was much too tired. Her exhaustion was a fact, like fatness or age. As long as he had known her, she had had no energy for him, no personality to spare. Why? It was all quite clear: because she was saving her game for the night, for those terrible talks. Sitting here in the kitchen pacing herself.

The day was cooling now with unnatural haste, with a night wind brewing round the river. Time to bring his father in. I mean, you can't leave him out all night, can you? Bloated and unrecognizable, his pockets stuffed with eels, hair green and impossibly long, we still have to bring him in. Why couldn't he have had a clean river to drown in?

Why did he choose drowning anyway? I really disagree with you about that, Father. A difference of character, I guess. Everyone knows that stabbing's best. Charles started drifting toward the dining room again, to the silver-box. There was no point putting it off indefinitely. If not today, then it would be tomorrow or next Candlemas, or his twenty-fifth birthday or his fortieth or his fiftieth, it didn't matter. His father's note, which his mother had not wanted to show him but which he had wheedled out of her (by convincing her that he *knew*) said simply, "I'm sorry, I can't wait any longer."

Charlie couldn't have that hanging over him for a whole lifetime. His father had been as strong as a man of that particular type could be. And he had had Mrs. Trimble hanging onto his wrist, doing a bang-up job. And yet, in the end, he couldn't wait. Couldn't wait for his son to be out of school and set up in business. Holy Mother of God. Charlie ran his hand right over the box, feeling the grain on each finger. Do it now while you're not afraid. Mother is too tired to care. She can't go through all that again for somebody else. She would say, Do what you like, dear. Be sure to clean up afterwards.

My God, this just wasn't real, just wasn't happening. Not to Trimble the snot, the snotty boy wonder. It was over, his father had taken his place. Get out of this house for a minute and you'll see what I mean. He made a fast break for the front door. The wind was rattling the loose glass, some day it would be scattered all over the Trimbles' rug. Good. Smash and clatter. The door whipped in against his hand, and he was wrestling with it like a nut. The wind held its breath long enough for him to get the door shut, then fired itself viciously at his bare head. He opened his arms like a cross and the wind smashed him backward against the door and pinned him there. A murderous wind. No, it only wants to play with you. Don't be afraid.

It slashed his eyes open like a paper knife and released the tears by main force. With these streaming down his cheeks, cooling him and curing some of the dryness, he bucked into the wind and shouldered his way to Miss Skinner's place.

Miss Skinner was sick again, perhaps she had always been sick. Charlie hadn't noticed. Lily the maid, drunk as a skunk, said he couldn't come up. But she was in no shape to stop him. He would have broken her jaw. He caught sight of himself in the mirror on the landing and was honest to God frightened by his own face: red and ravaged by the wind, but not just that.

She was propped up like a birthday cake. Expecting him of course—there was no surprising her. Charlie was trembling malarially. The thought of doing violence to Miss Skinner was an old, familiar one. A chair, a brutal-looking poker, the room was an arsenal, crammed with weaponry. Would she understand? or would she be very disappointed? if he mashed her brains in?

He sat at the end of the bed, not daring to look at her, telling himself that it didn't hurt what you thought if you didn't do anything about it. He placed his hands carefully between his knees and locked them there. His father must have done this many times.

"I'm sorry I missed the funeral," said Miss Skinner, "although I don't enjoy funerals as much as some old people I know. They are so proud of being alive, if alive is what they are, and a funeral shows them up to advantage."

Yes, yes. Is that so?

"I've seen so many people die by now that I'm sometimes not sure whether I'm dead myself. No one will tell you these things." Demonic strategy on her part.

"People make such a fuss about dying, so I suppose it matters to them. When Walter Pritchard died, Wendy Pritchard carried on as if nobody had ever died before. Yet he was a very dull man, and I can't believe it mattered much to him."

Charlie had to be infinitely cunning in his position, nothing less would do. Cooling things was her ace card. It might save somebody's life, time would tell.

"I was sorry about your father," she said, watching him like a fox. "Perhaps you'd like to hear about him, what he was like as a boy, and so on, if I can remember anything."

"Yes, please. That would do fine."

"Well, he was a great little fisherman, of course, in the days when fishing was possible. But I don't suppose you want to hear about that. He was very merry as a small boy." She leaned forward, farther than seemed feasible, and placed a cold hand on his forehead. "Try just to listen, not to think," she said.

This at least seemed like a good plan. To follow her ramble more intelligently, Charlie tried to imagine what his father must have looked like then. From movies and such, he assembled a pair of knickers, a straw hat, a brown jacket with a belt in the back, and a bow tie. He had no idea if this was accurate. A face and figure like his own, in full regalia, pacing the same garden; with women in long white dresses sweeping past, Miss Skinner among them—watchful even then, built to last. Some kind of paddleboat taking the bankers to work along the translucent Dela-

ware. Miss Cavendish trying to get into the Social
Register. This he saw under Miss Skinner's cold hand.

"I was quite old even then—I don't remember a
time when I wasn't old—but we were great friends.
He was one of those boys who enjoy older people. He
used to come through the hedge just as you do and
talk for hours. My own brother had died and I was
glad of the company. It's funny but he never came to
see me in these last months after you all came back
here. I should think that either you want the past or
you don't. You don't come back to Tewksbury and ig-
nore the leading monuments."

"Well, he was happy once, wasn't he?" said
Charles. "His whole life wasn't bad."

"Oh yes, very happy, one of the happiest little boys
I've ever known. I used to see him by himself in the
garden, actually laughing to himself. It's a shame that
one can't stay as happy as that forever. But one can't.
Of course, it was a very lively place in those days. A
lot of young fashionable people—where they've gone,
I don't know. You never notice the actual moment of
falling asleep, a person or a town, do you?"

Tewksbury, a boom town, bursting with colorful
people; his father, himself, rolling a hoop down the
main thoroughfare. Dodging carriages and ladies'
bustles. Suddenly everything stopping. The fashionable people piling into a train. Destination unknown.
The petrified fingers of Miss Skinner passing on the
story.

"O.K., he was happy here, and he was certainly
happy at Brookshire," he said quickly, quickly. "So
when did he stop being happy?"

Miss Skinner frowned. "I don't know about Brookshire. He was there such a short while. Only three or
four weeks."

"What happened?"

"He became ill, I believe."

Charlie writhed and moaned. This was terrible news. Ill indeed! Little Mr. Trimble sent home for flinging himself out of windows, burning, smashing, mutilating himself: delivered at Tewksbury station, bandaged like a mummy. With a dim memory of a debating team.

"He became, oddly enough," Miss Skinner and her disgusting wisdom, "a passionate alumnus. Rather like those war veterans who never went overseas." This was nasty medicine she was handing out.

"Was he really just ill?"

"So far as I know, yes."

"Where did he go after that?"

"He didn't go anywhere. He studied at home, with tutors, until it was time to go to Pennsylvania University. He did very well there, I believe."

Charlie flexed his hands within their prison of knees. "Is that all? Isn't there any more to tell?"

"Well, let me see. Cheerful, tutors, what else, what else? He became very serious about Tewksbury for a time, and decided to write an official history of the town. He asked me all sorts of questions—since I had practically founded the place, of course—and assembled a great many land grants and things. It was really quite fascinating, I daresay. I wonder what became of it all?"

"I don't know."

"When he graduated, he just stayed on in Tewksbury. This probably seems rather stodgy to you, but in those days it did not seem so necessary to leave places. I myself have never left Tweksbury in three hundred years or more."

He noticed, with that overdeveloped cunning of

his, the sturdy self-satisfaction planted deep in Miss Skinner, the way she worked in references to herself every few minutes. She watched people like his father come and go with enormous amusement. She was a good old woman and also an evil old woman. Could he trust her? She put the cold hand now on his wrist and pulled it gently from between his knees, as if it was safe to come out now. Was it? She would save you if she could, but if you fell she would be amused. Fair enough. Impulsively, he hunched closer and leaned against her. Her breast was withered under the nightgown, but seemed to give a small leap of life. It was not necessary to hit her, there were other things you could do with her.

She stroked his hair, but when she spoke, it was with absolutely no increase in intimacy: her voice was a stone that could not be warmed.

"I wish I remembered more. You know how you hear things and forget them. I daresay in the course of a life-time you hear everything you need to know. But one's attention wanders. For instance, there was something about the house. A fight with your Aunt Clara. But I don't know the details."

"When was that?"

"Let me see, let me see." She looked intentionally vague. She was keeping something from him. "He wanted to stay here forever and write his history and cultivate his garden. He took the train to work every day, I could see him from my window at first light, walking to the station, and then back in the dark. I don't know why, but I think of it as all happening in winter. It seemed such a heroic effort to be making in January just for the sake of keeping a house in Tewksbury.

"Then there was some sort of dispute about the will

and his sister moved in and he moved out, I never got it quite straight. She had been her father's favorite, of course." She spoke as if Charlie must remember all this, and just needed to have his memory jogged. "I suppose at the last minute he gave into his old feeling for her and wrote one of those peculiar wills on blotting paper, leaving your father's house to her."

"What did Father do then?" Not try to kill himself again, that was so boring and predictable; Charlie wanted to hear at least one other thing that his father had done.

"Well, he was very angry. I believe he broke some things. The house was quite bare when Clara arrived. And stayed so. She was a bit disturbed herself, you know."

Great. All he needed now was a crazy aunt.

"Her father may have alarmed her with his affection, she sometimes seemed frightened when he came in a room, smiling; but you don't want to hear about that, the big thing is that *you're* sane, Charles."

He gave a startled laugh. He was still hunched against Miss Skinner and he could taste her wool cardigan. She had overplayed her hand seriously, telling him rubbish like that. Her frosty fingers ground into the back of his skull. "These things do not run in families unless you let them," she said firmly. "There's a lot of craziness in old families that comes from just thinking about it."

Nice try, Miss Skinner. But let's not kid ourselves, shall we? The knives came first. Before the thinking. Remember?

"Your father should have left Tewksbury, there's no saving towns like this, he signed his death warrant when he came back."

None of that flashy talk, Miss Skinner. Charlie felt

himself slowly changing again, hair growing wild in his palms and nostrils, immense power in his arms. He didn't dare to move.

"I don't know what brought him back," Miss Skinner hurried on. "I talked to your mother just once, and she seemed quite terrified about something. But we didn't talk about it. We talked about—well, you know the things we talk about around here. So confining to the intelligence. And to the heart, of course. There was nothing wrong with your father but living here made it worse."

What was she talking about? Charlie was getting confused.

"Don't you like it here?" he mumbled.

She laughed. "It's different for someone like me. I'm old, you see, and quite possibly dead as well. Once you're dead, Tewksbury is a very nice place to be."

She's crazy, he thought. He tried to move and realized that he was pinioned to her. Her hands were incredibly strong, as if they were indeed a dead woman's. His own strength was illusory. He could not even move his neck. The cardigan tasted of verbena. "Did you ever do this to my father?" he muttered, knowing the answer quite well.

There was a pause and then he felt her nodding. Of course, of course. Her face, he couldn't see it, but he knew it was incredibly, incredibly beautiful. His body buckled. He embraced her for a long time and held her like a lover, and the poison ran out of his arms and buried itself in her and with the first slash of morning light under the blinds she released him, and he left without speaking.

His mother was more than willing to leave Tewksbury right away. Charlie was drowsy and relaxed the next day, as in his previous convalescence. But he was also more frightened this time, and wanted to get out quickly. He blamed it on the house. It had magic powers. He would be all right anywhere else.

He could not bring himself to see Miss Skinner, but he sent her a note. A silly note that said nothing. He wanted no part of her. He just said goodbye, Miss Skinner, we're going to New York. And by late afternoon they were gone, like gypsies.

They stayed in a hotel for a few days, in adjoining rooms. It was a noisy, well-lit place, full of drunken businessmen working on government contracts and soldiers rousting on leave: you could hear them out in the corridor searching for their keys, talking and whooping, occasionally glancing off a wall. Charlie relished every sound and was only sorry when their doors slammed, choking them off. He kept his blind up so that his room was flooded with neon until dawn.

It was agreed without discussion that he would not return to Brookshire. His uncle, Bonham Prescott, seemed to understand what was wanted. He boisterously enrolled Charlie in a day school, got him and his mother a bright airy apartment on Fifth Avenue, and pumped generous transfusions of rude health and money into them.

It was as if he had been standing by for years, waiting to do this. There was no sickness or dying in Uncle Bonham's world. He seemed to come from a different Philadelphia, a sunny, small town with large, open squares, white paint, and possibly even fountains. Once, Charlie was startled to see a death's head on Uncle Bonham—but that was a brief, isolated relapse. Uncle Bonham did not encourage that kind of thinking.

Charlie waited and waited for trouble, but after a while he knew it wasn't going to come. The devil had left him. He liked his new school almost hysterically. He liked New York, which seemed in a constant state of sunshine and high spirits. The fleet came in one day and sat in the Hudson River. Sailors in white starch poured over the city. Things like that were happening all the day. Christmas displays. Easter parades. Noise and light.

He was rewarded for his recent pains by a period of coolness. Interesting, because he seemed to be passing boys coming in the other direction. The world had no punishments for him any more. The onslaught of sex seemed like a small turmoil, a minor rising. Compared with what he had seen. As he sat, like a big pussy cat, at the back of the class, he felt that his "trouble" was over; other boys, with anxious faces, were just beginning theirs.

Far from trying to forget what had happened back in Tewksbury, he spent much time trying to reconstruct it—that seemed the healthier course—but felt it slipping away anyhow. He remembered things in set-pieces—Miss Skinner here, him there—instead of fluidly. But then, to make the scenes move, investing them with sequence and causality like a story. Unfortunately, his memory was the only record that existed.

His mother, to his annoyance, did not share his healthy candor about the past. She became, after her own convalescence, a busy, serene woman; lines seemed to drop from her face and regroup. New skin, new person. The past was dead, she lived in the present. This was supposed to be healthy too, but it didn't strike Charlie that way.

The only thing he ever got her to say about his father, in response to a brutal hammering of questions, was that the final move to Tewksbury was "for his health"; so Miss Skinner had got things wrong about that. Miss Skinner had thought that his coming back was a mistake; but it was really an act of desperation. As sole custodian of the story, Charlie made a note of this. "It was worse in Philadelphia," said Mrs. Trimble, who looked exhausted and dismayed at having said so much.

The other nagging questions would never be solved. Why the two of them had married in the first place, whether his mother knew what she was getting into, what kind of woman she had been before this. He pictured all kinds of horrible discoveries and adjustments. But Mrs. Trimble's new, bright mask would tell him no more. She was not responsible for what her old face had seen or heard.

She took up church activities in a fairly big way, which set Charlie to thinking on the same lines. He was not still angry with the Catholics for not burying his father—he guessed they had their reasons. There *was* something disgusting about a suicide. And contagious. If Charlie had killed himself, he would at that moment have been disgusting also. There was no getting round it. The Catholics were just protecting their ground.

On the other hand, he didn't want to get into that stuff again. The Catholic Church dealt in various fever points. If he started thinking about the things Catholics thought about he might find himself sliding down the chute again into the coal cellar. He wasn't altogether well yet.

So he settled for secularity, and if necessary, superficiality. No one should be obliged to think long and deeply if it hurt too much. Charlie was still a smart boy, but his school interests were factual-historical.

Mrs. Trimble, who was now his good friend, seemed to understand. But he sensed that she would understand just about anything at this point. She seemed to be following a policy of not upsetting him—which was slightly upsetting in itself. How much did she know? Had she seen him returning from Miss Skinner's in the early morning, shivering and drenched in sweat? He tried to pry the answers loose by indirection; but the mask wasn't saying.

It didn't matter. To be sure, he didn't like the idea of witnesses. He would tell other people about it in good time—but he didn't want them to know already. He had to have full control of the story. But it didn't matter, because she hadn't sent him to a doctor, she didn't think he was crazy.

By the time he was seventeen, the whole thing was beginning to be just an anecdote, something to tell when other people were telling things. It was a great period for that: the era of movies like *Spellbound*, and when girls said, "You're a very strange person," and you bust a gut to prove they were right. Charlie had a friend called Harold, for instance, who dreamed every night that he was flogging his father with a bullwhip. "Get out of that bed immediately, or I'll give you a touch of the cat." Charlie wondered in later life where Harold got this stuff. But at the time it was nice to know that he was not the only nut on the block.

Inflamed by the competition, Charlie finally told Harold, rather timidly, that he had once thought of killing himself. "Is that so?" said Harold, hardly listening. Harold also did better imitations of Peter Lorre. There was no topping Harold. So Charlie added the suicide caper to his repertoire of small talk, using it to fascinate women and at least to stay in the same league as Harold.

How far all this gabble was from the black dripping hedge and the poisoned river, he was to be reminded on his next and last trip to Tewksbury. He had often passed through the place since leaving it on his way to visit Philadelphia relatives, but always at the cleansing speed of an express train; and besides, he had never minded the part down by the station. The first time, he had childishly not wanted to look; but on later trips, he found himself looking forward to the flash of scenery, the hint of evil. A game.

This time, he had to retrace his steps all the way to the old house. Miss Skinner was sick, and this at her age meant, possibly, death. She had written him a note in spidery handwriting on violet notepaper, suggesting a visit. At first he was excited at being sent for like that. Boarding the train, buying a ham sandwich, peering between the grease spots on the window. But when he began to think about Miss Skinner, he realized that she had become a monster in his mind: a stone face, fifty feet high, with the sweet breath of a girl. A voice like something left in the attic. Hands with scales on them. A nightdress that would crumple like powder when he touched it.

He had to take the train into North Philadelphia, and then come out again by subway and trolley. She entered the train at Trenton and stayed with him the rest of the way, a few feet off, sitting up in bed staring at him. Her eyes were mean black rocks. Her cheeks were long and pale, made of some kind of furrowed marble. Her mouth was thin and angry. Or amused, he couldn't be sure which.

She could make cruel fun of him if she wanted to. She had a real memory of the past, which would stand up in a court of law, to put next to his phony one. She remembered exactly what he looked like as he came crazily blundering into her room. She *knew*.

He tried to keep all this in proportion, but it was a long, unreal journey (the trolley was especially unreal) and by the time he got to Tewksbury he knew he was in bad shape. His mind was wrenched out of line again, as by one sharp turn of the wrist. The smart thing was to go straight back to New York. Admitting that there was a crack in his brain, which would never quite heal. A Christian was supposed to avoid occasions of sin. So, too, occasions of craziness.

But he had already gone too far now. He had set foot in Tewksbury, and was beginning to pace out his steps. Under a new crowd of summer leaves, past several new houses that looked strange here, and several old ones that were up for sale. Turn right on Carter Street, where Mrs. Pritchard watched from behind her curtains; Mrs. Pritchard waiting for Miss Skinner to die, and a chance for another funeral. I may be able to help you, thought Charlie; and then, to get some kind of grip on himself, sat down next to a hedge and breathed deeply. And said some kind of incoherent prayer. These are just mental events, you have proved in the past that they do not affect your actions. (Yes, yes, but this time is different.)

He heaved up on his feet and continued on his way. The street was empty, he could have done anything, taken off his clothes, anything at all. Carter Street was a tiny section of a long road that ran all the way into Philadelphia getting cheaper and uglier all the way. He could almost feel his and his father's gorge rising over this. There was nothing approaching a sidewalk, and he noticed that the dust was accumulating on his shoes.

The short-cut, which he took automatically, went straight through the back of Miss Skinner's garden. He was annoyed to see how things had disintegrated back here. Miss Skinner must have laid off her gardener. The flower beds were snarled with weeds, the grass was lank and brown and came up to his knees. It added to an impression of approaching a witch's castle.

He climbed the porch, where the old wicker chairs were solemnly assembled, and pulled on the old bell. There was no answer for a while, and he thought the place might have been abandoned. Miss Skinner had been left to die alone upstairs. But finally, Lily came out looking sober and confused, in a clean white uniform.

The image of Miss Skinner swelled on him as he climbed the stairs. Angry and amused. Oh yes, she remembered everything. For instance, how you clung to me, Charles, and wanted to kill me, and to do things to my corpse, and how I held you off like a child. You and your father have really been too much for me. Much too much. Her mouth smelled horrible, as if she had been burning garbage in there. And she laughed and shook with rage at the same time.

When he burst into her room, she was quite small and ordinary-looking: asleep, with her mouth hanging slightly open. Looking small and ordinary was a shoddy trick. It would not affect his judgment in any way.

She stirred slightly, as if to welcome him, without actually waking up. He went over and imperiously kissed her. It was late afternoon now and the light was extraordinarily fine. He strolled, almost swaggered, to the window. He could see through the trees a sliver of water. He had come home now. All the time he had been supposedly getting well in New York, ice skating at Rockefeller Center and joining the Natural History Society, the other thing (disease was too tame a word for it) had been proceeding quietly. Until, by now, it reacted like a hair trigger.

After a while, he went downstairs and told Lily she could go out if she wanted to. Lily incongruously wanted to stay and talk. "She should have a nurse, but she hasn't any money at all. She hasn't paid me in six months. It's lucky she's dying, in a way."

"Yes, yes, of course." Charlie fumbled for his wallet. His allowance would run to a couple of drinks at least.

"All her old friends have died and she hasn't made any new ones. A lot of people think she's stuck up."

She looked at him with simple-minded cunning. She wanted to be in his good books, in case he dispensed some kind of patronage. A seedy, sniveling loyalty looked like her best bet. Charlie was disgusted. "You'd better get going," he said, handing her a five. She had frizzy red hair, and he wanted to plunge it in some kind of black dye. Along with her eyebrows. Give her some kind of definition. "I'll take care of Miss Skinner."

She left with a clumsy turn of speed, removing her white uniform and revealing a pink dress, which he also wanted to plunge in black dye. "I'll be here all evening," he called through the screen door. She seemed to be bobbing and weaving in anticipation: or perhaps she always walked like that.

When she had bumbled out of sight down the garden, he took out one of Miss Skinner's carving knives and sharpened it to a wild glow. This was something he had never had the courage to do before. He returned it glistening to the drawer, and felt luxurious about it; he could take knives or leave them alone. He had, in the past, made the mistake of tightening, of taking things too seriously; he should ride with these moods, humor them. Even enjoy them.

He was halfway up the stairs when he saw the fallacy of this. It was like humoring sex and thinking that that would be enough. He had touched the knife once, now he must touch it again. Such beautiful silver could not be ignored. There was a very sweet taste in his mouth right now as if a small duct of honey had opened in his cheek; humor me a little bit more, just one more little bit.

With the knife in his hand, he felt free to proceed up the stairs, and examine the other rooms, which he had always planned to do some time. They all seemed to be out of commission, with gray sheets thrown over the chairs and tables. Four-poster beds that you could cut the back of your knees on, a plush battle painting with two generals expiring at once, a landscape, a garden-scape. He looked at everything with a mild but feverish interest. The gray drop cloths had him almost shuddering.

He made it all the way up to the attic, where signs of Victorian childhood still lingered. Little old people at play, boys with side whiskers and hands that shook violently. There was an encrusted teddy bear, some peeling tin soldiers with arms, legs, heads shot away; a wooden sword. There was also a cache of real army junk, as if the Skinners had kept an arsenal up here to ward off the Rebels. Midgets deploying at the windows and out on the roof.

A real sword would be nice. But when he tried to lift one, it was unwieldy as a shovel. So he gave that up and went downstairs again with the dust still sweet in his nostrils: still carrying the carving knife: into Miss Skinner's bedroom.

She lay very still, with her long hard features drawn up in a kind of smile. There was something feminine, coquettish about her. He took her hand and studied the brown, mottled skin closely. It was a soft, half-dead hand, which could not fend him off for long this time. To think of what would happen after that was unworthy of both of them. He ran the knife across his wrist. With a little pressure, he could turn his whole arm scarlet. Then the other one. Then his white shirt.

But first, Miss Skinner, his companion. The correct thing was right through the heart. He looked at her chest speculatively: still not sure whether he meant any of this, or was just humoring his whim. With everyone dead or asleep, one could act out strange rituals, like putting on one's mother's clothes, desecrating holy pictures, etc. In a moment, he would know if that's what he was doing now, or something a little more serious.

He laid the knife on her chest, and realized how easy it would be to plunge it in and still not know whether he was being serious. He looked at her eyes, to see what she made of all this, and noticed that they were open: the cold blade on her skin must have galvanized her.

She was peering down over her folded chin to see what was on her chest. Her head dropped back and she seemed to resign herself to his next move. Unsurprised to the last. But then, with a great effort, she said, "Please don't, Charles. If you can help it." It sounded funny, even to him. "I'll be dead in a few hours," she added. "Can't you wait a little longer?"

It rather took the momentum out of things. He

said, impatiently, "What's the use, Miss Skinner? Next year or the year after—why not now? Together?"

"How about your mother?" she whispered.

"Oh, she expects it."

Miss Skinner seemed to sigh slightly, as if she couldn't think of any other arguments. "Look, please don't bother to talk if it hurts you," he said, suddenly genuinely solicitous. He wanted her to die happy, after all these years in this old house. He also wanted, urgently, to see what the knife could do. But he would wait if she liked.

He passed the time imagining, not dreaming, but painfully and awkwardly imagining, his father and Miss Skinner. Mr. Trimble was seventeen in this version, his costume still old-fashioned, with knickers, and a belt in the back; and his face was broad and troubled. In the movies, this boy would be telling his mother that he had just enlisted to give the Kaiser what-for. But in real life he was whispering gamier secrets.

Miss Skinner must have been powerfully persuasive in those days. Charlie could feel his father's indignation purring like a dynamo. Shoulders, hands bursting with strength. Of course, a drowning man would have certain problems that a knife man was spared. Charlie thought about this a minute. Miss Skinner was the key, she could tell him so much if she wanted to. Why was she lying there like that anyway?

He started to shake her shoulder, and then remembered that she wasn't well, and he patted it instead. This was a moment of slight coolness, like the eye of a fever. What was Miss Skinner's story? What would *she* tell the boys at school about her traumas and blocks? The Victorian midgets gathered round in a circle: tell us, Miss Skinner. What ails you? Why did you never leave this house, or get married? Why do crazy people turn to you so much? Miss Skinner wouldn't answer, and after a while the dwarfs began to grumble and plot. *This was not dreamed,* but laboriously imagined.

Her point about being dead in a few hours cut no mustard with him. If anything, it was an argument in his favor. Just so long as she was unconscious—he owed her that much. Her eyes were still glassily open: O.K., take your time, you old bitch. You old sweetheart. He understood now that his previous sessions with her had been rehearsals for this. Child's play. Now he was a man.

Another thing that seemed totally irrelevant was the question of why he was doing it. There were some things that were so clear, so right, that to explain them was coarse and unstylish. Miss Skinner would be the first to understand that. She taught him all he knew about taste. Hers was the only opinion that counted.

"You do understand, don't you?" he said. I realize you have to raise certain objections, but basically, you understand all right.

She was just staring at him now. The power of speech had gone, of movement gone, of thought probably gone. She was keeping her eyes open by main will power. She was stalling him. She was going to keep them open until she died.

He squeezed the knife, which still lay on her chest. But so long as she kept looking at him, it was hard to make his next move. All the life that was left in her had gathered in her eyes, which came at him now with physical force, nailing him, knifing him—not friendly, but quite malignant.

It struck him as he sat there at bay that she too had

a powerful gland of anger; perhaps this was what enabled her to deal with the Trimble boys. Hers against theirs, in silent combat. Of course she loved him—he had never questioned that. But now that she was down to her last gasp, she reached for the emotion that came easiest: rage.

He was locked in admiration, loathing, envy; cowering and snarling under the eye of the lion tamer. What terrible things had she conquered in herself that she could put him down so easily? Did she think she was stronger than the Trimble boys put together? Was that it? He wiped his mouth with his left hand, feeling he had to ask permission even for that, and it came away wet. He was dribbling or salivating heavily.

When the death rattle began, he didn't know what it was at first. He thought she was clearing her throat, snoring, or some combination of the two. It was very strange, observing her do this with her eyes wide open. A new fascination to keep him still.

At last she stopped, like someone plunging to a deeper level of sleep, and her mouth lolled open in a vacant grin of triumph. He reached roughly for her wrist, but couldn't find the pulse. Since he never could find his own pulse either, this was not conclusive. On the other hand, he sensed that he could not be moving so freely if she were still alive: thousands of golden threads had snapped, releasing his arms and hands. He bent over her chest and put his ear to both sides, not sure where the heart was supposed to be. No sign of it anywhere.

The old lady had foiled him. She might have to pay for this. He took the knife calmly and pushed it slightly up and in. It grazed the skin and a crimson freshet bubbled onto the blade. Dead or not dead? Where was the heartbeat anyway? In her eyes?

He wanted to do things with the knife now, things which he didn't even name to himself because they would have shocked him, but things that would come to him as he went along. But in another brief gust of coolness, he saw that one couldn't always be noble, one must make shrewd concessions. If he left her alone now, nobody would look at that scratch on her chest. Miss Skinner had died manifestly, overwhelmingly of old age. No super detective was going to look for murder weapons. I don't even want her property, which is also dead and worthless. They can't pin anything on me, if I stop now.

He must either do all those things with the knife, or none of them. He balanced the handle on his palm. He had drawn blood, was that enough? A pity some further compromise could not be arranged. He was tired, her death had tired him. Her body was heavy as old iron when he tried to move it slightly. She was dead for sure.

It dawned on him that perhaps the game was over. Miss Skinner had won quite fairly. He was drained of strength, hers and his, and wanted badly to rest. So he embraced her gently, kissing both cheeks, and went out in the hall. Should he keep a vigil till morning? Sit up all night with a dead woman? The idea suddenly gave him the creeps.

He was aware for the first time of being in a dark house with a corpse. The thing to do in that case was to get away. He bumped down the stairs and out the front door, flung the knife into some brambles—the place was a wasteland and you didn't need to look for a hiding place.

There was no transport at this time of night; he would simply have to walk the fifteen miles to Trenton and wait for a train. Good. He was too tired to do any more with Miss Skinner, but he had more than enough energy for that. He set out vigorously, cursing Miss Skinner and making gibbering love to her in the same harsh breath. All the houses looked abandoned, even the ones that weren't; but he imagined people sleeping in corners, under sacks, behind webbed, cracked windows; old caretakers, deserted children. He could make fast work of them, leave the place properly dead instead of half dead.

As he prowled along in the bright moonlight, he felt like a fox among chicken coops. He had the secret, he could do it. He could stop time, stop the world from turning. He knew, and Miss Skinner knew. But his momentum was set, toward the outskirts of town. And as he lurched along, he felt the brace on his scalp loosening. This goddam stinking cemetery was almost behind him now. New York, white and gleaming, was somewhere ahead. He gave a crazy howl, which carried back through the trees, and must have terrified the people crouched in their houses down on the floorboards. Charles Trimble had decided to spare them. Trimble, the Lord of Life.

He slept in the waiting room and a man in uniform woke him and asked if he was all right. Seventeen was what he was, and slightly overweight and anxious to get to New York. His mother would ask after Miss Skinner, and he would say, what? I think she died. Something like that. He would not go back for the funeral, to see the old ladies gloating. He would stay in New York, and take it very easy for a while.

Nowadays, whenever Charles Trimble reads about some child murdering his parents, or a teenager assaulting a crone in Prospect Park, he wants to present himself at court as an expert witness. But then he gets muddled. He doesn't know what he would say. He doesn't know what it is that he knows about it.

In the last twenty years he hasn't had the faintest relapse. For a while his memory resumed the business of shaping it into a story. Then, at age thirty-two or thereabouts, he felt he was finished. His mind froze on an official version, and he expects no further revisions.

During those years he has lived with his mother, become a history instructor at Barnard and developed a bad habit of falling in love with his students. He has not felt it quite safe to marry, so he has slipped into a seasonal routine of breaking off affairs and starting new ones. He is deft with girls, tender and slightly aloof. He is a man with a secret—perhaps he keeps a wife elsewhere, perhaps a humble attack of mumps has left him sterile. He isn't telling.

He senses at times that he has picked up some of the superficiality of the professional cocksman, but superficiality suits him fine. Knowing what he knows. Or rather, what he forgets. He never goes near Tewksbury, or Philadelphia for that matter, for fear he might remember. To remember a thing like that is to experience it again; there is no other way to remember it.

Recently, his life has changed. He has met a girl with a strong will who wants to marry him. She won't sleep with him on any terms. Exciting and tiresome. Furthermore, she wants to scour the morbidity from his system. He has told her most of his story—parts of it he can rattle off quite glibly, other parts of it, understandably, he cannot bring himself to say to any-one—but in any event: "Twenty years ago, Charlie, twenty long years ago. You're not the same person now. You are one of the healthiest people I've ever met."

In this she is backed up by a psycho-therapist whom Charlie frequented for a while. "The will to self-destruction in puberty is not uncommon. The need to expiate guilt takes different forms. No need to expect a recurrence." Charlie stopped seeing Dr. Mungo after a while, mainly because he had not brought himself to tell the doctor quite everything, so that their sessions were rather expensive charades, and partly because he thought the doctor had it all wrong anyway, and that they were both misleading each other. If his memory of Tewksbury was incorrigibly distorted, it was partly the doctor's doing: Mungo's inflexible Freudianism had worked its way in there, providing motives and even feelings that Charlie half believed he had had and half disbelieved: which added a religion-like vagueness to the whole affair.

What has convinced Charlie to go ahead with the marriage, outside of rampaging lust and boredom at breaking in a new girl, and fear of losing his job (all rather mild motives, oddly enough), is that he *feels* so healthy now. He has far fewer than the normal quota of hang-ups, is, if anything, "too sane." He is sure that other people have secrets as peculiar as his and are hiding them constantly. His fiancée also wants them to pay a visit to Tewksbury, so he can exorcise that too. She says, "Do you want to be some sort of funny old man, sleeping with a night light all your life, because Bluebeard is going to come and get you?" He honestly cannot see why they shouldn't go. Just a blank-looking house, in a blank-looking town. He cannot even remember what Miss Skinner looked like, let alone why he was concerned about her. His mother still has title to the house, so he might even stay there for a while and exorcise things well and truly. They are going down in a couple of weeks to look things over.

He is really exhilarated about his life at the moment. His fiancée hits it off famously with his mother. Charlie is going to church again, because Jane thinks that a man should have some religion; and the new ecumenical Catholicism has proved much less spooky than the older brand, so that so far he has felt no ill results. Jane is a strong woman, who can handle herself and him. She wants children and so, with faint misgivings, does he. He is anxious to know what he will make of a son.

Their friends, who live in the present, not the past, think it a fine match; possibly a little dull and frictionless. But again, it can't be too dull for Charlie, who still gets a kick out of ordinary spring days and minor historical discoveries, and thanks God every Sunday for he knows not quite what. He sincerely believes that everything is going to work out. As to that, we shall just have to wait and see.

The
Blacking
Factory

prologue

James Bannister III owns and operates two radio stations out of Salome, California, not far from Los Angeles. His audience consists mostly of old people who sit in the kitchen all day, drinking coffee and fussing with the dials. Ordinary radios do not seem to pick up these pinpoints of sound, the needle has to know its way; and even then it takes a deal of twiddling by a practiced hand to complete the mission.

Bannister talks on each of these stations for upwards of two hours a day. He is obviously an educated man and he knows that to many people small radio stations are a joke, like soapboxes. He also happens to believe in them. He says that radio listeners, for all their crotchets, are the only real listeners left, and he has the mail to prove it. Ardent, painstaking mail, wobbling above and below the lines, yet more carefully wrought, more soberly committed than anything in the whole lives of the TV watchers. "These are better people," he says simply. "Probably no less intelligent, and better, more serious."

Well, nobody wants to argue with Bannister, about that or anything else. He is a tireless arguer, fast on his feet and logical as a metronome. Every now and then, a fresh guest is ground up on his radio show—usually a guest who comes on believing that Bannister's politics are naïve. So unless you are very sure of yourself and very long-winded, you tend to concede him his point, along with his eyrie on the radio dial.

When not arguing, Bannister is on the shy side, given to sudden bursts of wit which sound harsher than they are because of his explosive delivery. At parties he is a notorious examiner of book jackets and stray magazines, if there are any about. Oddly enough he goes to a lot of parties, has never been known to turn down an invitation in fact, and has arrived at more than one with a high temperature and streaming eyes. He stands around patiently as if it were a church service, and is always among the last to leave.

He lives by himself in an old-fashioned apartment on the edge of town, keeping in excellent shape, with isometric exercises and a landlocked rowing machine. There is no visible girl friend, and you can never find an ashtray. His friendships tend to be decided for him on political lines, which he professes to deplore. He says that liberals are the intolerant ones—he likes them but they don't like him. He says he is sick of labels anyway.

The nastiest thing you can say about Bannister is that he has a slight English accent. (It all sounds the same in Salome, anyway.) This would be guaranteed to nettle Jim because he is actually the last of the great Anglophobes. It is his abiding belief that England has sold its soul in some particularly loathsome deal, and that Americans should keep clear of the stinking remains. "There is something sick there," he says. And again: "We're better *people* than they are."

His hatred of England flirts with being a fixation. When he gets within sniffing range of things British his voice ripens like a passion fruit. "Beatles," he'll say. "They're sending us their *beatles* now. Next they'll be sending us their maggots and their worms." "Latest word from the Funeral Home. Her Majesty gave an address today to the Royal Society of Perverts and Freeloaders. A gangrenous occasion, it was generally agreed" . . . Someone wrote in recently to say that the Redcoats, after all, were still some distance from Salome, and Bannister made a big thing of this on the air, saying that, what with the prime minister's hand in your pocket, who needed Redcoats—or perhaps the Redcoats were some new singing group? Robbing us blind that way. All in all, you have to think twice before you send a joke to Bannister.

Offstage, he is notable for a dogged sense of privacy. No matter how well you get to know him, he will not discuss his interior affairs with you. Nor does he care to hear *your* revelations. He seems to feel that there is something corrupt about all this self-exposure. Something dangerous to the Republic.

What is known is that he is the son of James Bannister II, the big New York real-estate man. Bannister II is a well-known ladies'-man, still active in his upper sixties: three times married and divorced, after a slow start (Hal Chester at the *Salome Sentinel* has the dates). The first Mrs. Bannister, Jim's mother, is rumored to spend most of her time in sanatoriums on some unspecified charge. If Bannister II has other children, the news hasn't reached Salome.

Jim never refers to either parent, but it is generally assumed that his America-first politics are not unpleasing to his father. At any rate, Bannister II is suspected of putting up some of the money for the radio stations. Mrs. Bannister is known only by her picture on Jim's piano, a curiously misty, old-fashioned one that looks as if it was taken before the First World War. Hal Chester's wife Clara believes that part of Jim still wanders the sanatoriums with his mother—but Clara Chester is another problem.

Jim Bannister's future is as clouded as his past. It seems unlikely that a man of his gifts will be content to keep his operation so small indefinitely. The local liberals consider him a real menace. They say that he is amassing contributions from the bless-you-son crowd and that he will break out any day now in a whole rash of radio stations, swamping the country in Bannister-style fascism. The local conservatives feel that there would be more chance of this (or its more favorably phrased equivalent) if he got off England for a while and turned his mind to local interests.

As a more or less liberal and a more or less friend, Hal Chester of the *Sentinel* spends a good deal of time defending Jim. "He is not your usual crank," says Chester. "He is a decent man who deserves a hearing." Chester's friends say, "Nuts to you, Hal—that's the kind of thing people used to say about Mussolini! . . . Suppose next you're going to say that he loves children." Chester: "Well, as a matter of fact . . ." As one of the few people in Salome who is relatively unsolved, Jim comes in for a good deal of discussion. Most of it to little purpose.

So there he is, still young (some place in the late thirties by the look of him), rich "nice"-looking, an uncertain quantity whose importance is what you make it. Some people feel he has the makings of greatness. Some who peg him a little lower than that are still happy to find a facsimile of a rational man on the right—compared with some of the others, Jim is a relatively civilizing influence, who helps to keep the yahoos in line. And still others say that's the most dangerous kind, the plausible kind. It is generally agreed that his broadcasts have been getting a little strident lately, but this can partly be put down to the medium. Jim is quite willing to discuss the phenomenon: he says that radio broadcasting has some of the effects of solitary confinement. He is manifestly not a common or garden nut.

Hear him on that for a moment: "This morning I got a letter from a man purporting to be a psychiatrist, offering me a free analysis. Very kind of him, I must say. A new concept in health service. He said that he was fascinated by the right-wing syndrome . . . Now why do you suppose my learned friend has discovered a right-wing syndrome, but no left-wing syndrome? Could one of his eyes be missing? Why analyze me when he might be analyzing a big man like Walter Lippmann?" . . . Well, maybe it's the setting. Lippman appears in serious-looking newspapers, whereas you usually catch Bannister on your Aunt Minnie's baling-wire set right after Jack Meredith's Hour of Faith or Doctor Price's attack on the cereal companies. There is a whirring and whining along the dial as Auntie gropes for inspiration; and the sound of bad acoustics in ramshackle studios. And finally Jim comes on.

"In this country," he might be saying, "and especially in the *West* of this country, Christendom has been given a second chance. People talk about Europe's wonderful postwar recovery, but to me this is no more than the last twitch of a corpse. No, I'm not talking about sex and I'm not talking about loose living. I'm talking about things like corruption of the heart; cynicism and snobbery and hypocrisy. I don't mind a girl in a bikini. But I don't want to hear that it's the Baroness Rotternburg. And I certainly don't want to hear that it's her *brother*. You have to apologize for even caring about these things any more. In the East, you are looked on as some kind of a yokel with straws in his hair. Yet what is more important than the quality of our national life? A little radio station in California may not be the ideal place to say it. But where else *can* you say it these days? Without being laughed at?"

Put like that, it is hard to disagree with. He takes you off guard by being literate. Bannister wins the arguments and loses the wars.

"The big Eastern magazines like to shed a tear now and then for the national morality. And you'll find that they usually shed it right next to a story about the latest pansy singing rage from England, or the latest trollop from Paris. You know, the one with the million-dollar death wish. What do they think they're doing? What do they think national morality is all about? . . . Let me tell you some of the things I think it's about. I think it's the way we talk to each other in the street, the things we laugh at: I think it is a quality of heart. We're not ready for decadence yet. We're not ready for old families with chinless children, or limp wrists, or boys who look like girls . . . Don't forget, there was a sweetness in this country once. There was joy in being a boy or girl in America at one time. You say to me, that's old-fashioned, and I can only say to you, is that bad? Is that really so terrible? It worked once. We liked it. Why this itch to change? Europe has changed and changed again. You can go over there if you like and see what change does for you. Look at the new houses outside Rome. Made of tin, chewing gum and adultery. They won't last as long as the Forum or the Coliseum. You can look at the stately homes of England. For fifty cents any pansy with hair down to his waist and a mind like a sewer can go and giggle at the past . . . I don't say we should have no change at all. But let us make our *own* changes. We're young. We don't need a senile old continent to show us how to do it. We don't have to learn tricks from a lecherous old duffer who has to find ways to stimulate his appetites"—your aunt purses her lips; but it is probably no better than those people deserve—"a clown with a painted face, a harlot that we fled four hundred years ago, and who is just beginning to catch up with us."

You listen to the country sounds through the window and the honest clack of the kitchen clock, and you think, yes, there is a sweetness here. Bannister may have something at that. It's silly prejudice not to give him a hearing: just because he talks at crank's length on a crank's medium.

"If I may be personal for a moment. You grow up in this country loving certain things. And you, as I say, grow up and people tell you, oh all that has changed—that was the twenties, or the thirties, or the war years, or the postwar years. You look around for the thing that you loved and it's gone.

"And in its place, what do you find? Some verminous import, some hybrid. Pop art—to show that we too can learn to hate beauty and life, 'Camp,' whatever that is. The 'jet set,' 'The Theatre of the Absurd.' I won't go through the whole list for you. You can get it from *Life* or *The Saturday Evening Post*.

"Anyway, when *I* grew up, I found I wasn't ready for this new country, this Lilliput. I wanted the thing I had loved, the freshness and joy of a young country, my country. And I came out here to the West. And here I stay."

And so on. At the end of it—after hearing him denounce cynicism and snobbery in that slightly affected accent (which he would probably give an arm to get rid of)—you can't help remembering that many country people consider him slightly Europeanized himself, hardly better than a limey. They may agree with him wholeheartedly, but there is a stubborn strain of mistrust—as if they would rather hear this stuff from one of their own. And that is, finally, the thing that may limit his effectiveness, and keep him, for all his gifts, in the minor leagues.

Hal Chester has been curious about Jim for some time, hoping some day to write a depth story for the paper, and he has done all the routine scratching around, trying to discover what makes Bannister tick. He managed to dig out an old profile of Jim's father in *The New Yorker* and from this morass of trivia was able to discover that Bannister II was, and presumably still is, a stout man with a long list of clubs, a chairman of many boards and a somewhat flashy dresser. Also, a self-made man, working off a middle-class base. The "II" after his name seems to be an afterthought. He made his big killing in the postwar boom—before that, he was a small, undistinguished operator in the New England area. Jim was mentioned only in passing, but whether this casualness was *The New Yorker*'s or Mr. Bannister's, Hal could not make out.

Interestingly, Bannister II was quoted as taking no special interest in politics, either at home or abroad. Perhaps his son has been serving as his mouthpiece in this respect. The elder Bannister gave the investigator an overall impression of shrewdness very well masked, clothed, as the writer put it, in coarse loud broadcloth. "I have never tried to run my son's life," was the only quote pertaining to Jim.

None of this has proved very helpful, at least to an amateur gumshoe like Hal Chester. Mr. Bannister II looks as if he might be a red herring altogether. Jim more or less follows the right-wing line on economics, which could be construed as a gesture to the old man, possibly even as part payment for the radio stations; but economic theory plays a comparatively small role in his rhetoric. He talks occasionally about the old village store balancing its books, etc., but this is filler material: he goes on about the smell of sawdust and the row of patent medicines and the salty old fellow bent over his ledger (*"balancing his books*, you'll notice") but has no time for statistics or economic *minutiae*.

Some people, including conservatives, say this is just talk anyway, that Bannister never saw a store like that in his life, "not where he came from." But some people will say anything to malign Bannister. Every time he carves up an opponent, they feel personally threatened, even if they happen to be on his side. And for all his charm, and his almost excessive politeness, there is this foreign thing about him that nags them. What does he want, what is he doing here? Although Jim has explained over and over that he is here because he believes in the West, etc., a lot of folk remain unconvinced. It doesn't sound like their idea of a reason at all.

Jim does seem to take this Western business quite seriously. He comes to Chester's office at least once a week (at first Hal had to go after him, but that has changed) and asks questions about local history, crop reports, real-estate developments . . . He is unfailingly courteous, although, like other public speakers, not unfailingly attentive. Clara Chester reckons he thinks he ought to know this stuff, just as he thinks he ought to go to parties—but again, that's a typical Clara Chester opinion. In fact, he does use a good deal of Hal's lint-picking as flavoring matter for his broadcasts.

On evenings when he isn't working or socializing, he sometimes plays chess with Hal. Clara Chester, doubled up with theories and suspicions, watches him closely for signs of insanity. Her husband tries to use their relaxed moments to ferret information. "What have you got against England?" he will ask casually. Jim shrugs, moves his pawn, suddenly asks for more coffee. Clara starts up as if from a trance: she has been staring at Jim for the last twenty minutes, baffled by his apparent normality.

Occasionally, Hal returns the calls. Jim's apartment is scrupulously neat, decorated with early American prints and lined with books on the Civil War, all as private and sealed off as himself. He does not drink alcohol, but offers some to his guest. They sit. Jim's voice is a little higher than it is on the airwaves. By God, it *does* sound English: Chester has a sudden crazy idea that it is meant to; that in some subterranean part of his mind Jim likes to be taken for an Englishman. This probably means that Hal has been talking to Clara too much lately. To change the subject he says, "I see you shaved your mustache, Jim." "Yes, I noticed it was the only one in Salome." "It looked, you'll pardon the expression, British?" "Yes, I guess it does out here. Although mustaches occur pretty frequently in American history, you'll find." Jim has an almost opulent sense of humor about himself. He pursues the joke like a terrier. "American mustaches have played their part on the world scene. Clark Gable's mustache, of course was one of the great mustaches of all time. And Teddy Roosevelt, *there* was a mustache for you" . . . there is no fire and brimstone in these conversations, just rather conscientious small-talk. He is impenetrably unpretentious about his work, if it happens to come up. "These things have to be said by someone," he explains. "And I seem to be the one." This from the man who is feared by the local liberals.

As Jim closes the ledger on mustaches, Hal feels unaccountably a kind of wistfulness for his own past —an attic smelling of fresh laundry—and he thanks Jim for it. In Hal's private book Jim at his best is one of the pleasantest companions he knows: certainly the pleasantest he has ever encountered on the nut-wing of the far right, where the conversation usually proceeds (so Hal believes) in grunts. He believes that Jim is a gentleman.

Yet for all his private charm, he can be a tiger on the Salome airwaves; only recently he derided the mayor, an alleged friend, in language that ripped and hissed like a cat. And perhaps he *is* getting more ambitious. There is talk of a campaign for Congress. Of a newspaper merger. Of more radio stations. This may be just the liberals up to their old tricks, frightening themselves, but Frank Strange at the bank says, listen to his voice. It's more eager than it used to be. He's about to make his move.

Jim is most comfortable talking in lengthy set-pieces, and when you have had enough of these you leave. His farewells are the most excessively polite things he does. It occurs to Hal on the way out that Bannister may be trying to acquire political charm, which has an artificial effect at first on anybody, like a set of false teeth. Whatever it is, it has not lost Jim any fans. If anything, his audience is growing. And some of the local rich people have begun to take him up seriously, inviting him out for weekends, etc. God knows what he will be like in twenty years' time if he keeps this up.

The only really revealing thing that Hal Chester has on Jim is something that came out unexpectedly on a recent broadcast. Jim was interviewing a genuine Englishman who was passing through on a lecture tour, a novelist called Walters. Walters sounded just like the kind of arrogant, petty fellow who likes to tangle with smalltown celebrities and remind them of their place. It was as if England itself had turned up, demanding an explanation. But Jim was totally unflustered by this. "I don't know why you pick on poor Europe. It seems to me quite the other way—that we are the simple wholesome people who have been corrupted by *you.*"

"Yes," said Jim. "I know that argument. It's the conventional one, isn't it? Of course, I don't like the things we've sent you very much. But they come back much worse, don't they? Rock 'n' roll, for instance, was simply country music, until you got hold of it . . ."

"Oh, come now, Mr. er . . . Bannister—you're not

going to blame us for *rock 'n' roll,* are you? This is really too much. England has been blamed for a number of things in her time, but really . . ."

Jim laughed good-naturedly. For a moment Hal almost forgot which of them was which. "It isn't just rock 'n' roll, of course," he said. "That was just a minor example. I'm talking about cultural decadence . . ."

"You mean the New York School of painting?"

"And amorality and cynicism and exploitation."

"You mean Hollywood. No, I'm sorry. Do go on."

"No, I don't mean Hollywood. A harmless rather touching aberration, that's all Hollywood is or ever was—and long gone to its reward, you'll find if you keep up with these things. I'm told that the nastiest thing in Hollywood is the English colony, but I'm not talking about that either. No—I mean the English press, which is fifty times meaner and dirtier and more cynical than Hollywood ever was. I mean mods and rockers and subdebs. The fungus that seems to accumulate on every fashion over there."

There was a pause. And then the condescending diagnosis. "Do you know what the trouble with you is, Bannister? I expect that some Englishman was beastly to you, at an impressionable age. We can be beastly, I don't deny it. It makes up for not having power, I suppose: And I've heard that some victims of English beastliness never recover from it."

"It isn't that simple," said Jim. There was a sudden harsh quality in his voice, as if he had been waiting for this man for years. "Apart from anything else, you people are not that effective. You think you've withered someone with an insult and he hasn't even understood what you've said."

"Oh? Then why do you hate England? If it isn't impolite of an Englishman to ask?"

Jim sounded almost surprised. "I don't hate England, Mr. Walters. I love it."

Fruitiest astonishment. "Excuse me—perhaps I'm on the wrong program? I hadn't gathered that at all. You *love* England, you say?"

"I don't love what it's become of course. And I don't want anything like that to happen here. But England itself . . ."

"I see. And how do you detach England itself from what England has become? You must be an extraordinarily subtle judge."

"I know England."

"Oh, indeed. Our films, I suppose. Our wonderful police."

"I was at school there."

"You were?" Lip-licking relish. "How extraordinarily interesting. How long, may I ask?"

"Long enough."

"Yes, but exactly *how* long?"

"One term and a bit, actually."

"I see." Sound of nodding. "What an acute boy you must have been. And what was the school, pray tell, that gave you this, mer-mer, microcosm of England?"

"Sopworth College."

"*No!* Not Sopworth College. I don't believe it." Sounds of gurgling amusement. Bannister is *right* about these people. "Well, of course. That explains everything! Sopworth College."

"What do you mean by that, Mr. Walters?"

"Well, of all the medieval institutions—no, *pre*-medieval institutions—Dark Ages institutions—no, *pre*-Dark Ages institutions—pre-Druidic, pre-Pleistocene, pre-creation . . . I hold no brief for any of the older public schools, but even among those—Sopworth *College*, oh, dear, oh dear."

"Come now, Mr. Walters. Pull yourself together. Pull your rhetoric together at least." Bannister sounded peeved, as if he cared about his old school.

"I exaggerate, of course. But you can't judge England by Sopworth College, old chap, honestly you can't. There's nothing else like it. I mean of all the creaking, middle-class, snobbish, imitation, mer-mer, pseudo . . . and of course I suppose you were there during the scruffy time just after the war. You poor blighter. You really have all my sympathy. On behalf of Her Majesty's government I should like to extend '. . . Had I but world enough and time, I dare say . . .'"

"It isn't that simple," said Jim in a bemused voice. "There are other things."

The Englishman had to rush and catch a boring plane after that, and the subject has not been referred to since on the Bannister programs. Hal keeps meaning to bring it up, but cannot quite bring himself to. Other people must feel the same way. There is something a little indecent about it, perhaps.

one

In the spring of 1946 James Bannister III moved across the ocean to England, with all his possessions, including a baseball glove, a pair of ice skates and a Bix Beiderbecke record that got broken in transit. It had been a high-speed decision, which hit Jimmy so sharply that he didn't feel a thing at first: a swirl of arrangements, passport photos, purchase of suitcase, urgent trips downtown, several light showers of good wishes, and suddenly he and his father were up in the air talking to a stewardess and down again, in a gray, quiet country, eating water-cress sandwiches.

When Jimmy came to, he found his father having an exploratory interview with a cadaverous school official three days before term started. Consciousness came back in cautious waves. Jimmy became seriously aware of his clothes, item by item, of the sports coat with the comb sticking out of the breast pocket, of the two-tone shoes; the room began to fill up with real furniture—a leather armchair which creaked every time his father leaned forward to make a point, a hardwood chair for himself—and not that snythetic airplane stuff; and the official had thickness, although not much. The people Jimmy had seen in motion had no thickness at all. The official sat with the light behind him, forming a stark outline, like an old turkey, against the black bars on his window.

For the moment Jimmy was tied up with these perceptions and not too attentive to the talk. The official turned out to be the headmaster: naturally enough, but Jimmy hadn't grasped this at first, in his travel bemusement.

"Back home, Jimmy was asking if he could start using the car next year," Mr. Bannister said. "So I thought it was high time I brought him over here." Jimmy noted a false heartiness about his father, sitting there in his gray worsteds. Travel had unhinged the two of them.

The headmaster nodded. "The English boy matures somewhat more slowly than his American counterpart." His fingertips drummed viciously at each other. His voice was the wildest thing Jimmy had ever heard.

"Well, youth is our most precious possession, isn't it? No sense growing up before we have to."

"Quite," said the headmaster. Jimmy had an idea that this was probably the wrong way to talk to this man. But the right way might take some finding.

"Of course intellectually and culturally British boys

are streets ahead of ours," Mr. Bannister said desperately, with a look of stark appeal at both of them.

"It's very kind of you to say so."

"Jimmy here is bright enough, but he could use some discipline. Don't be afraid to give him plenty of work."

Oh, this was ridiculous. Jimmy gazed at the window bars. Had anyone ever broken out of this place? he wondered. Or did the warden shoot them all down? The headmaster appeared to be smiling. "I think the boy will find his time sufficiently occupied."

Mr. Bannister talked with his son for a few minutes in the hall outside, in the same slightly hysterical way. "First-rate man that. Fine mind." He seemed to be trying to make a sale, "The British education is the finest in the world." Jimmy hoped his father would feel better when he got back to the hotel, or wherever he was going next.

They walked to the end of the quadrangle, where the hired car was waiting, and Mr. Bannister rather unexpectedly shook hands. Jimmy could not remember having touched his father's hand before. It had a pulpy feel to it. His father announced he was taking the next train back to London and clambered into the car, leaving Jimmy rather emphatically alone. As if some drawbridge had been retracted three thousand miles.

As he reviewed the data, Jimmy realized that in his fifteen and a half years he had had only a modest experience of being alone at all. He had been alone on a train to Florida two months ago, squatting among the GI's and their duffel bags, envying them their recent war. And he had been alone in a nightclub just last week with his friend Forrest Tuckerman trying to con the management into serving them rye and ginger ale. And of course he had been alone many times in the apartment while his father was out on his appointments. But this was aloneness on a new scale.

The best thing to do was to get moving. He decided to hang a left from the front door. The school was virtually deserted, and his feet crashed like wrecking balls as he moved off down a long, narrow hallway. "We are now in the death house in Sing Sing," he said, testing the echo. The walls were bare, except for an infinity of black doors with white numbers on them. He opened one of these at random and peeked in: desks and a blackboard facing each other in grim showdown. "This place spooks me, spooks me," he and the corridor said.

"Is that you, Bannister?" The headmaster's thin face and shining spectacles swiveted around the door at him. What was he doing in there? Would he have been behind any door that Jimmy happened to open? He spoke from the back of his long throat. An hour before, Jimmy had been introduced by his first name. But now it was the coldest of "Bannister's."

"I guess so."

"I guess so, sir."

"I guess so, sir."

"Getting the hang of things, are you?"

"Uh-huh."

"Did you speak?"

"Er—I mean yes sir, I am." The headmaster was making notations in a small black book. Numbering the desks, it looked like. There seemed no point in staying for this.

Out of doors all was gray and windy. But a change from the clammy old building. Jimmy rambled doggedly, to keep thinking at bay. Over cricket pitches, mildly wondering what the shaved parts in the middle were for (stomach operations, it looked like), past squash courts, into a genuine garden. The grass was dazzling, a shade of green he had never seen before.

He stepped over a flower bed as carefully as he could to avoid walking all the way round.

"Where are you going, you bloody young clot?"

A beefy boy in shorts (Jim didn't believe any of this for a moment) was lying on his stomach against a bank of tulips, clutching a pair of binoculars. He was of a shape Jimmy had never seen before.

"No place special. Just looking around."

"Well, you're not supposed to trample on the flower beds, like a bloody great elephant, and you're not supposed to go into the woods like a blasted young nymph. Otherwise feel free to come and go as you please." The boy drew a tired breath. "Until, that is to say, term time—at which point this becomes the master's garden and a prefect with a flaming sword and a busby hat stands guard over it. Any more questions?"

"No, your fatness," said Jimmy, whipping out a phrase Sam Pieper had once used on him, in his mysterious chubby period two years ago.

"And don't, I beseech you, try sarcasm. Your mouth is the wrong shape for it." Jimmy was puzzled: how did you answer a line like that? He groped for a riposte.

"Who are you, anyway?" he shot back finally.

"I just happen to be a prefect, that's *all*. Now buzz off and don't be tiresome."

"A prefect? Is that good?"

"Actually quite tremendous. Yes, oh indeed yes. If you fancy power, in ungovernable quantities."

"What can you do?"

"Just about anything, actually. What house are you in?"

"I don't know."

"What do you mean you don't know? Are you in Frisby, Upjohn, Cornwallis, or Farnsworth? Didn't Dr. Rabelais mumble anything to you about houses?"

"Who's Dr. Rabelais?" said Jimmy.

"Oh my God, impenetrable ignorance. Where does one begin?" He shook his head until the jowls rattled. "Buzz off now; be a *nice* little intellectual disaster area, won't you? Oh—and try to do something about that mouth, will you?"

"I don't have to take that stuff from you," said Jimmy.

"Oh, indeed you do, yes," said the fat boy, and he raised his binoculars to indicate dismissal. I could break him in two, thought Jimmy—but there was probably a rule against it. Some drops shook loose from the dark sky, and Jimmy returned to the gray building with his shoulders hunched, confused by the prevailing aimlessness and sorry his father had hurried off so quickly. He would have to find out from somebody whether he really had to take stuff from this guy. It seemed like a pretty obscene arrangement.

There were twelve boys in the dining hall that evening, bunched at the end of a long hardwood table: a table that cried out for a penknife. The meal was so bad that it had to be a mistake. Nobody could have planned all those potatoes. The fat boy sat at the far end chewing angrily.

"Who's that guy?" whispered Jimmy to a pale fellow next to him.

"That's the 'Brute,' otherwise known as 'Birdseed'

and the 'Yellow-chested thrippet.' You have a fairly wide choice."

"Has he got a real name too? Or haven't they gotten around to that?"

"Wagstaff—funny enough by itself, you might say. But we leave nothing alone around here, all must be embroidered. Fuss, fuss, fuss."

"I found him lying on his gut in the flower bed. Could that be right?"

"Yes, that's quite normal in his case. He comes here early every term to glare at the birds. Poor little devils. You're American, I take it."

"Yes. Listen— He says he's a prefect. What does that mean?"

"It means he can flail you from morning to night, if he feels like it, with the headmaster's undisguised approval. This is a thoroughly medieval country, you understand. Light years behind the civilized world."

"And I can't flail him back?"

"Of course not. That would be anarchy, dash it."

"And is Wagstaff one of the worst?"

"Well, one doesn't call a man the 'Brute' for nothing I suppose. But he's not brawny enough to be the worst. The 'Basher' in Cornwallis, now, is a true gorilla, and not one of your impostors," said the pale boy. "I have scars that light up at night from the Basher." He didn't seem to want to talk any more, and Jimmy finished his starchy meal in silence.

That night Jimmy slept alone in a barracks-like dormitory belonging to Frisby house. The sheets were like cold sandpaper, and a harsh wind raked him all night. It was a comedown from his father's apartment on Eighty-fourth Street but no doubt it was better than the Army. Jimmy's thoughts had been preying much on the Army for the last year. In the morning,

Wagstaff came and shook him awake and went away without a word. He appeared to be fairly boiling with anger and resentment: as if waking Jimmy was the last straw.

After the quietest of breakfasts, Jimmy went for yet another squishy walk on the grounds. He got as far as the woods, and sat on the wet grass that fringed the trees. There was nothing to see for miles, only the slate-gray buildings, and of course it was raining again. The school buildings did remind him of the state penitentiary, right down to the bars on the ground-floor windows. Sopworth College—even the name was wet. Well, it was all right if you liked a quiet life. The anesthesia of travel and novelty had worn off almost completely by now, and he tried to remember what the point was of his being here. "Fine education, first-rate mind." Was that all?

He pictured his father scurrying into the hired car and telling the driver to be off, before Jimmy came to and started asking questions. . . . It was really strange of his father to pull a thing like this without discussion. Usually he consulted Jimmy rather anxiously about decisions concerning himself. Yet there had been, Jim swore, no hint of this at the beginning of the winter. It had started out as an absolutely normal winter. His father had been working hard and nervously and staying out late, but there was certainly nothing strange about that. Jim was even working a little himself at that time. Wilbur de Forest was a mild private school that didn't expect much, but second-year high was a mite tougher than first.

To compensate, he really felt like a high-school boy for the first time, and not a displaced eighth-grader. He didn't know what he would feel like over here. Back at W. D. Junior High (two "rahs" and a Fig

Newton), he had felt well and truly entrenched. It was the first time since infancy that he had stayed in the same school for two years. His clique had formed and hardened. And with the war over at last, he no longer belonged to a nothing age group. The too-young-to-fight, too-young-even-to-carry-a-ration-book crowd. The pin-prick shortages which his father was always carrying on about were being lifted one by one. A great new day was dawning.

Come to think of it, this was kind of a lousy time to be leaving the country. It hadn't struck him before that he would not be taking part in the postwar boom; that he would have to sit the whole thing out in this peculiar place. He began to feel sorry for himself, the dampness was soaking into his bones. But surely, he told himself quickly, they would have some kind of boom of their own over here. He didn't know anything about the place, but peacetime must include some kicks.

He had two more interviews to get through with management. The first was with the housemaster of Frisby, a pipe-and-brown-tweeds man. A heavy breather with whiskery nostrils.

"Ah, Bannister." He consulted his lists. "Angel, Appleby, here we are, *Ban*nister." He puffed his pipe and made a tick on his lists. "Settling in all right, are you, Bannister?"

"Sure."

"I think you'll find that the word 'sir' does wonders here."

"Yes, sir."

"It will probably take you a little time to get used to our ways. Come to me if you have any problems. That's what I'm here for, you know . . . Oh, and we'll have to get you some respectable clothes. . . ."

"Yes, sir." What kind of problem would you bring to this man? The housemaster was back at his lists again, making little marks. He looked up. "Well, that's all, Bannister."

"Er, thank you, er, sir." The housemaster nodded, and Jimmy tried to pull the door open. "Push," said the housemaster.

He simply didn't believe it.

The second interview was at the school infirmary. He had to register with the matron, a burly character in white starch, stiff as knight's armor. She tested his heart and his blood pressure.

"From Yankeeland, are you?" she asked in a low voice growl.

"Yes, ma'm."

"That's why you have all those pimples, I suppose."

"Don't English boys have pimples?"

"Not the way American boys have pimples, not pimples the size of gooseberries, not pimples the size of soccer balls. Petted and pampered and stuffed with rich food," she said, flaring suddenly. "I suppose you'll be having colds and flu all term long. Yanks always have shocking health."

He was nonplused. Were Americans especially unhealthy? What was going on here? "We did O.K. in the war," he said, and then felt very silly.

"Absolute rot," the matron flared again as she clamped his arm in the blood-pressure sleeve. "Came in when it was all over, and then swanked all over the place—I believe your people went utterly to pieces in the jungle, my nephew was in the jungle, you know, and the poor darlings had to be sent home to their mothers and their psychiatrists and I don't know what all, to be petted and pampered back to a state of 'normalcy'—ugh, what a word. And then, and *then*, you had the cheek to make a flick about Errol Flynn conquering Burma." She had unraveled the blood-pressure sleeve and grunted at the result of the test. Confirmed her worst fears, no doubt.

"You guys wouldn't have won without us," said Jimmy. Part of his problem was that he couldn't make out whether she was smart or stupid, kidding or serious. Burma? What was so great about Burma? He had thought that the main part of the war was fought on Okinawa and Iwo Jima. Anyhow, it didn't much matter. He was not a great war buff, and had rather lost interest in the details. The dismal thing was the way it excited the matron. He didn't feel like talking to a crazy woman at this particular time. "What about Guadalcanal?" he said. "What *about* it?" she said. She had him there.

At dinner (another mistaken meal) he asked the pale fellow what he thought of the matron.

"You mean Lady Hamilton? She's all right. Heart of gold under the revolting exterior is her line. If a chap pretends to be sick, she usually plays along. I mean to say if one faints on parade, you know military parade, she doesn't report the blotting paper she finds in one's socks."

"What blotting paper?"

"Blotting paper, you know, makes a chap faint. Gets one out of two hours of squalid drill. A definite jape."

"Sounds great."

"It's all right if you don't cut your head open when you hit the concrete. The chances of war, you know."

"I didn't think she was so hot."

"Who? Oh, you mean Eva Braun. Well, remember, she's the only woman you'll be seeing for three months, if you care for that sort of thing. Or do your interests run in other directions? Or are you too young to have any interests at all?"

"No, I'm not," said Jimmy quickly. What other directions? He decided to let that go.

"Well, then, better get on the right side of Eva."

"I thought you said she was called Lady Hamilton."

"Yes, you have the option, depending on which-house you're in, what day it is and the color of your hair. As I say—fuss, fuss, fuss. She was named Lady Hamilton during the Napoleonic unpleasantness. You'll recall that, of course? Perhaps you'd prefer to call her, say, Dolly Madison. Feel perfectly free."

Nobody had talked to him so much since his arrival, if you could call it talking, and Jimmy felt that he might be making a possible friend.

"What are *you* doing here in the vacation?" he asked, trying to turn it into a real conversation and not one of these queer things.

"I'm one of those chaps who's all-brain," said the pale fellow. "They're preparing me for a scholarship to one of our ancient universities. Keeping me locked in a brightly lit room all day and all night, works wonders with chickens, so why not people? say they. If I win, I shall put the school on the map. The fees will rise like yeast. Dr. Rabelais will advertise in *The Times* for new succubae . . ."

"What are you talking about now?"

"Ah, I *thought* you were too young."

The pale fellow went silent, and Jimmy was left alone for the twentieth time that day with his thoughts and an unidentifiable green vegetable that tasted of wood. He had never found conversation so difficult. It must take years to make friends at this rate. And even if you made friends with someone like this, what would you have? The strain of watching him try to make every sentence clever would just wear you out.

He decided that in the vacation this place must function as a kind of funny farm, for misfits and basket cases. Tomorrow the normal guys, who weren't "all-brain," and who didn't watch birds, were due to arrive. There must be some among them who could talk more or less straight. The whole nation couldn't be like this, it was mathematically impossible. (And the food was mathematically impossible, too.) He went for a walk after supper and the air felt wet and gentle and moderately reassuring.

The next day the normal boys began to roll in. Jimmy stood in a corner under a staircase watching them come. A roaring horde swept past him down the main hallway. And this was the thing about them— they were all wearing *black coats and pinstriped trousers*. It was simply incredible: all scuttling toward the big staircase like a school of small bank-managers on the march, pink faces swimming along under a deafening roar. He had never in his life heard such a noise.

Jimmy began to cry. He hadn't planned it, or even considered the possibility. But that was what he seemed to be doing: wrapped as he was in his sports coat with the comb sticking out; watching two hundred or three hundred weird haircuts, odd shapes of skull, mild eyes. Realizing that no help was going to arrive. And those suits! So cry it was. He turned and ran up the stairs to the dormitory. There was nobody he could even discuss the situation with. The conversation around here was not for discussing situations in. "What did he think he was doing?" he said, being fully honest about it for just a moment. But his father

could not have known about the black coats. He could
not.

He lay on his bed trying to recapture his grip. To
find yourself crying at his age was much worse than
any particular thing you might be crying about. It
simply wasn't possible for him to cry. It was like a blow
in the back of the neck. The bank managers didn't
seem to notice or care, as they pounded past him into
the dormitory. They were probably used to people
crying at this time of year. But to Jimmy it opened
some great abysm—all the things he hadn't cried
about for years came roaring into it, saying "now!
now!" and for a moment his body shook with the
pressure; and then the tears were all gone, and he sat
up emptily on his bed staring at the bank managers
and listening to their high incredible voices and wondering how the human race had managed to diverge
so violently as to form a country like this one.

two

He went to bed right after supper, curiously exhausted, and only dimly sensed the bedding down of
the others around him. A flashing of lights which his
eyes resisted, and the jar of foreign voices—like trying
to sleep on a train; then sufficient peace. He awoke
several times during the night and was aware of a
light, low-definition homesickness, like a sneeze in the
back of the nose. If New York had such a thing as a
decent season, it was spring, and he had gotten a first
tantalizing smell of that just before leaving. Another
thing about spring was that his father usually came to
life around then and they bundled out of the apartment on weekends, and took ferry rides up to Bear

Mountain and Poughkeepsie, or before that, drove up to Gloucester, where they planned the summer and fantasied the future. The back of the school year was broken, and the long vacation was just an arm's reach away. Here . . .

He pushed past this, back to pleasanter ground. He had had good times with his father; to get mad at him now was to cut off an important source of reassurance. For at least four years they had been very close friends indeed. Jimmy could picture the round pleasant face, the hand clutching the tickets. Tickets to Radio City, to ball games, to the ice show. When his mother left home, his father moved from the shadows and became the great ticket man. The braces came off Jim's teeth and his piano lessons were allowed to cease: gestures of friendship. They moved from Bridgeport to Boston to New York. This English thing was hard to understand in that context.

As he drifted off to sleep he thought fleetingly, as one might remember one's night prayers, about his mother. Her face was so pale in his mind that it was hardly a face at all. He was really thinking about the apartment on East Eighty-fourth Street and the one before that on West End, and the one before that . . . and when he came to her picture on the mantelpiece he flicked over it like a duster.

His mother was nothing but a piece of celluloid. When the piano lessons had stopped, he remembered thinking that you don't question a piece of luck like that. That was his last serious thought about her. He wondered now what she would make of this place—well, that was a silly question. Photographs don't have opinions. Neither should he just yet, until he had sampled a classroom or two; he went to sleep sharply, for the fourth and last time.

Classes began the following morning and Jimmy found himself staring into the English education system. The first class was geometry, which Jimmy had never done any of before. There was a dryness in the classroom air, like the taste of prison bread: something to do with everyone's wearing black. The master said a few cryptic words, then called out accusinly, "Smith," "Carruthers," "Thomson"; and they bawled back their answers, until just about everyone had spoken except Jimmy. He wondered dreamily what he would say when they got to him, but it all seemed so unreal; and then the bell chimed and that was the end of that. "Do exercise 35 for prep," said the geometry master, and the boys surged out of the room.

"Where am I supposed to go next?" Bannister asked the master.

"I don't know," said the master.

Jimmy went downstairs to reconnoiter the notice board. Room 12 Arithmetic. That shouldn't be too difficult. Arithmetic was something he thought he'd seen the last of two years ago. Win a few, lose a few. He puffed into room 12, to find a class already under way.

"Smedley, you horrible oaf"—this one wore a black gown with green mold on it—"do you realize that your parents are paying good money to send you here, when you might be doing useful work in the mines or the factories?"

"Yes, sir," said Smedley, in a funny accent, as the class tittered subserviently. Jimmy edged his way in quietly.

"Who are you? And what are you doing in those revolting clothes?" The master had spotted him anyway.

"Jim Bannister, sir."

"Well, Jimbannister, or whatever your bally name is, perhaps you've been sent by some Higher Agency to tell our backward friend Smedley what the logarithm of 312 is? One must never despair of Divine intervention, must one?"

"The *what*, sir?"

"Logarithm, logarithm, logarithm. Oh, another cruel joke!" He bounced around in his gown. "Providence has favored me with another oaf."

"What's a logarithm, sir?"

"Whaat?" the master howled. "Oh my God!" And he buried his face in his hands. "It's come to this, then."

"I'm sorry," said Jimmy. The master sat motionless in an attitude of comic shock and bereavement. Years of disappointment with boys and now this. "Why do they send them to *me*," he moaned softly.

"I'm sorry," Jimmy repeated. It was all too ridiculous. What kind of an act was this? The heavy, lined face told him that this was a grown-up; otherwise there was no way of knowing. The other boys continued to titter on cue, but without much spirit.

"Well, it's no use being sorry." The master was suddenly business-like. "But there isn't much I can do for you if you haven't even heard of logarithms. Have you done any problems in mensuration, you loathsome boy?"

"I don't think so."

"You don't *think* so, eh? I imagine you'd notice if you had. Well, I'm afraid you shouldn't be in this class at all in that case. Jones Minor, perhaps you can fill in for our untutored American cousin? What is the logarithm for 312, you benighted oaf?"

"Do you want me to stay here?" asked Jimmy.

"Suit yourself," said the master, already absorbed in

his tilt with Jones Minor. Jimmy sat in a diplomatic limbo, thinking of other classrooms he had known, and wondering, furthermore, how this had ever come to be called arithmetic.

As the class broke up, one of the boys sidled over to him: "Don't pay attention to the 'Foghorn.' He's thoroughly uncivilized," and sidled away again. Jimmy frowned: the boy looked young to be saying things like that. But what was young and what was old in this country?

Outside in the corridor, boys were off and running again, this way and that. Jimmy gathered, from a blur of bulletin board, that he had to get to the other end of the school for his next class, and he joined a crowd which seemed to be sprinting in that direction. They all chuffered into the classroom together, squeezing through the door somehow, and a moment later a mild-looking man in a fuzzy brown suit was putting yet another tick next to his name. "Ah yes, Bannister. *Here* we are, *I've* got you."

This time the class was Latin. Jimmy had already had a year of Latin. The master seemed to be pretending to be shy—that was *his* routine. "What shall we do today? Perhaps a few sentences from English into Latin." He opened his book vaguely, and then looked up as if struck with a happy thought. "I heard rather a good story last night. I don't suppose it would amuse you chaps?"

"Oh please, sir," the cry went up, and the story was told. It was long, and some of it was in Latin, but the boys laughed anyway. One of them went into near paroxysms, flinging himself round like a dervish and slapping his desk. Oh come on, thought Jimmy. You don't think you're going to get away with that, do you? "That will do, Cornwallis," said the master: but he smiled as he wiped his glasses. The gnomes looked at each other in surmise.

"Sir, do you think Yorkshire will win the championship this season?" They probed at the loose tissue.

"Are they going to devalue the pound, sir?"

"Is socialized medicine really a good idea, sir?"

"Isn't it smashing to be able to travel again, sir? Where are you going to go first, sir?"

"Sir, sir, *please*, sir . . ."

He answered their questions with gravity and foolish precision. Fifteen minutes had gone already, only twenty-five remained. Maybe Jimmy would avoid entanglements this time. But at some point the master straightened his spectacles and summoned his woolly faculties. "That's enough now, you chaps. We've wasted entirely too much time." He looked at them as severely as he could and snapped his book open. "Why don't we try exercise 73? It looks like an amusing one."

One of the boys handed out paper for the class to write on. Jimmy searched through his Latin book for exercise 73. It consisted of five of the stupidest sentences he had ever seen in his life. "Caesar decided that if he had been told previously that the Gauls had encamped on the other side of the river he would certainly have moved his baggage back to the town from which he had departed at daybreak the day before." Jimmy chewed his pencil. "Regulus would have liked to disembark perhaps" . . . Yes, well. Very interesting. The other boys were already writing with beaverish determination, while the master appeared to be jotting down words on a crossword puzzle.

"Are you encountering difficulties, Bannister?" he said at last. Jimmy was sitting back with his hands in his pockets. He decided that this might be a good place to make a stand, before this madness went any further.

"Yes, sir. Great difficulties."

"Er, would you care to come up, Bannister? Perhaps we can solve them together."

Jimmy went up. The master looked at his paper closely, readjusting his spectacles. The paper started off "1. Caesar," and stopped. The master was profoundly disturbed.

"Is this all you've done?"

"Yes, sir."

The master peered at it again, and skewered his spectacles further into place. "This is distressing, Bannister." He squinted at the blank paper. Perhaps a closer look would turn up something, some words he hadn't noticed before . . . "Very distressing indeed." The master just sat and looked at the paper while Jimmy stood and looked at the floor. "Well, what are we going to do about it?" His face was close to agony.

"I don't know, sir."

"This isn't good enough, you know. Nothing like good enough."

He paused again. "Are you sure this is all you've done?" he asked. Invisible ink was a possibility. Jimmy couldn't make out what was the matter with this man: but he felt vaguely that it was up to himself to get them both out of the tangle.

"Maybe I should go see the headmaster," he suggested at last.

"Yes," the master grasped at the idea. "Perhaps that would be the best plan." He ran a hand through his thin sandy hair. "I'm afraid we can't be of much help to you here."

Jimmy strolled toward the door. He felt pretty

good; the man had simply collapsed. Perhaps they all would,

"Sorry," said the master.

The headmaster, "Dr. Rabelais" (real name Smyth, but that was beside the point), sat shrouded in a great black gown, nursing a cup of tea. For ten minutes he worked away at his lists, giving Jimmy leisure to look around him. The room seemed less strange today, although strange enough. On the opposite wall hung six little dandified walking sticks, which, Jimmy conjectured, must be for making mean little furrows on your backside; the rest of the room was dull with bright patches. Among the forbidding books he spotted several funny ones which he had read himself. His thoughts futzed this way and that; summer days, lying on his back reading. Flinging aside his book, or his violin like the man in the ads, and charging into the sea. New images struggled against the protoplasm: dancing on some kind of bandstand in a white tuxedo, with, let's say, Marilyn Jenkins in pink chiffon with her teeth freshly liberated (Marilyn's scaffolding had kept them apart until recently), and driving home together in the roadster Forrest Tuckerman had talked of purchasing. After all, America was his country, and he had a right to be in it, for better or worse. This place might be all right for the people who belonged here; it was hard to tell. Maybe he could make the headmaster see all that. He was supposed to be a big brain.

"Infernal nuisance running a school these days"— Dr. Rabelais interrupted his thoughts—"ration books, identity cards, shortages, *et* cetera, *et* cetera. It's worse than the dashed civil service. Can I help you, Bannister?"

"Yes, sir." He gestured with his hands. "It's no good. I just can't seem to make it. I think I'd better just go home."

Dr. Rabelais looked uncomprehending. "Can't make what?"

"Anything. The school. The grade. Anything."

"Ah, I see. Don't you think you're judging the situation a trifle prematurely, Bannister?"

"No, I don't think so. Look, I went to three classes today, and I was made to look like a monkey in two of them. Now I don't mind looking like a monkey . . ."

"Excellent, the beginning of wisdom."

"If it's in a good cause. O.K., maybe I'm stupid, and can't help it. But don't you think it's a little bit unnecessary to spend a whole term proving it?"

"What exactly do you mean by that, Bannister?" The headmaster plunged deeper into his burrow of vagueness.

"Well, if I'm not mistaken, my father wrote you a letter last month describing my qualifications. Didn't you get the letter?"

"Yes, I think I have it here somewhere." The headmaster fished about on his desk.

"Well, then, how come you just throw me in over my head like that? You know I don't know any geometry . . ."

Dr. Rabelais looked terribly, terribly tired. On the evolutionary cycle, the human race had barely begun its journey. And now, here was this boy. "We must have patience," he said. "Rome wasn't built in a day, you know."

"Yes, so I've heard. The word gets around, about things like that."

"I don't believe that impertinence will help us

materially in our quest. Restrain your native exuberance, I beg of you, or I may be required to restrain it for you. Now what was I saying?"

"That Rome wasn't built in a day, sir."

"Ah, yes. Now I agree that the analogy may seem remote in your particular case." His voice reminded Jim of old curtains. "Nevertheless it is not altogether without pertinence. We must make haste slowly, building slowly but surely. Labor omnia vincit, if you'll excuse a rather colorless paraphrase."

Jimmy could barely remember what he had come here to say. He was being woofed more and more tightly into the headmaster's endless tapestry: pinned by velvet threads, tenuous syllabic filaments.

"I just don't feel I belong here. I admit I'm stupid."

"Ah-hah." Dr. Rabelais wagged a much-wagged finger. "You can't get away with that, my boy. I've seen all your school reports from the age of five, and I've also had special recommendations from several old teachers. We know quite a bit about you, you know."

"I didn't think you cared."

"I warmly advise you to think very carefully before you venture another impertinence. Yes, we feel the utmost confidence that you can, as you say, 'make the grade.' Otherwise you would not be here, depend upon it. Now, as to your classwork, we can't very well put you in with boys of twelve and thirteen, can we? As it is, most of your colleagues are no more than fourteen, and backward to boot. There's a chap called Smedley in one of your classes who knows even less than you do if that be possible—another American as it happens, but that's neither here nor there. Now, it's simply up to you to make up the difference with stern applications of native wit. I believe you Americans call it 'Yankee ingenuity.' I knew some Americans during the war, you know."

"But the Latin teacher sent me in here because he didn't know what to do with me."

"Ah, Mr. Moore. Brilliant classicist, but not used to boys. I'll have a word with him. By the way, shouldn't you be somewhere at the moment?"

"I guess so, sir. I just don't know where."

"Well, out of respect for your frayed nerves, you might as well take the rest of the morning off. It must have been quite strenuous, settling in like this to a strange environment." He paused, hoping no doubt that Jimmy's hash was settled forever. "Morning off should fix things up."

"Thank you, sir."

A happy thought struck Dr. Rabelais.

"You may be a little daunted by the famous English reserve. Could that be it, do you suppose? I find it singularly relaxing myself, but my American acquaintances inform me that it tends to make them a trifle jumpy. If that's your trouble, I'm sure that time will take care of it. There are several quite pleasant chaps about the place, whom you will doubtless get to know in due course. Perhaps in the camaraderie of the cricket field . . ." His voice trailed off.

"Yes, sir."

"Is that all, Bannister?"

"Yes, sir, I guess so." He stumbled out of the room, assuming that his question must have been answered at some point, and that the answer was no, or yes, he was staying here, and continuing the farce. In his present state of brain fog, he was happy just to get out of the office.

That afternoon Jimmy was introduced to cricket. His fellow competitors in game number 16 were all

playing against their wills. They were a squinting,
shambling crowd, who detested cricket, and played it
as badly as possible, partly as a protest, partly because they had no choice. Appropriately enough, Mr.
Moore, the Latin master, was in charge of the game,
and to him fell the gloomy task of preventing the
players from fielding the ball with their boots, and
heaving it willfully into the woods. ("Oh, I say chaps"
was his formula for this.)

The game lumbered along, and Jimmy was glad to
find that his own incompetence was lost in the general confusion. In fact, as a fielder he was somewhat
above average, and he flung himself at the knobbly
red ball with crazy abandon, because it seemed a nice
straightforward thing to do.

Later he found that he was sitting next to Smedley
while both awaited their brief turns at bat. Smedley
was on the plump side and sluggish-looking, and easily the worst player of any game that Jimmy had ever
seen: three reasons for slight contempt, as far as
Jimmy was concerned.

"You had a bad time this morning, didn't you, Bannister?" Jimmy recognized Smedley's strange accent
as simple American.

"I guess so," said Jimmy.

"Well, welcome to the club. I've been having a bad
time all year."

"Gee, that long? How do you stand it?" He
wouldn't have liked this guy back home, but here you
took what you could get.

The fat boy gave him a long, solemn look. His face
was American too: bulbous and open. Well, that was
one kind of American face.

"Passive resistance," said Smedley at last. "The
madder they act, the dumber I get. I'm trying to give

them the impression that I'm too stupid to bother about. And I'm gaining."

"Don't they beat you?"

"Sometimes—when I overplay my hand. That's all they can do, though. And you get used to it. Especially with a figure like mine. Besides, there's a growing body of opinion that says I'm a real idiot, one of God's holy people, and maybe it's bad luck to push me around."

"But won't they kick you out someday?"

Smedley gave him the look. "And what do you think I've been waiting for?"

Jimmy thought this over for a second.

"Hey, Smedley, you're a great man." He'd need time to work this thing out in detail, but it looked, offhand, like a way to beat the system. Smedley gave no indication that it was meant to be a joke. It just seemed to be the way his mind worked.

Jim walked back to school with some of the old Bannister bounce. He figured that he might possibly try to do it the Uncle Tom way for a while, pay attention in class, and wait for the camaraderie of the cricket field, whatever that was. But if that didn't work, he would use the Smedley plan. Act dumb. Act obnoxiously dumb, swinishly dumb, and find himself on a boat to Marilyn Jenkins in no time.

He found himself for now just behind the headmaster, who was trudging up the slight incline to the dressing rooms and who looked unusually vulnerable in a pair of baggy tennis shorts. Rabelais was whacking his spider's legs absently with a squash racket, and Jimmy felt something like friendship, at least for his dilapidated back view. The front was something else. A slingshot aimed at the left calf would produce the most endearing little dance.

Jimmy pulled abreast, and smiled a greeting. Probably not the thing to do: but Rabelais let it go for now. "Settling in all right, are you, Dannister?" he said. "Not such a bad country, perhaps. I expect you'll find that we have our moments." And they both tunneled into the school, on a wave of rather freakish good cheer.

three

The characters seemed to change. The boys he had
seen in those first few days receded, dissolved; and
new ones appeared. The pale fellow with the brain
was nowhere to be seen. Wagstaff the bird watcher
lorded it over another house, so was somebody else's
problem. Jimmy was shuffled out of Mr. Moore's class
(a clerical mistake in the first place, he gathered) and
into the Latin equivalent of cricket game number 16.
Dr. Rabelais clearly wanted as little to do with boys
as possible once term had begun, and withdrew bit
by bit into that all-purpose vagueness: his eyes empty
as a blind man's, his legs seeming to whisper to each
other, "I'll get you past these boys, never fear."

The boy in the bed next to Jimmy's had a Norman skull, which was depressing at first but later became a comfort like a tea cozy or an old piece of china. He didn't say anything to Jimmy for two whole weeks, but padded modestly to and fro with his tooth mug and his washcloth, and one night he cried in bed softly and politely, which came as quite a pleasant surprise for Jimmy.

Those first two weeks were incredible in a whole new way: Smedley plans, modified Smedley plans, were of no avail—because for that whole time nobody talked to him at all. It was like the first day of kindergarten prolonged indefinitely. Nobody looked at him or asked who he was. If they wanted the salt, they reached across him. If their arms weren't long enough, they went without salt. At night Jimmy was obliged to troop with them for their nightly wash, where they jostled him mutely to get at the basins. This was an awful scene. Flannel dressing gowns, the dismal swoop of slippers, and the boys rolling up their pajama legs and dunking their feet awkwardly in the washbasins—he didn't know why, but this was the low point of the day. Later in the sandpaper sheets he would lie grimly still, his hand between his thighs for comfort, like a drowning man clinging to driftwood. He felt he must be changing, losing his bearings, as men do in solitary confinement. He considered masturbating but was restrained by two thoughts: one being that it would induce the most violent melancholy in this setting and the other that any displacement of these impossible bedclothes would be noticeable for miles around. So he lay still like a knight on his coffin.

It was better in the morning. He could hear farm noises, the crunch of heavy boots on cobblestone and above that the shriek of the school crows. There was one man who always said, "Morning, Harry," and stopped to talk under Jimmy's window in a comfortable Midlands accent about weather prospects and such. Jimmy had never heard such a pleasant voice. Inside the dormitory the boys snored or muttered or went sniffing into the bathroom. When they were all in place they formed a line of gray mounds like a Druid graveyard. Jimmy lay there watching and listening to the voice through the window.

One evening, at the end of two weeks exactly, the boy with the Norman skull came and sat on his bed and said, "Do you like jazz, Bannister?"

"I guess so," said Jimmy: surprised at the sound of his own voice.

"I do too. Very much indeed. Do you know 'In the Mood'?"

"By Glenn Miller, you mean."

"Yes, that's it. I think it's super, don't you?"

"Yes, its nice."

"Do you know 'Frenesí'?"

"I don't think so."

"It's Artie Shaw. Quite first-class. He hummed a few notes.

Jimmy was delighted to talk, on anyone's terms and this fellow, who had seemed so shy, went at it now with the utmost composure.

"We have a jazz club, you know. Your compatriot Smedley has furnished us with some of his records, and we also get speakers in from time to time. Last term we had a super talk on discography. By a Frenchman."

Discography? Jimmy didn't like to ask.

"Yes, several Glenn Millers. 'The Man I Love' by the Benny Goodman quartet— That man can really play the licorice stick, can't he? All in all, quite a good collection."

Jimmy stared at him solemnly; it wouldn't do to laugh.

"Anyhow, we were talking it over and we wondered"—there was a sock-picking pause and the fellow suddenly looked unspeakably embarrassed—"if you'd care to join us."

So Bannister joined the jazz club and listened that Thursday evening to the several Glenn Millers and to Benny Goodman's licorice strick. The whole Smedley collection, in fact. Smedley had changed his own *persona* for the occasion, slipping out of his banker's uniform and into a purple sports shirt and double-breasted suit, as one was allowed to do in the evenings. As the records spun, Smedley combed his wet hair into a lounge-lizard coif and snapped his fingers, while the others looked on with admiring interest.

It seemed that this deviant music room, with its bust of Elgar and illuminated manuscript of William Byrd, was the one place in the school where it was good to be an American; and Smedley had decided to be American to the hilt. It was obviously he who had taught them to say "licorice stick," and to nonchalant their smuggled cigarettes. "Gimme some skin, man," he said gravely as they entered. "Shake it but don't break it." "Tell you whut I'm gonna dew." His language seemed to have been purged of all but the most conspicuous Americanisms.

Jimmy felt a slight contempt for the records on principle—licorice stick indeed!—but they got to him after a few rounds. Glenn Miller, he thought. Billy Butterfield plays George Gershwin. Gershwin equals penthouse. Penthouse equals Fifth Avenue bus. Girls jumping on and climbing to the top deck with skirts swinging. Waiting for reviews at Sardis. He missed it all so much. He didn't want to stay in this nuthouse another minute. "Frenesí" unraveled him completely. Play it again, Sam, he thought. Purple shadows and blue champagne. And outside, all those English boys. His throat seemed to constrict with some rich substance; but the sight of Smedley combing his hair steadied him.

He didn't like that. Americans don't behave like that. And he didn't like the way the other boys were looking at Smedley: a group of rich Romans inspecting the muscles of an African slave. It kept him from acting American himself. When they got to the end of the set, they played them all again, tapping their feet and scrutinizing Smedley. "What do you think, Bannister?" asked the boy with the Norman skull, whose name turned out to be Ryan. "It's very nice," said Bannister.

Several others looked around—let's hear from the other American chap. So Jimmy said, "Well, you can't really call this stuff jazz, can you? I mean I used to go down to Eddie Condon's and listen to Muggsy Spanier, and that was . . ."

"You went to Condon's? You heard Muggsy?" A clamor went up, chairs scraped forward. It was all so queer. "Tell us about Muggsy. Does Condon really drink two quarts of whiskey a night, or is that just propaganda? What about Peewee Russell?"

Something about the way they pronounced Muggsy —Jimmy felt as if he had played right into their hands. He had actually been to Condon's only that once, with Forrest Tuckerman, and had had to concentrate so hard on looking eighteen (squint, cigarette, flickering jaw muscle) that he hadn't noticed much else. He remembered that it was awfully smoky, and that, because the waiter had put him and Forrest maliciously close to the bandstand, the trombone had rent his skull in two.

"Hey, Jimmy, you been to Condon's, I hear," Smedley chimed in. "That Condon is a character, isn't he? And Peewee and Wild Bill . . . I and my buddy used to go there on Sunday afternoons and buy them a few rounds, just to get them talking, you know . . ."

No, no, no. Jimmy just couldn't cope with this. Jazz should have been his subject; yet these finely trained bank clerks were outflanking him even there, Two weeks of silence had rusted his tongue: so he left the exposition to Smedley, affirming with occasional grunts and looking as detached as he could. Ahead of him lay the long dark corridors back to Frisby house, the piping good nights ("Night, Smedley," "See you guys on the campus," "Right-oh, Smedley.") The boys teetering at their washbasins scrubbing their pale white feet.

On the way back to the Frisby dormitory with Ryan, he heartily denounced the records, and Ryan said meekly, "It's the best we can do, I'm afraid," Ryan, at least, accepted his authority in the field.

The corridor outside Frisby was dark enough to trip in. And as Jimmy edged along the wall, jangling with trumped-up outrage, he nearly stumbled into a dark pair of hands. A tall boy was standing there in dressing gown and pajamas, smiling apologetically and holding out his hands in a kind of supplication. "Are you all right, dear?" He reached for Jimmy's shoulders, and Jimmy twisted away.

He ran a few steps to keep up with Ryan. What had happened, nothing had happened. (*Dear?*) As he looked over his shoulder he saw that the boy was still standing there, still smiling. His face was quite luminous, fair and thin, but the rest was blacked out in shadows. That was the first friendly gesture Jim had encountered since coming here.

"Who was that?" he asked Ryan.

"That was Padgett," said Ryan. "He's a shocker, isn't he? Out there every night, rain or shine. I don't know why he hasn't been caught yet."

Jimmy honestly didn't know what Ryan was talking about. And he didn't much want to. He simply decided that he must leave this place as soon as possible.

On afternoons when he wasn't playing cricket, Jimmy went for long walks in the country. The other boys did military drill but as a representative of a foreign power he was excused from that, and he didn't much care to watch it. The shouting and the clump of boots presented the school at its bleakest, and he saw no point in punishing himself. So he took walks, along the exceptionally gentle paths that wound loosely round the school, and he got in the habit of composing imaginary letters to his father, all on the theme of "Get me out of here. A joke is a joke. *Now get me out of here.*" Sometimes he added, in his head, the words "before it's too late," although he had no idea what he meant by that. The other morning at breakfast, Ryan had said, "You just said 'actually.' Listen, chaps, Bannister said 'actually.'" But he didn't think it was that.

At fifteen I should be spending my time with my father, he thought theatrically. Time with Mr. Bannister. He'll be an old man when I get out of here, possibly dead. Certainly remarried. Remarried. To Gloria whatzit—that was the best he could hope for. The worst? . . . Jim had the uncanny feeling in the back of his mind that Padgett had been wearing make-up the other night, to make him glow so.

The imaginary letters lacked force, because he didn't feel so bad in the afternoons. The countryside was friendly, compared with the school corridors, and he was getting used to the hanging, motionless drizzle. He even liked the taste of the grass when he sat down on it to brood. He tried to remember how he would feel later in the day, and to borrow some of the night's agitation on credit, but the fields and the cows and the broken-down hedges left him hopelessly becalmed. There was a bowlegged farmer who rode a lady's bicycle down whichever path Jimmy happened to be taking and who always tipped his cap as he wobbled by, and Jimmy liked him in the same way he liked the voice under his window in the morning.

After the misleading afternoon there were several more hours of classes to get through. By some mystery of scheduling, he kept landing in the Foghorn's class, where he felt the was being kept from learning arithmetic by sheer terror. Not just terror for himself, but terror for the Foghorn as well. For Jim had formed the idea that Mr. Withers was literally going crazy. His ranting seemed to get more and more absent-minded and hysterical as the term wore on: everyone was an oaf, everyone was a cause for despair. His eyes emptied out and he looked, in some curious way, like a man lost in a railroad station. Jim got a feeling that Mr. Withers had completely withdrawn from the scene and was railing at phantoms; private terrors.

After the Foghorn came geography, presided over by a dwarf called Smiles, who paid close, ferret-like attention to everything and who made a stylish needle point thing of his bullying. He had decided from the first to make Jimmy a scapegoat because "Americans don't know the first thing about geography. You people have inherited much of Great Britain's power since the war and yet you haven't the remotest . . ." He seemed personally affronted by postwar developments and talked as if the shrinking red patches on the map were Jimmy's doing. "Bannister, come up here. I wonder if you could indicate to the class the whereabouts of the crown colony of Singapore. I suppose you know what *ocean* it's in, do you?" Titters. "You know, your president made us give a good deal of this away. I devoutly hope that his geography was better than yours." Jimmy hated standing up there, not only because he confirmed everything that Smiles said about America and geography, but also because Smiles seemed to be drenched in nicotine from head to foot. Even his rusty hair smelled of nicotine, and the fingers with which he seized Jimmy's arm impatiently, to guide him to Malaya and Borneo, were outrageously long, yellow and fetid.

The last class of the day was possibly the worst of all. The French teacher posed a unique problem in that he took a rather florid liking to Jimmy, based on a notion that Jimmy was basically a first-rate student who had come upon bad times. "Ban-ees-tair—thees ees not op to you ol' standar," he would say sadly whenever Jimmy handed something in. He had been teaching a long time and had doubtless had a gifted pupil called Bannister in the old days. Now Bannister was back with his gifts gone.

Jimmy, of course, knew no French to speak of, and while he was getting reasonably inured to the steady diet of embarrassment in the other classes, he found Monsieur Necker's false hopes ever-freshly excruciating. He worked hard at French, but was so far below the original Bannister's standard that he continued to disappoint in about the same measure all the time he was in the class.

That was how the days went now—rounded off with godawful suppers and homework and the thwack of pingpong balls in the Frisby common room; and then, trying to avoid Padgett on the way home. Padgett was, he now understood, a joke and nothing to be alarmed over. Old Padgett never actually did anything, but just stood there, smiling and whispering, "Good evening, dear," to anyone who would listen. "I think he's barmy," said Ryan. "If he wasn't a scholarship candidate, he wouldn't be here at all."

So much for Padgett. Still the Sopworth hallways at night seemed as strange as some underwater kingdom and Jim was happy to make it to his sandpaper bed without incident. The fact that Padgett was a joke was strange because he had never encountered a joke like that before. And how many other jokes lurked in the night? Even by daylight odd things could happen.

To wit, the Sprague caper, which showed him in a lightning flash how much he had changed since coming here. This was at the end of his first month, and he was so used by now to solitude that conversation seemed like a bizarre exception. He was on his way to Monday lunch, the culinary ass-hole of the universe, when Sprague happened. At first, all that registered was a distant cry of pain. "Hands out, you squalid little man. Hands *out* . . ." Jim looked around vaguely: he had just had forty minutes of the Foghorn, whose anonymous bellows had a dulling effect, like the guns on the Western front. "You—who are you, anyway? What's your miserable name? What's your unfortunate house?" Spam and boiled potatoes, Bannister was thinking. Thick flour on the spuds, bread pudding and custard. After such a morning, it wasn't much.

"Look here. You can't just walk past when I speak to you." A smallish boy stood now directly in Jimmy's path. "*Get* THOSE *hands out of* THOSE *pockets.*"

"Are you talking to me?"

"Who do you think I'm talking to, you verminous creature? President Rooosevelt? *Get* THOSE *hands—*"

One curious thing was that the boy's hands were wedged deep into his own pockets. It must be a local joke. "Look, I've had a hard morning," Jimmy said.

"This is plain, dumb insolence. You'll take those hands out of those pockets immediately, or I'll—" He stopped because Jimmy had already taken his hands out some moments before, without thinking, simply to make a despairing gesture. He continued to glare at Jimmy—quite meaninglessly as far as Jim was concerned. Two other boys had flung themselves against the wall, to watch in an agony of languor, their hands very much in their pockets. Jimmy squinted at his challenger. Two stringy blond whiskers corkscrewed from his chin, and his upper lip was a downy shambles. Five feet five or at the most six. I can take him, Jimmy thought. By why? "Look, if you don't mind—" Jimmy tried to edge round but found himself blocked again. "What is this?" He stared down at what seemed to be the gravitational focus: striped trousers stretched to bursting. Absently, Jimmy put his own hands back in his pockets.

"My God!" Jimmy took them out again, still without design. People who were late for lunch didn't get served. He tried sidestepping the other way, to get to his custard, but again his tormentor skipped with him and this time butted him lightly in the chest. The two friends against the wall looked suffocatingly bored. As if they had to contend with this sort of thing every day. The custard wasn't much, but suddenly Jim couldn't get it out of his mind.

"Look," he said. And he put his own hands inquiringly on the boy's chest. "I don't know if this is supposed to be a joke. I don't know who you are, or what you want—" He felt his stupid lip trembling. He couldn't think of anything to say, that was why. The lip gave a violent shudder: he hadn't cried for seven or eight years before coming to this crumby place. Here he never seemed to stop. To crown it all, the chest was harder to push than it looked. Embarrassment had weakened him. Jimmy tried one more quick breakthrough on the left and the little fellow darted across silently and blocked him against the school bulletin board. It was like a game in which use of the hands is illegal.

What Jimmy had forgotten about this kind of crying was that eventually it exploded on you like hiccups and you lost control of it. It was the *incredibility* that got him down. He thought of past fights—challenges he had met without enthusiasm, but met. But this wasn't even a challenge. He bent against the wall and tried to pull his nose and mouth together. If there were three people in the world he didn't want to cry in front of, it was, at the moment, these three snots.

"I ought to report you to your house prefect," said the boy, all business now. "However, perhaps I'll let it go this time. All I can tell you is, don't ever behave like this in front of a school prefect again. Here, try this on your nose." Reluctantly he pulled his hand out of its nest and thrust a huge handkerchief at Jimmy.

Jimmy handed the handkerchief back without

using it. It would have been the final disgrace. The little man shrugged and went over and joined his friends, and they strolled together to the dining room, their hands still firmly entrenched. They were laughing, but Jimmy had a queer bad feeling that they were not talking about him at all, in fact that they would never refer to him again.

The best thing was to forget it. But Jimmy was too hungry for that. It festered on his empty stomach. Apparently it didn't matter when prefects got to the dining room, but it was certainly too late for him. He ran upstairs to the dormitory, ravening for the custard that might have been. He remembered seeing his father truckle to a traffic cop once, and feeling ashamed. But this was much worse. He had, in his quiet days and nights here, lost his ability to cope with a verbal crisis. He had just wanted to get out of there, at any cost. He took out his writing block and began a real letter to his father, imploring him to end this foolishness: but found that his grievances had suddenly become too delicate to mention. He sat on the bed chewing his pen, and in a moment the bank managers came pounding in again from lunch. Unless you locked yourself in the toilet, there was no question of privacy around here.

"I didn't see you at lunch, Bannister," said Ryan as he began to forage for cricket boots under his bed. "Didn't you feel well? Or were you devouring a food package from America, you greedy swine?" Ryan had chosen this moment to advance their friendship.

Jimmy looked up and without a moment of warning the tears came back. They didn't match his mood at all now—he was so angry that he wanted to belt someone. But the whole duct system was out of kilter.

He hated to admit it but he was also moved by the fact that Ryan had spoken to him again.

"Do you know a little blond guy who goes around with his hands in his pockets? He wouldn't let me go in the dining room—" Jimmy sniffed this out somehow. "Wait till I catch up with that runt."

"What will you do to him?"

"We'll just see."

Ryan giggled. "I wouldn't make any positive plans if I were you. That sounds very much like Sprague, who only happens to be our beloved boxing captain —peerless lightweight and all that. He loves bashing people into the bulletin board. I don't know what he sees in it. You're lucky he kept his hands in his pockets."

Ryan's voice was surprisingly warm and sympathetic, as one of life's victims to another—they could be friends now. "You Yanks are headstrong, I'll give you that. Imagine tangling with a chap like Sprague. He plays soccer too, you know. He could have had you beaten to a jelly."

"I wouldn't have cared."

"You Yanks!" Ryan laughed again and said, "Have you seen my other boot?"

In Ryan's eyes he had behaved with headstrong dash, but in his own he knew better. He had wanted all the way to slug Sprague, but his nervous system had simply refused. It was like blowing a fuse. If someone else had described such a scene, he would have said, why didn't you just hit him? Well, you couldn't fight for the right to keep your hands in your pockets. That was the only answer he could think of. A fight required a cause. You couldn't race your motor over nothing.

That evening he saw Sprague again, patrolling the

corridor with his two friends, like the Queen inspecting a new garbage-disposal unit. Jimmy thought once more of hitting him, but decided against. Who knew what crazy point of etiquette the scene would turn on this time? He could see himself blushing, stammering, unable to raise his hands—because he was *wearing the wrong color socks*. Good God, man. He wanted to slip past before his pants, shirt, garters caused comment. To miss another meal would be catastrophic. Sprague appeared to have forgotten him completely, looking round him and through as celebrities do; but as the blank eyes swivelled round, Jimmy whipped his hands from his pockets; and felt a smaller man for it.

So what with Padgett and Sprague, the terror by night and the arrow that flew in the day, the classrooms came to seem almost like sanctuaries. The school corridors were booby-trapped with embarrassment—could *that* be the secret of English education? To make your classwork the only sane part of the day? From the fourth to the eighth week of term Jimmy went through his educational period. The teachers were definitely more rational than the boys. They had to do their acts, it was expected of them, but they never departed from the script. Once you had gauged any particular master's sound and fury, had probed to the outer limits of his ferocity, you could set your panic quotient with confidence. Example, Mr. Quince, his new Latin teacher. "Bannister, you erk"—a typical Quince-ism, nothing to worry about there. "I wish you would give some thought to that glazed expression. It's getting on my nerves." Good. Humor. Sir? "Page 58, you clod. Unless you use a different system of numbering in your curious country." The storm would pass by today in the distance.

But other days Quince would ooom really to care, and Jimmy would care too. "Bannister, this is a disgrace. Bannister, you're not trying." His features would fold over like a bloodhound's. And Jim would feel, please stop that, I'll try again.

Too late now for the Smedley stupidity plan. What a disaster that had been. He had tried it just once on Mr. Smiles in geography, a bad choice, and Mr. Smiles had almost broken his elbow with his fingers, while taunting American education at the same time. Since then Jim's nerve had deserted him. At the last second he would always shrink from acting stupider than he had to. It required a kind of verbal confidence, of a negative order. So he said, "I'm sorry, sir," to Mr. Quince, and meant it. Jimmy lived in the limbo of the half stupid and would never be one of God's holy people like Smedley.

Smedley, meanwhile, kept pursuing his own plan with a heavy-faced fanaticism. Jimmy sat near him in arithmetic and marveled at the way he never flinched or brightened up in face of the Foghorn's roars. As a result he became a dumping group for the Foghorn's excess bluster, and this had somehow worked itself into a privilege. Occasionally Mr. Withers would wing him fondly with a piece of chalk or a blackboard eraser. "Smedley, you *clown*, Smedley, you ineffable—no, don't bother to look it up. What would be the use? You would probably look it up under 'f.' You ineffable, as I say, transcen*den*tal oaf." There was actual warmth in his voice; he had reached with Smedley some empyrean of insult where they were alone in mystic union.

After that, Jimmy only got the Foghorn's second-best shot, joyless and mechanical and actually much harder to take. As term wore on, Smedley seemed to become the only boy worthy of the great man's powers, and then finally even Smedley roused him only rarely.

The only comfort about all this was that Smedley's plan did not seem to be getting him to America any quicker. On the other hand, his denseness had made him something of a culture hero among the boys. There was something grand and incorruptible about him, like a Western hero. His wooden expression could almost be construed as tough. And he was doggedly and systematically stupid. His ignorance was so intricately dovetailed and cross-referenced that he could never be caught out knowing something today that he hadn't known yesterday. And he presented his poverty so solemnly and with such reverses of dignity that even Jimmy was almost taken in by it. (He couldn't really *be* stupid, could he?) "What page was that? The green book, sir? I don't have any green book. Oh—you mean this one?" He fumbled at the very portal of the question. The Smedley plan had sounded so simple; but in practice it called for almost excruciating heroism. Jimmy felt that it was also, probably, the most honorable response to this place— but he just wasn't up to it himself.

A man wearies of ping-pong eventually, and Jimmy took to slipping out for short strolls after supper. As usual, he didn't find out that this was against the rules until too late: until yet another outraged prefect had pointed it out to him with a virtuoso display of sarcasm. But by then these discoveries were becoming a fact of life and Jimmy found that honor was satisfied by waving a cautious middle finger at the prefect after he had disappeared.

This was some weeks later, and by then Jimmy had already managed to put in a number of quite satisfactory walks. The cool night air on his face kept the spooks at bay, and the thickening twilight made for a richer texture of reverie than the gray afternoons. The gaunt school buildings looked impressive in shadow. The school chapel blew up to a cathedral and the gymnasium could have been the rear end of a fortress. Through the downstairs windows he could see boys playing ping-pong and chess. Not so bad.

One of those evenings he chanced to bump into someone who was making the tour counter-clockwise, and braced himself for the inevitable roar. He was bound to be doing something wrong. On closer view, it turned out to be Mr. Withers, the Foghorn, so he double-braced himself.

"Enjoying the night air, are you, Bannister?" said the Foghorn with treacherous pleasantness. Jimmy's hands were at least eighteen inches wide of his pockets on either side. Nothing to fear on that count.

"Yes, I guess so."

"It's nice at this time of year, isn't it? I believe we have longer evenings than you do in your country. But of course we pay for it in the winter." His voice and what Jimmy could see of his face were rather anxious, as if he had been working out some personal problem. "It's particularly nice in this part of the world," he said. "That's why I moved here, you know. The air has remarkable tonic qualities. And the earth is marvelously fertile if you go in, as I rather do, for gardening. You can grow absolutely anything down here. Which is why the school never wants for fresh vegetables, of course. Well, I won't be keeping you,

Bannister. You'll want to be getting on." He began to drift away. "Evening, Bannister."

For a moment Jimmy had a curious feeling of sweetness. He was to remember this moment the next time the Foghorn wailed at him.

Another time he thought he saw the ghostly Padgett standing in his usual shadows. But Padgett, he reminded himself, was a joke. After that, when the prefect came out and told him he wasn't allowed to go outside by himself after supper, he wasn't all that sorry to hear it.

On Sunday afternoons there was a letter-writing period and Jimmy wrote his father: but not the wild letters that still shrieked through his mind like express trains during the week. He described the conditions at length, but found himself pulling his punches as if he was embarrassed to let his father know what a crazy school he went to. Mr. Bannister's letters usually arrived on Saturdays and, after Jimmy's heart had leaped at the first two, began to seem quite a bit flat. Jim wearied of being told that he "seemed to be settling in" and that the headmaster was a fine man. When his own turn came on Sunday, he would iron out his father's latest, and try to find something to respond to. But there was nothing there, his father seemed to be sending the same letter over and over.

This at least kept his homesickness in bounds. (Could that be the old man's strategy? Unlikely.) On those lank Sunday afternoons in the big blank study hall, his father almost seemed to join his mother on the piano—two old photos, peering at him under glass. He certainly didn't sound like the old friend on Bear Mountain; he didn't answer Jim's questions about the summer or how his business was going. He almost seemed to be copying the letters out of a letter book.

But then—his father didn't set up to be a man of letters, in any sense. He dictated whatever he could, and added a small uncertain signature at the bottom. He was a smart man, but most of his business was done through personal contact, and he took to his pen with reluctance and suspicion. There was no point drawing conclusions from his letters.

Without noticing how it happened or when, he suddenly found himself friends with the two boys on his left in the dormitory—Ryan and Philpott—and the one across the way—Samuelson. These three spent much time devising ways to sneak food out of the dining room and ruses for dodging Army drill, and Jim found himself first listening and then throwing in suggestions: and then suddenly his tongue snapped back into place, and he was their friend. Slight concessions were called for on all sides. For instance, they seldom talked about girls, but listened politely enough when the mood was upon Jimmy. Philpott usually giggled. "You Yanks are all oversexed," said Ryan. "Smedley's just the same. On and on he goes . . ."

"Don't you guys have any interest at all?"

"Well, some, I suppose. But it isn't the whole life, you know."

"Worthington is interested, and Peters." Samuelson ticked them off solemnly, as if they were the boxing team. "Smedley is really the ringleader. He brings in all the new jokes."

"Do you know 'Roll me over in the clover?'" giggled Philpott. "I heard Smedley sing the whole thing the other night. An astonishing piece of work."

Jimmy almost had trouble remembering what girls looked like by now. You could scarcely reconstruct them from the matron, and she was the only woman he had seen lately. Hence he found it difficult to sustain any kind of erotic fantasy. The girls had a way of turning into something else. He had lost his normal expectation about faces since coming here. His vision of Marilyn Jenkins, for instance, might suddenly turn quite fat like Winston Churchill, or thin like Dr. Rabelais. Or even grow a mustache. The picture-making faculty was disordered by this onrush of English faces.

So this was one more reason to curtail masturbation and hurl himself into whatever nighttime activities were going. This meant in effect a quite endless pilfering of food, and two pie-beds a week for a boy called Jamison. Jim got surprising pleasure from this latter. Jamison was the dormitory butt, a mild boy with thin hair and glasses, and the teasing of him was as orderly as a minuet. Every third night or so Jamison would shuffle the length of the dormitory to complain to Meredith, the resident prefect, about some fresh indignity. He and Meredith would then shuffle back together through the gloaming and there would be a brief interrogation, with Meredith trying to look stern and the witnesses embroidering hotly. "Now look here, you chaps, this was simply got to stop. You're not in a junior school any more." "I think it was a raid, sir. From one of the other dormitories." "Oh now, Philpott, come on." "No, honestly, sir." "Yes, I thought I saw a chap skulking. It wasn't one of our chaps, different sort of chap entirely," said Ryan. "I suppose he was wearing a mask, was he?" "Yes, that's right. A mask and a hat over his eyes, sir." Jim held his breath, shivering with amusement; he doubted if anyone found it as funny as he did. Afterwards Jamison would plod about repairing the damage: not upset, to all appearances, but seriously puzzled.

The dormitory came to life as term sank into its third month. Meredith had seemed at first as brutal as the other prefects, but he showed now a slack, gentle side. He allowed the boys to read books under the sheets, and even to get in a little furtive visiting. The Ryan-Philpott axis took to staging brief picnics of bread and jam: at first in whispers, but then, as Meredith failed to respond, more and more raucously. Ryan would sing a few bars from *H.M.S. Pinafore,* and everyone would shush him and Philpott would giggle as he shushed. Then Samuelson would start things up again with one of his huge burps (he had the gift of burping at will) and Philpott would begin to laugh helplessly, hysterically. "Wrap up, you chaps," someone would groan from the far corner, the end near Meredith's cubicle, and eventually Meredith himself would come out and shout "Silence!" and wave his flashlight about listlessly. Then Ryan would have a hand clamped over Philpott's mouth and Jimmy would be shaking silently in his bed; laughing to himself over nothing, a burp and a snatch of song.

One day as he sat waiting in his cricket pads Jimmy found himself describing one of these affairs to Smedley. It really had seemed awfully funny, there was no doubt on that score, and Jimmy told it exuberantly. Samuelson's burp going off like a howitzer; Ryan yelling "ouch" as Philpott bit into his hand; Meredith's flashlight reluctantly playing on them and then swooping off again before it could get involved.

"I had the jam pot under my pillow. Ryan had the bread under his *sheets,* I think it was. Anyway he was halfway out of bed trying to keep Philpott quiet . . ."

Jimmy suddenly realized that Smedley wasn't even slightly amused. And he didn't have to be told why. Jam pots. "But still I'm called, burp, Butterfly." He looked at Smedley closely. There was no expression on the fat boy's face. By God, I'll get you, Smedley. For this I'll get you. Smedley shook his head slightly and didn't say anything. He wasn't mocking Jimmy, just being true to his own lights. He had a kind of integrity at that. He would never sell out to this place, as a lesser man might.

Smedley walked out to bat, his hips rolling suavely. A self-made man. An American. He missed the first ball bowled to him, with an incompetence verging on grandeur, and began to walk back, unbuttoning his batting gloves.

Jimmy resolved then and there to cut out the dormitory capers. Pie-beds, for God's sake. At this time of life. That evening Ryan said, "What's the matter with Bannister?" "Bannister has a tummy ache. It's all that rich American food he gorges on secretly!" "Smile, there's a good chap." "Cut it out." Jimmy pushed Ryan's hand away—Ryan was actually squeezing at his cheeks. "There's no need to be ferocious, Bannister." (Murmur of "Yanks are so blooming violent" somewhere down the dormitory.) They backed off and left him alone. They had moods themselves sometimes and were quite considerate. He perched morosely on his pillows, deaf to the giggles and the snatch of *Pinafore*. Of course, he reasoned, Smedley wasn't grown up either: on the other hand, you had to pass through Smedley to get there.

The loneliness came back slowly, an inch at a time, on caterpillar treads: rolling from the back of his head and occupying his sinuses. He realized that the fooling around had at least kept that away—a pity it was childish. Just for the sake of someone to talk to, he had sold out completely. Smedley, on the other hand, was taking the trouble to keep himself American. Making little sacrifices. When he got home, he could say, "I kept the faith." Jimmy would have turned into an English schoolboy by then. He groaned and turned his back on the invitation. Imagine thinking that business was funny. He absolutely agreed with Smedley. Practical jokes in the dormitory —two months ago he would have said it was impossible. Almost sixteen, almost driving, sipping his father's beer, narrowing his dates down from double to single—and here he was, hiding jam under his pillow. What had happened to him?

The voices twittered like sparrows, with a swiss-swiss-swiss of whispered s's. They were just as silly as Smedley said they were—but what else was there? Without the foolishness, it went back to being an empty barracks, damp, sniffling gloom, solitude, a druid graveyard, a waiting room—for what? For nothing, for seeing his father again. He got out of bed. He dug for his slippers without looking down. He felt instinctively that he must raise his head. A strange wave of sweetness that absolutely must be ignored in this place fanned across his loins, hardening his decision.

Now that he wasn't inside it, the laughter sounded harsh, exclusive. There were boys farther down the dormitory who would have felt privileged to join the picnics, as he could, at will; the laughter must sound to them like laughter through the Colony Club window. In this kingdom of gnomes he had social stature.

It was really the depth of shame. Worse than yielding ground to a blustering prefect, worse than groping for loagrithms that never came. But there was really no choice, no other life around here. And maybe if you kept reminding yourself that you *knew* it was silly, kept part of yourself outside it . . . He knotted the tassle on his dressing gown definitively. It was this or the horrors again.

"Here comes Bannister. Everything all right now, Bannister? Have you brought some lovely American Spam?" Jimmy bowed his head and submitted to the feast.

four

Toward the end of June there was a sharp change of air pressure all over. The last month of the summer term was in fact a startlingly mellow experience. One of the prefects stopped Jimmy in the corridor and asked him a serious question about American horse racing. The masters seemed to slacken, doing their various routines from memory (the Foghorn even got Jimmy's name wrong on one occasion, and bawled out a fictitious boy called Manwairing in his place). Half the boys seemed to be sitting for various public examinations, and this took the heat off the other half. Ryan explained that the masters had a professional stake in their pupils' performances and that they tended to become pleasanter and more human as they watched and waited; as if when the Day of Judgment came they would be able to say, "At least I was a nice chap. For instance, I was kind to that dreadful American boy."

The classrooms were wheezingly jocular. Homework was assigned and then forgotten. Mr. Smiles, the geography teacher, seemed to make his peace with America and took to reminiscing instead about rock-climbing holidays in Scotland. Dwarfish scamperings. Some classes were canceled altogether in deference to the exam schedule; and the masters spent the long afternoons playing squash, stalking butterflies, grubbing for leaf mold.

Thus ended Jimmy's educational period. All his friends were sitting for the school certificate (an exam which seemed to be the watershed between the middle and upper school) except for Smedley. So the logic of the situation threw him toward Smedley; but Smedley made him nervous these days. As fellow Americans, they kept a diplomatic connection alive, with exchanges like "You guys should taste some real ice cream. Right, Bannister?" "Right!" But there was a basic mistrust. Jimmy's failure to pursue the Smedley plan had something to do with it. Jimmy's choice of friends had a lot to do with it.

His new circle of Ryan, Samuelson and Philpott was quite outside Smedley's world. Smedley obviously thought they were little twits, especially Philpott, and of course they were, by any normal standards. Jimmy felt Smedley's eyebrows going up every time their respective convoys clashed. Why didn't Bannister hang out with Worthington and Peters and Featherstone? These were the logical companions for a high-stepper from across the pond. When

Smedley wasn't mooning around by himself, looking detached as hell, he was observed swapping prurient one-liners with these three. Worthington was reputed to be one of the reasons the school had stopped using maids in the kitchen a couple of terms back; Featherstone was said to keep a motorcycle in the neighboring village, which took him to parts of London where pimples were no handicap. Peters at least kept pictures.

Maybe if Jimmy had been aware of them sooner, he would have gone the same way as Smedley. But now he was used to his little friends and there was no combining the two groups. On afternoons when they weren't working, he hiked with his claque of twits to outlying teashops, or to farms which supplied real boiled eggs and homemade cider. Ryan trudged be-him in a monkish stoop, while Philpott would bound ahead and catch at leaves. Samuelson always wore a neat little raincoat with a belt. Their conversation was babyish in the main, full of nagging jokes and sexless chatter about the holidays. But then suddenly Ryan would say, "Do you believe in God, Bannister?" or "Do you think it was a ghastly mistake to nationalize steel?"

In general, Bannister found that he was treated as a man to respect in matters of experience, but as rather backward intellectually. It was understood, on the few occasions the question arose, that Jimmy had already lived a definitive sex life and was totally reliable on such matters. But when he was asked about politics and religion, less was expected. The question about God or nationalization was simply a polite introduction to the questioner's own thoughts.

Philpott, absurd, childish in every other walk of life, was deadly sober about his politics. "I am High

Church in religion and Tory in politics," he would say, all seriously. Samuelson was also conservative. "One must have order" was his thought on this, and Ryan would jump up and down and say, "Yes, yes, yes. That's the whole point. That's why one must vote Labour." If they brought Jimmy in at all, it was only to say, "Of course, you Americans have a mad system, don't you?" Once they asked him to explain this system—the machinery of primaries, delegations, etc., and of course he couldn't; and Samuelson, who had never been west of Bath, had to explain for him.

He didn't really mind. He rather liked being considered the crude man from out of the West with little formal learning but much savvy; a chap who knew the right moves in a nightclub or the back of a movie theater. Compared with, say, Philpott, he was a shrine of experience. Compared with Smedley and Co., he was something else. With them such claims had to be proved and updated. Being American started him off with a certain amount of credit. He knew how to play seven-card stud, and the other variations that Smedley had brought over, and he had been to Eddie Condon's. But where was his motorcycle or his girl in London? And why did he go around with twits? Judgment seemed to be permanently suspended in his case, and he began to see these boys as a vague threat.

The evenings now were impossibly long, and boys played cricket patiently in the twilight after supper. Jimmy had learned more or less how to bowl a cricket ball and he liked the gentle plodding about in the half dark. He could not bring himself to miss a ball on purpose (another weakness of character) and so, inexorably, he moved within range of the under-sixteen cricket team; and then, on a day when half of the side was laid up with examinations, into the side itself. He scored three runs and almost made a running catch and was complimented on his keenness, which was in truth considerable. At one point he saw Smedley lounging past the boundary, stopping, gazing without expression like a Hereford cow, and thought, Smedley, I've betrayed you again, here as elsewhere. And yet the funny thing was that Smedley never said anything disapproving, never looked anything worse than stolid. It's all in your mind, Bannister. He continued roaring after the ball and firing it back to the infield or whatever they called it.

As he trailed back to school, with his cricket boots scuffing to the seven o'clock chime of the church bells, he asked himself why he was still allowing the concept of Smedley to bother him. The answer was of course that Smedley stood for America in some way—rather as the matron stood for women. He had no very special personality of his own, only a great undifferentiated Americanness. To lose touch with Smedley, to lose favor with Smedley, was to cut yourself off from the source.

Jim had in his pocket a fresh letter from his father and that seemed American too, which was odd. For your father to seem any nationality was odd. The voice that had always been neutral as water would probably have an accent the next time he heard it—a grotesque accent, if he didn't keep in tune with Smedley.

Anyway, there were only two weeks to go now. Ryan had begun to count off the actual hours till the end of term, 236–235 . . . By the end of July, Jimmy would be back home, swimming, boating in the Sound with his father, smelling the fresh paint on the boats. He could picture the white sails, hundreds of them, bobbing under a flawless sky: an honest-to-john blue sky after three months of scattered showers, unsettled conditions, depressions in the Midlands.

When he got to the changing room, he took out the letter for the fifth time since breakfast and read it again, with the sailboats in mind, hoping to hear a friendly twang in his father's voice, some promise of a good summer ahead. But Mr. Bannister had nothing to say about the summer. His voice came through faintly, like the metallic sound of a long-distance phone call. He had been receiving still more satisfactory reports about Jimmy's progress; seemed to be getting the hang of things, popular with the boys. By next term he should—next *term?* Well, we'll see about that, buddy boy. He put the letter away and looked around at the empty shower stalls. Who was watching him getting the hang of things? Who saw him being popular with the boys? Nobody ever seemed to see him at all, nobody but his little cubicle of friends: and yet his father kept getting these wonderful reports . . .

At supper Samuelson said, "I hear you distinguished yourself on the cricket pitch this afternoon?"

"I wouldn't say that."

"He was the absolute linchpin of the side," said Ryan. "Of course he kept dropping his bat and tearing over to mid-off and shouting, 'Let's get 'em, gang,' but apart from that . . ."

"Yes, and spitting on the ball," said Philpott. "Wonderfully expressive people, Americans. Marvelous athletes, I hear."

"It's the food, of course. Limitless Spam." Samuelson flexed his biceps and belched. "Peanut butter, milk shakes, vitamin-enriched plastic meatballs, the lot! My father's been over there this year and he says you wouldn't believe it, my dear. He says Americans are all at least six foot six by this time, in their plastic socks, and weigh a minimum of twenty stone . . ."

"Of course, take baseball," said Philpott suddenly. "It's just a form of rounders, isn't it? There's not much science to it, is there? You just slog the ball, don't you? It's not like cricket, is it?"

"My father says it's much more exciting than cricket," said Samuelson.

"Pooey on cricket," said a boy farther up the table, which started a familiar digression. Ryan leaned out of this to say, "Are you jazzing it tonight, Bannister?"

"I haven't thought about it."

"We have a new record."

"That's nice. We could use one."

"It's by Duke. 'Take the A-Train.' Smashing." Now that he was attuned to finer distinctions, Jimmy found Ryan a somewhat incongruous figure at the jazz club. As term wore on, he seemed to become ever more bouncy and zestful, developing a tendency to roll his eyes and tap his foot ferociously, as if it had gone to sleep, whenever the music got the least bit hot. The others glanced at him from time to time with something like embarrassment: as if to say, "Please! Not in front of Smedley!"

But then everything had turned upside down. At the first meeting of the club Smedley had seemed almost like a comedian: using his Americanism as a clown would use a physical deformity, to raise a laugh and ward off disgust. But now Smedley seemed absolute master of the scene, poised, sure of his audience; the slang phrases sounded quite ingenious, even to Jimmy, who knew theoretically that they shouldn't be mixed half so thick. As for himself, he was now the other kind of American; the laconic, underplayed kind, trafficker in surly monosyllables. He wanted to explain that he had misled them about this, but he found that it was too late, he was stuck; with this particular group, he *was* laconic.

In some curious way this one room where it was good to be an American had become one of his worst rooms. He was expected to live up to something here; he was Bannister, the other American. A tone-setter. His facial expressions were studied covertly. Notice how Bannister does it, notice how he listens. Yet the music sounded a little foreign to him now, accustomed as he was to the dormitory voices, Philpott's selection from *Pinafore,* and the "Sir, sir, *please* sir!" of the classrooms.

The New York scenes that had hit him with such poignance two months ago had lost almost all their flavor. Had he really felt sentimental about a Fifth Avenue bus? Yes, and an IRT subway as well. He felt like a monk clutching a lost faith. The holy pictures meant nothing anymore.

The twelve members of the jazz club came from all corners of the school. Jimmy didn't know any of them in real life except Ryan and Smedley. So he was slightly surprised when one of them wheeled on him and said, "Wasn't that you I saw playing for the Colts today?"

"Yes, you might have."

"I thought so," the fellow said. "Yes, I thought it was you."

"I didn't know that Yanks played cricket," said someone else.

"They don't," said Smedley.

"Oh."

Jimmy could still feel the tingle of the afternoon's game and of the cold shower afterwards. He would have liked more silly conversation about baseball and cricket, but this was hardly the place for it. This was Smoky Joe's saloon, the bust of Elgar notwithstanding, and Big Dwight Smedley had just dropped in to touch bases with a bunch of the boys. The A-train was off again and they were all tapping their feet rigorously. Smedley snapped his fingers softly and muttered, "Yeah, yeah. Well, all right then." The smoke from the mandatory cigarettes hung like fog. Why was he sitting in this stuffy room when he could be out practicing his cricket? He looked at Ryan with his cozy Norman skull: the only face he liked was the only face that didn't belong here. Ryan, grooving like a madman, because he was Bannister's friend and felt safe, under the wing of a real Yank. Ryan, stay the way you are. It's better than this.

Yet this was America, or a groping fascimile thereof, and Jim sensed that if he began enjoying cricket better than this, he would be in some kind of trouble when he got back.

Well, American wasn't just jazz, of course. There was also fishing with his father, and the like. The next day he began counting off the hours with Ryan, although this made them go more slowly of course. Which was perhaps the point. At night he got into the habit of conjuring American scenes just to keep them clear in his mind: Huckleberry Bannister afloat on his raft. Dead-End Bannister, swimming bare-ass off Pier 19, rustic Bannister and urban Bannister all combined and intermingled. America was a series of colored slides, dates 1935–45, deeply engrafted on his retina: some based on fact, for his life had contained equal parts of city and country and he came by both his wienie roasts and his sunsets over Manhattan legitimately—but some just things that he thought he had seen, and everything just a little too bright and sunlit in the un-nuanced Technicolor of the period. With his picture machine slightly on the fritz, he found it helpful to overexpose his fantasies. And since the slides were made in England, his American sky overcompensated by being a gross, undeviating blue. The light was so strong at times that he had to open his eyes and bathe them on the darkness of the dormitory.

One night when he was either awake or asleep he received a visitor. He had been trying to conjure up Marilyn Jenkins—or, if he couldn't get her, at least Paulette Goddard—when soft as a moonbeam, the ghostly Padgett slithered between his sheets. He knew it was Padgett without looking. It seemed quite inevitable, almost expected.

"How are you, my dear?" said Padgett.

Jimmy didn't turn round. He was too tired to scream. Too embarrassed for Padgett.

"You've been avoiding me. You've been very cruel, you know." Jimmy shut his eyes and blocked off the nerve ends. He was not going to think about this. He began to sense a restlessness behind him, a dry heaving of sheets. "Well, that's all I wanted to say."

When Jim looked round a moment later, Padgett was gone. Jim fell asleep, or perhaps had been asleep all along. He honestly never knew which. (There should be a rule about people like Padgett, he thought.) The memory bothered him for several nights after that, mainly the memory of his not screaming. But he managed at last to drive it away with American prints; and—perhaps the thing had been an exorcism—he never saw Padgett again. Ryan told him that Padgett had been sent home early, sick or something. So that was the end of that.

Dr. Rabelais suddenly came back to life in the last

two weeks—as if his real life was lived in the vacation and he slept like a koala bear through the terms. He would be observed regaling knots of older boys in the corridors: the guffaw of the eighteen-year-old Englishman would probably echo in Jimmy's head forever. Dr. Rabelais arranged two-minute chats with every boy in the school, making up thus for three months of paralytic inattention. Jimmy must have been about 230th on the list, because he sensed a certain languor beyond the usual in the headmaster's style when the meeting finally eventuated.

"I hear you've been settling in very well, Bannister" —so that was where all that talk came from. "Mr. Worthing tells me that you're quite popular." If there was anybody Bannister had seen less of than the headmaster, it was Mr. Worthing, the housemaster of Frisby. All the petty house discipline was funneled through the prefects, and Mr. Worthing spent most of his time tinkering with his baby Austin, wiping his hands on oil rags, climbing in and puttering off through the gates.

"Scholastically, the picture is not quite as grim as it might once have appeared. Mr. Withers informs me that you have apparently mastered the mysteries of logarithms and should be prepared to sit for the school certificate a year from now; Monsieur Necker seems to feel"—Dr. Rabelais looked puzzled as he read this bit of the report—"that your French has gone off slightly? But that you are still one of his most satisfactory pupils. Well." Dr. Rabelais hurried on. "Mr. Smiles says that you have taken significant strides . . ."

There was simply no listening to this stuff. Jimmy gazed round, his eye pausing at the little white walking sticks. He wondered once more what they felt like. Bee stings? Razor cuts? They were part of the life of the place, very much so, and he was curious about them after listening to the veterans compare notes.

He had come within inches of finding out just two nights ago. Meredith, the dormitory prefect, had decided for some reason to reverse the general thaw in labor-management relations. Possibly wishing to make up for a lackluster performance through the balance of the term; possibly because Ryan and the chaps had simply pushed him too far; possibly from some discontent of his own, about leaving school forever. In any event, he swung his torch flush onto the picnic for once, and then surprising everyone by not swinging it away again.

There was the usual ratlike scurry, for which Meredith seemed to allow sufficient time. But Jimmy was held for a second or two by a strange torpor, mixed with a wish, perhaps, to test himself against an easier prefect than Sprague. What would happen if Meredith caught him? He hesitated, still on the edge of Ryan's bed, with a large coconut cake on his lap.

Somebody told him the next day that the cake possibly saved him from a charge of moral turpitude. But at the time it seemed to incriminate him further.

"Hello," he said to Meredith, who hovered a few feet away now, a dark lump of anxiety. Meredith waved the torch at him in a wild gesture. "Bannister! What the devil do you think you're doing?"

"Nothing."

"Devil do you think you're doing with that cake?"

"Nothing. Just sitting."

"Well, you don't just sit with a *cake*, Bannister. In the middle of the night! Do you?"

"Yes, Meredith. I mean, no, I guess not."

There was a breathless silence. Meredith had his torch beam leveled at the cake, lighting it up as if for a celebration. He, too, had face to save. His difficulty was obvious, and one could sense the other boys working it out quietly to themselves. Meredith did not lack for courage; as a rugby football player, it was said to be his strong suit. But this was a poser. Jimmy was close to the age where, by unwritten custom, beating stopped. Beyond that, he was an American. Did one beat Americans?

No one spoke. Meredith swung the torch around, and Jimmy half expected him to say, "Ryan! What would you do?" Jimmy sat and waited while the plate grew heavy on his knees. Meredith, he suddenly realized, had enjoyed the dormitory childishness as much as anyone, although he must be all of eighteen. He was now making a stern effort to grow up.

Finally Meredith spoke. "Put the damn thing away, will you?" And they heard him stomping slowly back to his eyrie at the far end of the dormitory. In its way, it almost made up for Sprague.

"I have been in correspondence with your father, and he quite agrees," Dr. Rabelais droned, "That it would"—Jimmy was barely listening—"be beneficial" —it was like being in church—"for you to stay with us a bit longer and do some leisurely tutoring, tone you up, so to say, for the hard road that lies ahead . . ."

Jimmy's immediate reaction was one of only mild interest. He understood in a general way what the headmaster was getting at, but nothing said in that voice could have consequences in the real world. Besides, the thing was manifestly impossible. The words must have a different meaning over here.

"I have arranged for you to have a private room.

You'll like that, I expect. And you will eat your meals . . ."

"You don't understand. I'm flying to America on the twenty-seventh. It's been fixed."

"Yes, the plans have been altered slightly. You're to stay here for the first two weeks . . ."

"No, it's impossible. Father told me himself the twenty-seventh."

"Perhaps a subsequent letter has gone astray. The mails have been in an infernal chaos since the war. I remember when you used to get a letter . . ."

"I don't believe it. It's a mistake. I'm flying on the twenty-seventh, you see."

The headmaster fished around for the blue air letter. "Very handy little things, these. Ingenious. American, I daresay. Yes, here we are." He handed it to Jimmy.

The typewriting, the tone were authentic. Mr. Bannister was delighted with his son's progress, concerned, fully cognizant, willing to leave it up to, eternally grateful . . . Jimmy looked at it blankly. At this point the thing that bothered him was his reservation on the twenty-seventh. It was all fixed, you see. He knew the ticket by heart, knew that his name was spelled wrong on it (Banester), knew that its powers were unchallengeable. It sat in his pocket right now, as solid as the crown jewels.

"It's only for two weeks," said the headmaster. "As you observe, your father has made a reservation for you on the"—he peered at the letter—"twelfth."

"The summer will be over by then."

"Surely not. In any event"—the headmaster became wearily stern—"it is absolutely imperative that you have the extra tuition, and two weeks is the absolute minimum if it's to do you any good at all. The school certificate is far from a certainty in your case, you know. By next summer you will be"—he shut his eyes and pondered—"sixteen . . ." He went on like this for several minutes, or perhaps it was hours, demonstrating in the course of it that Jimmy's "wonderful progress" was just a manner of speaking; that, in fact, if Jimmy had done any less well, he would have been out of the ball game altogether. "It will be quite a *coup* if we achieve the school certificate after such a very unpromising start."

Jimmy noticed that the office seemed to have become much darker, so perhaps he *had* been in there for hours; or perhaps it was the snuffing out of his ticket. The latter had become completely worthless. He could imagine a man in a blue uniform frowning and scratching the name Banester off his list, and then the steel door shutting without him, and the plane rising. The ticket was right here in his jacket *pocket!* Worthless—

"Here, here, don't do that." Dr. Rabelais moved clumsily, pulling out the inevitable white handkerchief. Jimmy shook his head. It had become a point of pride never to accept these things.

His mind was temporarily deflected by the crying problem. Leaky Jim. He had supposed, after the stupid, hands-in-pockets affair, that his crying days were really over this time. Not so. Just beginning. He turned his face from the headmaster and tried to wrestle with it privately. He could hear impatient voices through the door: a long line of boys were waiting to see the headmaster and their voices had become shriller as the study had become darker. He would have to pass them on the way out.

"Well, Bannister." The headmaster was embarrassed now, tapping his finger. This seemed to be an aspect of the job he would never be able to cope with. He began to rise, and Jimmy had a strange feeling that he was going to swoop across the desk and pound his back. Jimmy made one last attempt to compose himself. He tried feeling angry, and the only result was a withering snort that startled both of them. He stood up and more or less bolted from the room.

He ran past the line of boys, trying to look determined and overdue somewhere else: but he was betrayed by another rending snort just as he had cleared the end man. He decided not to try the dormitory, which would be full of boys packing and skylarking, but veered off through a side door in the building, past another group of shrill, happy boys—the whole school reeked with happiness now—and out to one of the quiet lanes, where no one could bother him.

Another two weeks here wouldn't be so bad, he told himself. His father not telling him wasn't so bad. His father not telling him—he crouched down by an old stone wall in a last paroxysm: a lead weight squatted behind his eyes, in the bridge of his nose; and fresh tears were swimming around in his chest. The mails were, of course, a perfect chaos. But still.

He stopped crying, but stayed in the crouch for safety's sake. The talk about his progress had undoubtedly softened him up. That was one thing. Another thing was his . . . his . . . oh, this was ridiculous. He focused bleary eyes on the lane. The old man on the woman's bicycle would be by at any moment and one wouldn't want him to find one crying.

Look at it this way, Bannister—up till an hour ago, one had actually had mixed feelings about going home at all. One had actually . . . He must force himself to talk American. The stone wall across the way was supposed to be five hundred years old. How

about that, sports fans. Behind that was a meadow
with some stupid cows. Brown and white, which kind
was that? Jerseys? Alderburies? The cows are taking
over, men. Behind the cows a white farmhouse. Built
by the Romans in 10,000 B.C. Utterly destroyed by the
Vikings, restored, *utt*erly destroyed, restored . . .
Only two weeks actually.

He saw now quite clearly that America was better
than this stupid place would ever be. One aspect that
hadn't occurred to him before came to mind now
with the impact of something quite important. And
that was that all the good ballplayers would be back
from the war this year. Joe DiMaggio, Tommy Hen-
rich, King Kong Keller. He had already missed more
than half the season. He could see the bright grass of
the Stadium, the white ball flying around like mercury; and hear the harsh mumble and smell the mustard as you went up the ramps. Cricket, for Pete's
sake. Time out for tea, fellows. Effort, chaps.

Anger was good. He straightened up cautiously. He
could probably stand now without crying. He had a
grip on it. His crying days really were over. He suddenly knew it for a fact: but he wasn't going back to
the dormitory to watch them pack. That was too
much to ask. Instead he wandered farther into the
country, raging at cricket and old farmhouses. Throwing stones at the trees or bouncing them along the
road. Crumby old country.

Well, why didn't Father tell me? He looked at the
thought with dry eyes, drying heart. Really, so what?
It might bother him again later, but right now it
didn't matter too much. His father wasn't that important. He had banked too heavily on that, that was
why he was always crying. Two stupid weeks. He
could survive it, he guessed. They wouldn't get much

work out of him, that was for sure. After five hundred years they could use some new walls around here.

His feet got tired and he turned back. As he neared the school grounds he saw a dejected figure slumping toward the iron gates—from the other direction, as if he was coming out to meet himself. No, it was Smedley. Smedley, what ails you, boy? Smedley waved weakishly and sidled through the gates.

"I saw you crying outside Rabelais' office," he said.

"Yeah, I guess so."

"Things are tough all over. Whatsamatter, Jim—they keeping you another year?"

"Uh-huh. And not only another year. Two weeks of the summer as well. Can you beat *that,* sports fans. They really love me around here."

"That's too bad. Just can't get enough of you, huh, kid?"

"That's right. Love that Bannister."

"Well"—Smedley kicked the ground—"you have my condolences. I'm only sorry I won't be around to watch you suffer."

"What do you mean?"

"I mean I went right in after you and got canned. It seems that in spite of all those good American dollars my father pays them to keep me they don't need the guy men call Dwight Smedley."

"Well—that's great, isn't it?"

"I guess *your* father will have to support the joint by himself." Smedley rambled. "One American to a school."

"It's great, though. Isn't it just what you wanted?"

"Yeah, I guess so." Smedley suddenly looked like a boy again, as he had the first time Jimmy had seen him. His face was round and gentle and desolate.

"Good luck, Jimmy," he said.

"You too, er, Dwight."

Smedley shuffled off to commune with the country lanes Smedley-fashion.

The packing seemed to last forever, and Jimmy got used to watching it eventually. There were jolly accusations of who's been pinching my this-and-that, and scuffles in the bathroom over unidentified soap and toothpaste. From being such a stiff place at first, the school had lapsed into feebleminded carnival. Even the matron conducted her final business in a pepper-and-salt suit, with a Tyrolean hat plainly visible on the rack outside.

"Going back to Yankeeland, are you?" she said.

"Yeah, any year now."

"I'm told it's rather lovely around Arizona," she conceded. "Is that where you're going?"

"No."

"Pity." She released the blood-pressure sleeve, which was sort of her trademark, and waved him on.

Seeing the school empty out was almost as bad as seeing it fill up. The boys chuffed along the main corridor lugging their outsize suitcases, with the cricket bats and the tennis racquets and even in one instance a pair of oars strapped to the sides: putting the whole mess down, breathing hard, and then heaving along again and out through the main door.

Outside, they piled into taxis and chartered buses, giggling and crowding. Jimmy strolled outside to say goodbye to his friends. Samuelson was rather abstracted, already halfway home in his mind. (A really nice little home for Samuelson, with a neat apple-pie bedroom, prints, boxes full of colored stones, sea shells.) Ryan gave a very warm handshake. "I'll see you in the autumn, I trust," he said. Philpott was running around the bags, trying to hide Ryan's under somebody else's mackintosh. All three were going to London to begin with, before heading their separate ways; and it would be a hysterical train ride if Philpott had anything to do with it.

In place of the crushing undifferentiated sadness he had become so used to, Jimmy experienced something new, which he called immediately by its right name —melancholy. The quadrangle was silent, except for the soft crunch of the matron's boots. "Cheerio, Bannister. Have a nice holiday." The door of Mr. Worthing's baby Austin clicked shut: "Crank-case" Worthing was giving the matron a lift to the station: they chatted together in the front seat like old friends. Again silence, except for the distant shriek of the crows. A curious sweetness flooded him, like a special sweet kind of blood. His bones felt light and there was even a sweet taste in his mouth. This feeling had approached him several times before, but he had shied away from it. The doorman at his apartment building was subject to fits of epilepsy. The man had told him of a strange, gorgeous elation that came on just before his attacks . . . But nothing had happened now. Jim circled the quadrangle twice, floating slowly like a soap bar, savoring the silence.

His drift was interrupted by a clatter at one of the side doors. A boy he didn't know came crashing out with suitcases under both arms. "Have they gone? *My God!*" cried the boy. "Have they actually left?"

Ha, ha, you're trapped! thought Jimmy, and it was all he could do not to laugh a sweet evil laugh at the way things were going.

It was arranged that he should have breakfast every day with Dr. Rabelais and his wife. The doctor read

The Times. Jimmy read the *Telegraph,* and Mrs. Rabelais brought in cold toast and pungent, peel-ridden marmalade (strong enough to drown the taste of the margarine). The breakfasts were large and slow, and Jimmy got used to browsing through the pictures of King George and his daughters reviewing, inspecting, standing indefatigably by, and of the Queen Mother being handed things by small girls, the mellow endless court calendar. And when he had read almost every word of the *Telegraph,* he would squint at the pictures on the back page of the headmaster's *Times* —the Duchess of Kent assisting at the all-England croquet championships, the passing out at Aldershot (whatever that meant), the Queen Mother launching a new library.

Imperceptibly, he and the Doctor would slide into the morning's work. The curious thing here was that Rabelais now treated him as an absolute equal, asking his opinion, deferring to his judgment. "What would be your rendering of this word? Chambers allows a third possible meaning, but his only reference is to Pliny, which is rather late for our purposes. What say you—shall we take a chance, or shall we follow the path of prudence?" "Let's take a chance, sir." "Very well, Bannister. A chance it shall be . . ." Jimmy was getting to like this kind of talk.

They pottered their way through all the subjects in the syllabus, and although he couldn't see that it was getting him any closer to the school certificate, Jimmy did at least begin to understand the headmaster's musty enthusiasm for learning: and, just in this peculiar context, even to share it a little. Rabelais made it seem like an extension of *The Times.*

Jimmy had the afternoons pretty much to himself and was allowed to borrow Dr. Rabelais' barnacled bicycle for sorties to the nearby villages. There he would dismount and, having parked his bike in whatever passed for a municipal center, cruise the streets slowly on foot, like an old man with nothing better to do, ruminating into shop windows, front parlors and even into back gardens. Nobody seemed to mind, or even to notice. At four o'clock he would seek out a stationer's and if there was a new issue of *Film Fun* or *Picture Post* to be had, he would carry it off to a café and read it over a large, solitary tea.

When he got back, the headmaster's wife would encourage him to take a bath, and he always made a business of it, stewing interminably and then drawing pictures on the steamed-up mirror and examining himself from various angles, keeping abreast of developments. (Philpott had asked him one day if he thought he was handsome, and he had said yes, and Philpott had giggled. It had stuck in his mind.) He had reached the stage where he thought he needed to shave, but nobody else agreed. The pimples which the matron had sneered at had temporarily leveled off: but shaving would undoubtedly cause some confusion among them.

When the mirror had cleared all the way, it was his pleasure to stand in front of it swinging an imaginary bat in some indeterminate game, or to pitch, bowl, make faces, sometimes even to do a soft-shoe in his bare feet on the bath mat—until Mrs. Rabelais would knock on the door to ask if he was all right, and he would reach for his trousers in a reflex of embarrassment.

He always left the bathroom with regret, as one wakes from a good dream. But most evenings the headmaster would have him down afterwards for an orange squash or possibly a sip of sherry, so the prospect of evening was not as gloomy as it might have been. At dinner Dr. Rabelais had a tendency to make puns (surprising, because he never made them at any other time: it was like family prayers), after which he would retire to his study, leaving his wife and Jimmy to do the dishes and listen to the wireless.

So it turned out that the two weeks he had dreaded so much were among the happiest he had ever spent. Leaving the school at the end of them was not unlike leaving the warmth of the bathroom. He packed his ice skates and his baseball glove and jogged to the station in the headmaster's prewar Morris. The train ride to London was drafty and long, with no Philpott on hand to hide his suitcase and dash up and down the corridor. The only people who talk to fifteen-year-old boys in transit are people fifteen-year-old boys don't especially want to talk to. He liked the train itself, though, and enjoyed the lunch of sausage and mashed potatoes and the fields jogging alongside.

He was met at Paddington Station by a friend of his father's, a man called Soames, in a big American hat and a broad-shouldered topcoat which looked very strange. "Hiya, Jimmy," Mr. Soames said, although they had never met before. "Your dad told me" —his voice was as dissonant as his hat. He seemed friendly at first, but after a while Jimmy felt that he wasn't friendly at all. He paid no attention when Jimmy talked—and very little when he talked himself —but kept looking around and around to make sure that everything was going smoothly. "I bet you'll be glad to get home," he said.

"I guess so," said Jimmy. "I only wish I was going back for longer. *You* know, I'll just be getting used to things and then I'll have to turn round and come right back here."

Mr. Soames didn't answer: he apparently wasn't the man to discuss delicate points of sensibility with. He said, "Have you got your ticket? That's a mighty heavy suitcase, what have you got in there anyway? Bricks? Your dad will be glad to see you," etc. Driving in a taxi with this man through the dingy London streets lined with mustard-colored overcoats was one of the drearier things he'd done lately. Was Soames a typical American? He couldn't remember for the life of him.

It was probably possible to explain Mr. Soames, without dragging America into it. Mr. Soames worked in the embassy and saw thousands of people a day and he had developed a personality like a swinging door. Jimmy slumped back in the seat. There was no point in getting used to Mr. Soames, or even to London: he was flying away from both in the morning.

"You know you have a slight English accent, Jimmy?"

"I do?"

"Yes, you do. Your dad will be tickled."

The phrase "your dad" jarred more than anything Mr. Soames said. Of all the phrases he couldn't imagine Dr. or Mrs. Rabelais using, "your dad" surely came first. "Your father has been in touch with me, Bannister." The grave music came back to him, like the memory of a perfect croquet game or a really superb crossword clue. "Your father informs me that he fully concurs in my own view of the matter, which was not arrived at lightly, I assure you, where was I, Bannister—oh, yes"—that was the way to talk. It was like a chapel at twilight with shafts of blue sunlight falling on the preacher's smock and the begats falling like rain—so I have an English accent, have I?

They had supper together in Jimmy's hotel, and

Mrs. Soames, a listless blond woman who reminded Jimmy of a woman in a knitting pattern, made further comments on Jimmy's accent (It's cute. Your dad will love it") and told him no, she didn't think he needed a shave, did he, Ted? He looked perfectly fine; and he went to bed early, glad to get away from the two of them. His memory could not have capsized completely: Americans were not all like that. He thought about his friends, Harry and Forrest and Vince; but as he dozed off, each of these friends seemed to take on a certain Soames-like quality, their clothes and voices and haircuts. "Your dad told us you'd be here, it's great to be back in the U.S.A., five'll get you ten, gimme some skin man"—a grinning chorus of Smedleys and Soameses waited on the dock waving flags and frankfurters; he drifted by on his raft, in blinding sunlight; *rocketsredglare*, boom, *bombs bursting in air*, boom . . . The P-49's flew overhead in endless volleys while the President talked total victory. Noise, war effort. Miss New Jersey drove her ten-millionth rivet while the bulbs popped and the new battleship slithered down the causeway. He twisted away from the racket and banged his head against the old brown cabinet that housed the porcelain chamber pot. Oh, brother, this was going to be great.

As a result of his restless night, he slept a lot on the plane through the long day of a westward flight. When he wasn't asleep he read a detective story and chewed on the mints and bits of gum that the stewardess kept priming him with. (She had been especially asked to look after him, and this seemed to be the only thing she could think of: Jimmy in turn didn't like to refuse her.) The man next to him was contagiously shy, so that it was all very nice and quiet. Jimmy became uncomfortable just before the end, because he wanted to go to the bathroom, and this shy man next door had a way of jerking his knees nervously as Jimmy passed over and then half rising and getting pinned on the arm of the chair, and Jimmy was reluctant to set all this in motion. Then, when he could stand it no longer, the *fasten seat belts* sign went on and he was trapped for another twenty minutes or so. Outside of that, it was an uneventful trip.

five

Dad was the right word for him after all. To eyes accustomed to Dr. Rabelais, Jimmy's father seemed large, streamlined, all the bugs removed from the 1946 model. He had on a sky-blue summer suit and a broad silver necktie, a brown straw hat and two-toned shoes: not a single item that Rabelais could have worn to one's wildest dreams. Had he always dressed like that, or was it the postwar boom? The customs official was very large and smooth, with manicured fingernails. He welcomed Jimmy back to the country and winked solemnly at Mr. Bannister, who unfortunately winked back.

"Which of these bags are yours, sonny?" asked the colored porter.

"These three, actually," said Jimmy.

The porter laughed, his father laughed. "Are you quite positive, old boy?" said the porter. His father laughed all the way into the cab. Jimmy felt a multiple embarrassment. Was this going to happen everywhere he went, and every time he opened his mouth? Tiresome, as Rabelais would say.

His father certainly shouldn't have laughed. It was all right for the porter, but his father had sent him to the darn school and shouldn't make fun of him. He found it preying on his mind as they drove into the city. It put him at temporary odds with his father, who was also fatter than he remembered.

"I have to go to the office this afternoon, Jimmy. I guess you could use some shut-eye."

"I slept on the plane."

"Oh, well, that's not like regular sleep, is it?"

"I guess not."

His father had been laughing to please the porter, not because he was really amused. Oh, well. Jimmy was glad to see him anyway. He was a nice comfortable man whom everyone had a slight urge to tease. Jimmy knew that the teasing was on sufferance; his father had a hard streak and would hit back if he felt he was being gotten at. Why am I telling myself all this? Jim was sleepy after all, and he faded off right there in the cab.

The plan was for Jimmy and his father to spend two nights together in town and drive out to Long Island the afternoon after tomorrow. This involved sharing a hotel room, because Mr. Bannister had given up apartments for good, now that he was living by himself. That evening Jimmy was seriously appalled at his father's large, slug-like belly, which flung out mountainous over his floral pajama pants. You would never have supposed that all this lurked under the smooth blue jacket. A gentleman's corset lay panting on the bag rack. Jimmy could hardly bear to look at it: although of course he could see nothing else in the room.

His father walked into the bathroom . . . Jimmy didn't want to think of him *as such.* He talked quickly, trying to sneak back into friendship that way.

"You know, when you travel from one place to another place you keep seeing things like it's for the first time."

Mr. Bannister was brushing his teeth already but gave a muffled sound of agreement, or anyway of interest.

"Like the cars. They really look crazy, don't they? You see one little guy in a great big car. What a waste of space, huh? And the food in the dining room tonight—I saw a lady leave a steak on her plate that would have fed four people in England." He got into bed and pulled up the sheet. "Did you ever eat powdered eggs? Take my advice. Don't." He felt his old voice coming back, forcing its way exultantly. "Powdered milk. That's even worse. They put it in your tea, and they say—now, I'll bet you can't tell the difference. Ach, ptui! *Can't tell the difference.*"

His father came out of the bathroom drying his ears.

"It's been an interesting experience for you, hasn't it, Jimmy?"

"Yeah, I guess so."

"I'll try to send you more food next term. Give you a change from those powdered eggs."

"Next term? Hey, I don't really have to go back next term, do I?"

"It's a wonderful cultural experience."

"Yeah, but enough cultural experience is enough."

"A fine educational system . . ."

"Very handy if you happen to find yourself in ancient Greece—" But the threat was still a long way away and he argued weakly. At the moment it was hardly even a threat; he rather liked the prospect of roaring along the drafty corridors again, with Ryan barking like a machine gun and Philpott crumpling against the bulletin board, or of drinking tea with Mrs. Rabelais, and reading the back of her husband's *Times,* and weaving into the village and bicycling home for more tea. He let the argument go for now. He could bring it up later if he felt like it.

His father sat on the side of Jim's bed, and told him how it was. "In years to come, you'll be thankful. A lot of the kids around here could use a taste of powdered eggs. Our kids are a lot too soft if you ask me."

What did he know about this man anyway? Jimmy shut his eyes and prayed for sleep. But he couldn't help thinking, just before he lost the thought in blackness, that Mr. Bannister sounded just like one of his own letters.

His wild remark to Rabelais, that he was getting back to America "too late for summer," had a certain truth to it. The summer had its own rhythm, and it had been pushing along all this time without waiting for him. Marilyn Jenkins, for instance, had left for Cape Cod. He called his other city friends the next afternoon and listened to the wrangle of telephones in empty apartments; or found himself talking to thick-voiced cleaning women, who always let the phone ring twenty times before answering. "He's out. They gone away, didn't say when they'd be back. O.K. You welcome." Strange, strange voices. The worst blow was getting no answer at Forrest Tuckerman's; he was really looking forward to gassing with Tuck.

His father worked late the next day and Jimmy finally fetched up at a movie: Cary Grant, neither English nor American, a way station or oasis . . . Jimmy was relieved to notice that some of the men sitting around the theater were dressed like his father. That was one embarrassment the fewer. In fact, Mr. Bannister looked a lot better by dinnertime: his face was creased and friendly, stamped with little red crow's-feet, and he had lost some of his accent. Jimmy almost asked about the two extra weeks in school and why his father hadn't written to warn him: but again he was suddenly *embarrassed* for his father, afraid for what silly thing he might say.

Instead he asked about the pennant races and what kind of year Phil Rizzuto was having for the Yankees, what it was like in general having all the prewar stars back from the Army. It occurred to him part way through the conversation that he didn't really care very much; and he wondered whether his father cared either. Well—it was something they could talk about.

His father's whale belly had lost most of its terrors this time around. Remind me never to let myself get fat, was all Jimmy thought about it. Mr. Bannister's night talk was more relaxed than it had been yesterday, reminding Jimmy of their previous bouts of summer friendship. He realized that he had indeed missed his father, it was just a matter of getting his land legs. He asked if his father had made any big sales lately, and Mr. Bannister began to describe one particular coup that had pleased him; and Jimmy suddenly felt a bone-crushing boredom, and decided then and there to keep this kind of talk to a minimum. His father sounded like a stockholder's report.

The next morning Jimmy went down to a drugstore for breakfast, with a crisp five-dollar bill in his pocket, and felt, as he sliced through a pile of soggy, mottled pancakes, the first pure and delicate joy at being back. All this food—you couldn't stay mad at it for long. *The New York Times* was spread out on his left and the baseball information was suddenly as enthralling as it had ever been. He read every report of every game and then the box scores, noting how many hits Johnny Pesky had made (he liked the name Pesky) and how many chances Lou Boudreau had accepted. Five assists, three put-outs, no errors. How about *that*, you American mothers? He was so elated this morning he could have shouted.

His father left the office early that afternoon and, perhaps sensing that Jimmy was in a good mood, launched into a discussion of some girl he was seeing these days, Lorraine Somebody-or-other. Jimmy preferred to study the postwar cars through the side window. He didn't care to hear his father talk about girls.

"The Cadillac is the only car that looks any good," he said. "The new Chryslers stink."

"You'll be meeting Lorraine this evening and I hope you—I know you'll like her."

"I expect I will," Jimmy said politely. "I liked the last one: Gloria. The Studebaker looks kind of interesting in a morbid kind of way."

"Yes—Gloria was a fine girl, but she was never more than a friend. Lorraine is something special."

"Yeah?"

"I'm thinking of asking her to marry me."

"You are?" They passed a low-slung Mercury. A mustard-colored mess, in Jimmy's opinion. Mr. Ban-

nister was gunning the car in his excitement, and
Jimmy thought, oh for Pete's sake. Here we go again.
A few months ago Mr. Bannister had been gunning
his motor just as hard for Gloria. Then something had
gone wrong in mid-winter, there was that sense of a
mute scuffle, of voices late at night nicking at his
sleep, and his father was free again. Right after that,
Jim had been whisked off to England. He simply refused to take his father seriously in this area. The
DeSoto was sort of pointless . . . he shut his eyes and
opened them to the smell of fresh fish and the signs
advertising fishing tackle and fried clams, and the
stout men strolling the boards in T-shirts and peaked
hats and sandals, details to be stored up for some
winter or other.

They drove to the old summer house in Queequeg.
His heart jumped a full inch at the sight of the dusty
white clapboard. They went through the rooms open-
ing the windows, expelling the must and letting in
gray briny air. His father was still flushed and a bit
absent-minded, and Jimmy had to face the fact that
their last friendship, and the one before that too, had
been abbreviated by girls. For several weeks each
time he would see less of his father; and once he even
wound up with his aunt in Brockton. But it always
worked out. Meanwhile, he liked the stripped-down
house. The bare floorboards and the empty closets
with wire hangers dangling. Some of the best things
about being back were odd things like this. A stack of
old comic books stood by the bedside, looking wonderfully inviting, and having nothing better to do except unpack and make his bed, he squatted down on
the mattress and began to leaf through *The Phantom*.

Thump, crunch, the clockwork collision of ill-drawn
bones. About five comic books later he heard voices

being piped through the floor, shrill cocktail-hour
voices that pierced the planks like hot rivets, a
woman with a wide mouth, a man showing off. He
hoped this wasn't going to louse up the summer. He
rammed through a couple more of the comics, although it was frankly an effort by now. More whirling
capes and flashing feet than he had bargained for. He
tossed *Flash Gordon* aside. Give me the Queen
Mother any day—and went reluctantly downstairs.

His father was gently agitating the martinis, like
holy water. Martinis usually meant a bad evening,
worse than bourbon, much wild laughing and jokes
that didn't make any sense, followed by midnight
swims and mysterious excursions; and for him, the
house to himself, a house that looked like an unmade
bed, with ashtrays slopping over and glasses on the
mantelpiece and even teetering on the back of the
john—well, why go on? To the last giggle and door
slam? It wouldn't be as bad now as it was a few years
ago. During dinner he would at least be ignored. He
was too old now to be haphazardly manhandled and
flattered. ("You're a fine boy, Willy." "Name is
Jimmy.") Many dank evenings came back, just from
watching his father's small hands on the martini
pitcher. ("Willy here is going to be *all right.*")

The second thing he noticed was, my gosh, it's Mrs.
Soames. There's been a terrible mistake. A stringy
blonde with long heavy lids was drifting toward him,
circling Mr. Bannister, and she was just like the
woman in London. What a depressing development.
Something had happened to women in his absence.
She shook his hand and he felt long golden nails
skimming against his palm. "I've heard so much about
you," she said.

"You have?" he said—he had never worked out an answer to that one.

"Yes, your dad is always talking about you."

"He is?"

"Yes. He's very proud of you."

"Huh."

Having finally worked out how to talk to Englishmen, Jimmy had clean forgotten how to talk to Americans. No doubt it would come back in a day or two. But for now, "I'm very proud of *him*" was the only thing he could think of saying, and that was manifestly not the thing.

So he sat down quietly and listened to them instead. Their voices didn't sound quite so bad down here, but they were still awfully loud and scratching. Lorraine talked in a Seven Sisters drawl that sounded suspect to Jim (although he knew this accent sounded fake even when it was done right), and this brought out a trace of latent North Boston in Mr. Bannister's answers. It was like being able to look into people's skin through a microscope. "Can't you hear that she's a phony?" he wanted to tell his father at one point: and then: "Can't you hear that *he's* a phony?" to Lorraine. Can't you hear that we're all phonies? When Jimmy chimed in himself, his own voice sounded just as silly as theirs, and the thought of having to listen to the three of them all summer became really quite depressing.

The martinis went on and on, sizzling cold and smoky, and when dinner finally came along, Lorraine didn't eat any of it, but kept right on smoking and drinking and talking about the Wheeler estate, which had recently come on the market. As soon as he could, Jimmy slipped outside. They were getting affectionate, jamming two or three honeys into every sentence, and fumbling intermittently for each other's hands: the hairy arms of an out-of-shape tarantula groping for a daddy-longlegs. Jimmy also couldn't help wondering how his father disposed of his stomach during the act of love: and felt a bubble of nausea forming around the thought. He was happy to get out in the night air.

This summer was a big fat nothing so far. He hoped tomorrow to dig up some friends, but meanwhile he had to settle for this ugly, overtrained woman. She wasn't funny or interesting. She was an account executive, whatever that meant, and she had a niece about Jimmy's age—probably a junior account executive, another cross for him to bear. (Lorraine was dying to get the two of them together.) He just didn't like the feel of things—to tell you the truth, he could hardly wait to get back to England.

The next day he went to the Club with his father and Lorraine, and watched more martinis go down on the Club verandah. They had only joined the Club last summer, but already his father sat with the dullest people, which made him seem like an old member. "You remember Mrs. Vanderpatch, and Mrs. Fredericks. My son, Jimmy. He just returned from England. He's in school there." Two flabby, bathing-suited women, purple across the top of the chest, and startlingly white just below that. "Where's Dave?" he asked Mrs. Vanderpatch. "He's spending the summer in camp," she told him, thus eliminating one more friend from the running.

Rather than witness another scene of degeneration like last night's (Lorraine had finally kicked off her shoes and plunged into a South American dance with Mr. Bannister), he pulled out and went for a quick swim. The Club pool seemed to have been commandeered by the eighteen-year-old set, so he headed for the beach. He really didn't care for the basic American face as represented at the Club. Americans had never had faces before, of course, but they certainly had them now. Just look at the mouths on those women: huge red rings like the big end of a megaphone. Teeth like sharks. And the heavy stupid jowls on the men. He suddenly realized that he hadn't seen a single English person that you could seriously call fat. Here you hardly saw anything else.

"Hey, Jimmy." He looked around, and there was a human face at last. Forrest Tuckerman, dripping wet from the sea. Forrest! The guy he had been looking for, without much hope. Not just an American but a friend. The last time he had seen Forrest had been at his farewell party in March. They had each been allowed a beer for the occasion, and they had clinked the heavy glass bottles solemnly in a toast. So—here was Forrest.

"How you doing, Tuck?"

"Fine! I see you got back."

"Yeah."

"How was it?"

Jimmy shrugged. How was it? He shook his head. "They tell me I got an accent over there."

Forrest inclined his head and seemed to listen closely, although Jimmy had stopped talking. "Say something," Forrest said after a moment. "What do you want me to say?" "Anything." "It's a nice day." "You haven't got an accent," said Forrest.

Tuck was blonder than he remembered and his bones looked bigger. He was tanned through and through. Jimmy felt suddenly that he had missed three crucial months of growth and sunlight.

"So how was it really?" said Forrest.

"Very queer, very strange. I couldn't describe it."
They walked slowly to the beach. Jimmy remembered
Forrest as being all dressed up for winter with an
outsize overcoat and a long unwieldy scarf and a
small, man's hat. It was hard to recognize this gawky
stripped-down version, sniffling and dripping sea
water, stepping from winter into summer. "Did anything happen when I was gone?" "Not much, I guess."
"How's Sambo?" "Fine, far as I know. I didn't see
much of Sambo lately." "How's Harry?" "I guess he's
O.K. His family moved to Connecticut, you know."

The group at his party had seemed indissoluble, a
scene he could rejoin at any moment. "See you fellows in three years," he had said on the way out. "See
you, Jim," see you, see you . . . And here they had
fallen effortlessly apart. "Vince is changing schools
next year. He didn't do too good in English." Forrest
smiled and his darn teeth had grown an inch. "You
gotta do good in English, you know what I mean, *pai-
san?* You gotta talk it right."

Jimmy was still wearing his English clothes, a dark
blue blazer and gray flannel pants. He felt funny
standing on a beach like this, the sand lapping his
trouser cuffs, as if he had arrived there in a dream.
He said, "I'd better find a bathing hut."

"Yeah—well listen, see you, Jimmy."

Forrest had scented the sea and went loping toward it. Jimmy was relieved not to have to talk to
him any more. Accent or no accent, they talked different.

He found a bathing hut and got changed very
slowly, staring at the dry gray wood of the door and
the wet sandy slats on the floor, not thinking about
anything special. The sea air felt good anyway.

He stood outside the hut for a moment, squinting

across the dunes. It was very strange being here. The roar of the breakers, the glare of the sun. For a moment he couldn't place where he was or how he had got here. In the middle distance stood Forrest, shivering from his latest dip, talking to a girl. Jimmy supposed he had better head in their direction, because Forrest was the only person he seemed to know around here. The unnerving thing was that, just like that, he felt he didn't much like Forrest. Friendship couldn't be like that, could it? Ah, he'd get used to Forrest again, by and by.

He tiptoed across the sand, finding it painfully hot. His eyes were on the girl now and she looked awfully pretty, but as he got close she moved away, leaving him with Forrest again.

"How's it going, Jimbo? You look as if you could use some sun."

"Yeah, I guess I could."

"They tell me it's always foggy in England." Forrest suddenly got excited. "You can't see where you're going or what you're doing, it's so foggy. Your candle goes out and you feel these slimy hands on your throat. Aargh! Oh, so sorry—I thought you were Carruthers. Is that right?"

"No."

"All the English movies I've seen take place in the fog. I guess thay wait for a foggy day before they start shooting, right?"

"Maybe that's it."

"Playing cricket in the fog is what they do over there. 'I say, old boy, that's my wicket you're standing on'—" Jimmy wasn't getting used to this guy at all. He was forming a real loathing for him. Forrest must have sensed something was wrong. "Well, that's what they tell you. I don't really believe it. They make jokes like that about all the countries."

"It's a stupid custom," Jimmy said sharply.

"Yeah, I guess so." Forrest seemed embarrassed. His old friend had lost his sense of humor. Lost it in the fog. Jimmy wanted to explain—look, it isn't my sense of humor; I just wish I could show you how stupid all that stuff sounds, fog and cricket and the rest of it. He wasn't angry, just a little impatient. But Forrest didn't get it at all. His pale blue eyes blinked. "You coming in for a swim?" he said quickly. "All right." They started jogging the last few feet. "Oh, by the way—" Jimmy thought of a happier channel—"who was that girl you were talking to just now?"

"Her? That was Carol. Carol Fletcher."

"She looked nice."

"Yeah, you think so?" He sounded surprised.

"Well, I was pretty far away. Isn't she nice-looking?"

"I don't know. I thought she was kind of homely."

They stood uncertainly at the sea's edge, each willing to defer to the other's judgment about Carol Fletcher. Jimmy could have sworn she was good-looking, but he had made mistakes on this point before.

"Well, how *is* she? I mean, has she got a nice personality?"

"She's all right."

They looked at each other blankly. Jimmy's jaws were locked from the cold water round his shins. As for Forrest, the sea and the salt seemed to have washed his eyes away, the way the sea air bleached the trees and shrubs along the shore. Are we supposed to be friends? thought Jimmy. Is that why we're standing here?

They ran together into the breakers and the first

big one seemed to blow them apart. Forrest shot through it expertly. Jimmy was flipped backwards. He sat in the oozing sand and the sea came shouting at him again and hit him in the mouth and spun him half around. His mind was on Carol Fletcher. She was *his* idea of good-looking anyway. Forrest was not necessarily the last word.

He spent most of the rest of the morning looking for her, mainly to pass the time. Forrest had emerged from their joint plunge in a chillier mood. He must have been thinking it over in there and decided that he didn't much like Jimmy either. It was for the best. Jimmy sat on his towel in lonely grandeur, gazing at the horizon but with one eye out for Carol. Forrest encamped with some friends about fifty yards away. Jimmy didn't want to meet them. ("You have something in America called teenagers, I believe," Ryan had said. These boys looked like what Ryan had in mind.)

By lunch Carol Fletcher had become a second-degree obsession. He wasn't quite sure what she looked like any more, but he had a general impression of utter loveliness. He imagined walking quietly along the beach with her, throwing stones, laughing. Her in a white dress, him in a black tuxedo, her face a little vague in the twilight, and all the prettier for that. His difficulty in fantasying girls had righted itself—all it took was seeing one occasionally. Forrest and his friends got up to go and Forrest waved goodbye. He would have come over with a little encouragement, but Jimmy simply wasn't in the mood.

When he did see Carol again he had to be slightly disappointed. She was sitting in the Club lounge with a strange-looking mother, reading a movie magazine. Her hair was an ordinary brown, stiff with salt and pulled back tight. It took Jimmy a moment to readjust his feelings. But he had gone too far with her to turn back. He would love her now whatever she looked like.

He was sitting with his father again, and some other people he no longer bothered to register—more big mouths and flabby skin, creased red thighs, spongy, weak-looking arms—waiting for them all to finish their drinks and go into the dining room. Where they would undoubtedly have more drinks. This country was really one big pigsty, you know that. Slurp, slurp, slurp. His father had certainly made a lot of friends since last summer, but he hadn't been very choosy about it. Jim hoped nobody noticed the way he kept looking at Carol—he knew the kind of awful big-mouth kidding he would be in for if anyone did. But nobody noticed anything and finally Carol and her mother got up and left the lounge, and there was nothing to look at at all. Except the woman with the pendulous biceps scratching for a cigarette, and her husband's thin fingers drumming on the glass tabletop. (He said he was on the wagon, and he looked pretty desperate about it.)

At lunch Mr. Bannister asked Jimmy if he had had a good morning. "O.K., I guess. The water was colder than I remembered."

"Did you see any old friends?"

"Yeah. Forrest Tuckerman was around."

"I remember him. He was a nice boy. Fine manners."

"Yeah, he's all right."

Lorraine said, "I think Jimmy's losing his accent already. It's amazing how fast they pick things up at that age."

After lunch he went looking for Carol again and

found her right away, sitting with her strange-looking mother on the verandah. He wasn't quite sure what to do next, so he just sat down on a rocking chair and looked at her, as long as he decently could. She didn't look round, so all he could see was a piece of one cheek. But it looked great. He watched her for half an hour, until she and her mother got up and stowed their stuff into beach baskets and left.

His father came out and asked him if he was having a good time and he said sure and his father ducked back in. He was playing bridge with his scaly-looking friends, so that was that for the afternoon.

Jimmy wandered back to the bathing hut and got into his wet trunks. He noticed that his chest was turning pink. By tonight his shoulder blades would be pillars of fire. Every year it happened, without fail. Whether it was worth going through this baptism of fire in mid-August was a question.

He draped a towel round the pink area and went back and sat on the sand. Carol had driven off somewhere with her mother, so there was no point in looking for her, although he did anyway, out of habit. It occurred to him that he should have brought a book: but to get one now he would have to change his clothes again, find the book, and get back into his bathing suit, and no book in the world was worth all that.

After a while the inevitable Forrest Tuckerman appeared again (he seemed to be everywhere, like an official greeter) with his little band of spear carriers. Forrest had obviously been reviewing the situation one more time—or possibly had discussed it with an older relative—and he came over with some determination and said, "Jimmy, I'd like you to meet my friends."

They squatted around him and Forrest called off the names. "Hi, Jimmy, hi, hello." They were all very tall. Jimmy had this fooling again of having boon de prived of his summer's growth, his regulation three inches.

"Jimmy's been over in England."

"Yeah, how is it over there?"

"It rains a lot."

"I hear that."

Forrest was writing his name in the sand and making a big thing of the "T" in Tuckerman. "Jimmy says it isn't that foggy," he said diplomatically.

"Is that right?"

"I guess they wouldn't get anything done if it was, they'd keep bumping into each other, right?" Jimmy laughed politely this time. Fog jokes were something he would have to learn to live with.

"*You're* in enough fog already, Judson." Judson reached over and pushed the speaker out of his squat and onto his back. "Enough out of you, Pinhead," he said.

"Hey, they talk funny over there, don't they? Eh what, sniff sniff. Ripping, old boy."

"You get used to it."

"Yeah, I guess so. Say something in English, Jimmy. I mean in limey. 'Ow har you, old bean. Ain't it a nice die, old bean.' "

"I never heard anyone talk like that."

"How do they talk then?"

"Like me. I've got an English accent."

"Cut it out. *You* haven't got an English accent. You don't say 'Pip-pip, old chap!' " They all laughed.

"I *assure* you I have," said Jimmy—and they laughed again. "I guess you have at that," said the one called Pinhead. "That has real class—'I *assure* you.' Why can't *you* learn to talk like that, Judson? Your English is a disgrace to all of us. Ain't you got no education?"

"Duh," said Judson, scratching himself like an ape. "Whudjusay?"

It was like being hit methodically with a cushion. Jimmy hoped they would get onto something else in a minute. But Pinhead was still working the possibilities. "You really should teach Judson the King's English, Jimmy. Honestly, it's embarrassing. Any place you take this guy, it's a social catastrophe. He says Pop-pop when he ought to say Pip-pip; and when anyone else would say 'Beastly weather, what?' he says 'Lookada lousy rain.' "

"I guess you sound pretty funny to them too," said Jimmy. "I mean, to English people."

Again the effect was wrong. They looked down and around. "Yeah, I guess that's right," somebody murmured. Cheezt. Why didn't you tell us this guy had no sense of humor. That is a minimum expectation. Besides, it isn't like he was English himself. What does he care?

And Jimmy wanted to explain again: It's all so stupid. That's all I mind about. And he wanted to say, I've only been gone a few months, let's talk about the kind of stuff we would have talked about if I'd been here right along. But something had happened: there was no subject matter any more. Jimmy had never been exactly shy in his life, but you had to have subject matter.

"It looks like the Red Sox have a chance this year," he said tentatively.

"Yeah, I haven't looked at the standings lately," said Forrest. "Howie is a baseball nut."

"Not so much this year. I got more interested in tennis."

"Well, Judson is a baseball nut, and I mean *nut*," said Pinhead. "Aren't you, Judson? You just have to nod, don't try to say anything." Pinhead danced out of reach. "Judson is a typical Dodger fan—isn't that right, Judson? A dirty old bum." Judson jumped up and began to chase his tormentor toward the ocean. The others rose and joined the dance, pounding over the west sand with wild eagerness, almost as if they wanted to get away. Jimmy ran after them, but again the sea scattered them, and when they came out he was alone again.

From an infinite distance Pinhead seemed to smile apologetically; we'd like to have you in the club, but you understand how it is—these things take time. Maybe we can process your application by Labor Day. The others toiled up the beach to the clubhouse, tugging at their bathing suits and sniffling. They had been making the awkward first moves of friendship back in June while Jimmy was still polishing his cricket. From behind they looked so much alike that they could have been brothers; that was from being together all summer. Jimmy felt that his own real view had lagged behind and that he couldn't even *walk* with them any more.

He made a routine check on Carol Fletcher's whereabouts and was surprised to see her sitting up the beach a ways with her mother. Mrs. Fletcher was camped in a deck chair, in a gray print dress and sturdy stockings, as if it didn't make a bit of difference to her that this was a beach in summer. This reminded Jimmy of his own ripening skin and he pulled the towel round his neck, only to find that the grain of the terrycloth ran the wrong way wherever it touched down. His flesh had been burned raw.

The only thing to do then was to go inside. He was loath to leave Carol behind but he couldn't sit in the sun and he couldn't sit under the towel, so there was no choice. With so many rear glances that he was virtually walking backwards, he retreated to the bathing hut. One of the glances was picked up by Mrs. Fletcher, who looked annoyed, as if she was being spied upon through a knothole. She said something to Carol, who turned toward him and shrugged.

He spent a long time in the bathing hut, just diddling around. He thought of the bathroom at the headmaster's house, with the steamed-up mirrors and Dr. Rabelais' shaving brush and the tweezers Mrs. Rabelais used on her chin. And he remembered how he used to sit in the long thin tub (long and thin to fit the headmaster) and dream about America. And here he was in America dreaming about England. Making up color slides of it, the way he used to of America, only softening the light instead of hardening it. The pictures were straight from the tourist bureau—country walks, tea shoppes, cows everywhere, lots of greens and browns. He saw himself in a belted raincoat, strolling with Carol Fletcher, pausing to stare at a thatched cottage—but there *were* no thatched cottages near the school. He had never seen one in his life. He wondered where these pictures came from anyway.

He hated to leave the hut and go back to that wretched clubhouse, but there was no avoiding it. He found his father where he had left him, still playing bridge. "Are you having a good time, Jimmy?" said Mr. Bannister, a little uneasily.

"Uh-huh."

"That's good. There are some nice young people in the Club this year."

"A lot of families have bought houses out here just since the war," said his partner. "I'll bid three diamonds."

"Pass. That's *right*. This place used to be practically empty." It was hard to tell whether they were pleased or not with the expansion of the town. They seemed equally elated and depressed as they discussed it between bids. Recognition was sweet, bustle and boom were of the essence; yet they didn't enjoy losing thir sanctuary. (What difference does it make, if you play cards all the time, thought Jimmy.) The new people were of course top quality, the very best available; they added a lot to the Club, took part in things; yet there was something dubious about them too, something faintly unpleasant. Being new was dirty and tasteless—he had had the same feeling himself with the boys this afternoon.

His father said nothing during this discussion, being not only new himself but also a real-estate man who was helping to bring these scoundrels in; and for a minute Jimmy thought, watch out, they're going to spot you. But then he saw that his father wasn't nervous. He was more confident than last year, no doubt about it. He knew that talk was cheap, but they all needed the real-estate man—along with the divorce lawyer and the kidney specialist. Jimmy had never supposed before coming here that real estate was anything to be ashamed of. But last year his father had been more diffident about it, showing his card reluctantly like a rubber-goods salesman.

The talk got more specific, and Jimmy realized that his father had indeed made some big sales out here recently. The Asbury estate was his masterpiece—sold to Godfrey Farnes, the hotel magnate, a deplorable intruder and a valuable asset all in one. It was a funny conversation, because even Mr. Bannister seemed to have caught the elegiac note about what was happening to the place: he the literal agent of change. Oh, well.

Business never interested Jimmy for more than a few minutes. He began to wander off again and his father looked at him quickly and said, "Jimmy—how would you like to go sailing tomorrow?"

"Great!"

"You would?"

"Yes, I really mean that."

"Good." It might be agony tearing himself from the card table but he would do it. Jimmy felt that summer could now get into gear. The best dream of all, the white sailboat—surely nothing could go wrong with that one.

six

The sailing was O.K., although actually he spent the whole time thinking about Carol Fletcher. This obsession had developed feverishly during the night, along with his sunburn. He had filled the emptiness of drinks and dinner and Lorraine's chatter with thoughts of Carol; and then in bed he found that there was nothing else he *could* think about. His shoulders burned for her, and he even hallucinated her fitfully against the gray curtains of morning. By breakfast time, he was well and truly possessed. His father took him to church and he saw Carol there in person, and for a moment he was disappointed again, but by now he was even in love with his disappointment. Mrs. Fletcher sat next to her of course, looking just the same in church as she had on the beach, unsuited to any setting, and Jimmy began to fear that his dreams of Carol would soon start to include her mother, if he never saw them apart.

As he sat staring at Mrs. Fletcher he found himself thinking for the first time in his life about middle age as such. The stark ugliness of his father's friends, and let's face it, of his father too, had struck him the day before as simply a series of unfortunate accidents. But now as he gazed around he saw that it was no accident. The people in his pew were like a row of church gargoyles, with scraggy skin and coarse, unhappy features. The minister's skull was red from modest sun-bathing, and his face was dry and bony, as if his skeleton had already begun to assert itself triumphantly against the flesh. The point was that this business was at work in everyone, even him and Carol. Even *Carol.*

So that was his meditation in church that day. Later he realized that he hadn't seen many older people for the last three months and had lost his natural link with them. If you excepted the masters at school, who were freaks and would have looked funny at any age, he had seen nothing but super young English complexions for three months. So this sudden onslaught of defective American flesh had simply overwhelmed him.

The vision nagged at him all day—gray skin, sagging, dripping off the bone—whipping his thoughts back to Carol from one more direction. His father and friends flubbered about the boat in striped T-shirts, trying to look like sportsmen: carrying bottles of beer and talking in loud pilot-to-navigator voices; Lorraine was wearing denim shorts and her thighs were blue in the back, a switchboard of worn-out veins. He thought, Carol doesn't have to get like that. Some movie stars don't get like that.

This was not the kind of thing he had expected to think about on his first yachting day. He tried for a while to concentrate on the mechanics of sailing, but he was past the age when people said, "Here, Sonny, you take a turn," and Mr. Ogilvy and Frank Small and Mr. Bannister plus the little guy in glasses were more than enough crew to keep the small sloop tacking along. He had been introduced all round, with what seemed like a mixture of pride and embarrassment, as "my son Jimmy—from England," after which he had been ignored in a manly sort of way. So he sat back and looked out to sea, tossed between two banks of thoughts: the physical and spiritual decay of middle age, and the antidote represented by a physically fit Carol.

He imagined taking Carol to meet Dr. and Mrs. Rabelais. All four sat in beaming silence—since Jimmy had not yet heard Carol speak, these sequences had to be silent. But Dr. Rabelais obviously approved of Carol, pouring her cups and cups of fresh tea, and later taking them both on a tour of the house, tromping cheerily about the attic, pointing things out. On the way down he clapped Jimmy on the shoulder in soundless approval. You've picked a winner, my boy.

The English style of not saying the obvious certainly had its points. As he listened to the hearty chat of his father's friends, he pictured Rabelais grimacing slightly over, oh, a marmalade sandwich: raising his eyebrows, murmuring, "Quite, oh yes, quite."

Unfortunately, when they spoke to Jimmy he found his jaw locking again. What was the answer to "How's it going, Jimmy?" anyway? He got so tired of saying "fine" to everything. "How's the boy. Your dad tells me you've been to England, how was it, how's the rationing. Your dad certainly picked a nice day." After each silly question they waited politely for an answer, and would not be fobbed off with a mumble or a gesture. They looked right into his eyes until they had extorted yet another "Fine," or "He certainly did."

"You know something funny, Mr. Small?" he said when they had pushed off. "I was just thinking how many times people say 'How' in this country. 'How you doing?' 'How's tricks?' Isn't that what the Indians used to say too? How?"

"I guess it is," said Mr. Small.

"Do you think it might be something to do with the weather or what? that makes Americans say 'How'?"

Mr. Small chuckled uneasily. It did sound awfully silly, but it was the kind of theory that Dr. Rabelais used to throw out at breakfast, to start a whimsical discussion. "Maybe that's it," said Mr. Small. "I hadn't thought about it."

That was his last attempt at bright commentary. Mr. Small obviously thought he was some kind of pervert. He retired to a corner of the bow. Maybe they really preferred him just to say "fine." Or maybe there was a kind of clever talk that was acceptable from his age group which he had forgotten about. He could imagine Forrest Tuckerman and his friends doing it right. Diving off the boat with a final sally; and then the grown-ups could talk about wonderful kids, fine boys. "That boy of yours is going to be something, you must be proud of him." The speech patterns were unnaturally clear to Jim—he could see them in bright blocks, like subtitles in a movie. "Jim-my is quite a boy. We-'re ver-y proud. Proud of

Jim-my. We-'re ver-y proud." If *he* dived off the boat, there would be a puzzled silence.

So he tried to keep himself unobtrusive, even eating lunch by himself. Making a neat pile of his cellophane wrappings. Contemplating the great American slurp. He gathered these men did not belong to the Club but were down here looking for houses or for better houses: beginning the slow climb to the Club. Real estate took over from navigation during the lunch hour. As for himself, there were, as everyone knew, two kinds of teenagers, glib ones and sullen ones: and although it wasn't his natural type, he would have to settle for sullen right now.

Behind his wall of plexiglass, he watched them spooning their potato salad, chewing it like horses. His father's associates had always been on the dumb side, hadn't they? Gloria, Mr. Bannister's previous companion, had teased him about it sometimes. "Really, James—those *truck* drivers." "I can't help it, dear. Those are the people I work with." His father himself was not dumb, but he had to pretend. Maybe they were all pretending. It was better to think about Carol, who was obviously highly intelligent in a quiet sort of way.

When they dismounted late in the afternoon, Jimmy noticed that a couple of the men affected a slight sailor's walk on the jetty. Honestly. It was too bad Gloria wasn't still around to make fun of them. *You should have piped them on shore, James.* He was parched for mockery.

"Did you have a good time, Jimmy?" his father asked. There was a slight anxiety in his eyes, as if he too had remembered Gloria. "I haven't had much time to talk to you—looking after the guests. And keeping us off the rocks."

"I had a great time."

"You did?"

"Yes, I really did." His tongue was loosed. "I used to dream about this at school, you know. Just sailing around and having lunch and sailing around some more."

"You weren't bored?" His father looked almost grateful.

"Oh, heck no. It was just the way I remembered it. Sailing around, taking it easy, wearing old clothes. This and going fishing were my two best memories."

"That's great. We'll have to fix up some fishing one of these days."

"You know, those are the things you miss in England, the old-clothes things." Saying made it so. "You know what I mean, lighting out for some place in an old car. With a gun or some fishing equipment— things you can do by yourself, or with just a friend. And cooking your own meals."

His father clutched his arm. "We'll fix up some fishing real soon," he said.

His father didn't have to go to work the next week, so they stayed out in the old house and Lorraine stayed with them. Jimmy had gotten used to her face and her voice by now but that was about all. She wasn't a friend and she wasn't an enemy. She was always saying, "What was that, Jimmy?" as if they literally spoke different languages. Well—none of that mattered. But his father wasn't himself in her company. He was more of a, well, banker, his humor was louder and slower, and the quotient of business talk was way up. As a by-product of their separation, Jimmy was plagued with all kinds of insights into his father this summer. He was forced to realize that the old man's character had actually been drifting about in strange ways for a long time, possibly since his wife had left him. Jimmy saw absolutely no point in thinking about his mother. He had no idea why she had left or why she had so lightly yielded his own custody. It didn't matter. But he found himself thinking about her anyway in relation to his father. While Mrs. Bannister was on hand, his father had been one of those fixed middle-aged men with a closetful of blue and brown suits and a repertoire of blue and brown jokes. Jimmy could see him perfectly; it was as if Mrs. B. had held him in place for all to behold.

Somehow all that had come unstuck with her departure. He and Jim had become friends, that was good, that was good: but then his father had begun courting these girls. Which got his *age* unstuck. He began behaving youthfully, but in fits and starts: thus putting Jimmy on a sort of sliding scale. When Mr. Bannister was in full caper, Jimmy was his old buddy; when he reverted to middle age, Jimmy was lowered into childhood with a swift thud.

Next his father's weight came unstuck. He began going on and off diets, in tune to some mysterious urgency, becoming now a jolly fat man, now a determined thin one. Even his clothes began to look confused. The girls all wanted different things, Jimmy supposed. Mr. Bannister's taste in women had been tentative from the first, as if he didn't really know what he was doing: one week it would be a loud-mouthed blonde, the next a language professor from N.Y.U. Now he had found a businesswoman from Radcliffe. There was no design to any of it. And with each girl his father's character would float loose again, and Jimmy would go shooting up and down the scale from small boy to young man to confederate. And his father's cheeks would go slack and hollow as he whipped his way through a new diet. The point about this summer was that Lorraine herself was a tentative sort of girl who didn't know what sort of Bannisters she wanted, father *or* son, so there was nothing to stabilize the old man at all, and every evening was a groping about.

With so much time to burn away, Jim now found himself remembering his mother a bit in her own right. After years of being content to be an old photograph, she began to move around a little. He remembered her saying, "There'll be plenty of time for girls later." That was one of her phrases. And "your father isn't feeling well this evening." She was taller than her husband, at least in high heels, and she had a tendency to walk around in her dressing gown. There was no point to these recollections, they just slipped in between thoughts of Carol, and sat there.

. . . As for Mr. Bannister, he would settle down presently. There was only so much to say about real estate. After all of the, say, 100,000 houses in Long Island had been discussed fully, he would get onto something else. Save us all from businesswomen, thought Jim. Lorraine was to blame for this sharp narrowing of focus. She managed to combine a snobbish interest in the holding families with a cold concern for the property itself: and the wretched Mr. Bannister fell in with her mood.

So the early part of the evenings at least was rather drippy. Jim wished he could play the piano. Those lessons he had been so happy to shuck off at the time of his mother's evaporation would have come in handy now. There was an upright in the summer cottage and stacks of withered sheet music in the seat, with pictures of forgotten singers and band leaders;

and occasionally he tried to pick his way through a
number or two. But there wasn't much to it. By the
time he had mastered one of the wooden arrangements, he was usually sick of the tune. As the evening
thickened, his father and Lorraine liked to play records, but then they wouldn't listen to them, which ir-
ritated him. (They insisted they were listening, which
made it that much worse.) He would crouch down
next to the victrola to drown their voices. Eventually
they left him in charge of the record selection, and
then imperceptibly this became a form of duty. "How
about putting a record on, Jimmy . . . How about
putting *another* record on, Jimmy?" They didn't care
what he played, but they did notice the silence when
he stopped.

The supply was only slightly larger than that of the
jazz club at school, and the records were chipped and
scratched, but there were some good ones. Jimmy
Dorsey's "I'll never say never again again," brother
Tommy's "I'm getting sentimental over you"; Bunny
Berrigan, Claude Thornhill, the big boys of the late
thirties. After his father and Lorraine had gone out to
wherever they went, taking their voices with them,
the records made a ripe background to the latest
thoughts of Carol Fletcher—strolling through tall
grass with Jim at her side, dabbling her feet in lily
ponds (that was a weird one), staring at him with luminous eyes in darkened nightclubs: he had at last
eliminated the episode with Dr. Rabelais. That was
just silly.

Since there was no automatic record changer, he
had to break off every few minutes and attend to the
machine. Which kept him just busy enough to feel as
if he were doing something. The spinning ten-inch records ground their way into his bones: he supposed

he would never forget a word or even a bit of instrumental business on a single one of them as long as he lived. Sometimes he turned out the lights to heighten the effect, which led to some awkwardness with the record labels: he would peer at them by moonlight or, failing that, hold them against a splinter of light from the bathroom door. Once that was taken care of, he would fumble the record over the little knob and sit back for three minutes of meditation. He felt splendidly lonely in the dark, collar up against the world, Carol at his side—his father walked in and found him like this one evening, and a spooky exchange ensued. "Jimmy? Is that you? Are you all right? . . . It's Jimmy, honey." Four large bewildered eyes when the lights went on. "I often listen to records in the dark." "You do?" Mr. Bannister looked as if he were about to seize Lorraine and shelter her against this madness. "You'd better get to bed, Jimmy." Jimmy ground out his cigarette and stumbled off.

The only snag concerning his idyll with Carol Fletcher was, of course, that he still hadn't met her and wasn't likely to. A year ago, even a few months ago, he would have gone up and blithely introduced himself to her—mother and all. At least, he thought he would have. But now as he edged closer to his sixteenth birthday he found a certain tendency to postponement, a not-today attitude. Mrs. Fletcher had taken a strong optical dislike to him—well, let's be frank about it, she obviously thought he was nuts, staring at them through the Club window as they rocked on the porch—and, in fact, it was really Mrs. Fletcher he shrank from meeting. Carol still showed no awareness of his existence, unless those occasional shrugs she gave her mother had something to do with him.

He supposed he must be a premature victim of mother-in-law trouble. If he didn't make his move pretty soon, his nuttiness would be permanently established in both their minds and his cause would be hopeless. He had been here for ten days now, and already the summer was beginning to pack up and shift out. The boys were talking fall talk. Labor Day was the great watershed, and that was suddenly just a few days away. So—do something, Bannister. Stir yourself, you idle boy.

He tried the radical move of sitting in the next rocking chair and waiting for them to come out, but that only made things worse. He could see how he must look to them—that peculiar boy who comes out and sits in the next rocking chair. He thought of trying something through Forrest Tuckerman, but the lines were down with Forrest. He passed the gang every day on the beach and exchanged greetings: and they stopped courteously and chatted with him. But he might as well have been a diplomat from Africa. They talked as if he had never heard of football or high school or even girls: he almost began to wonder whether he had.

"I guess you'll be going back to England soon, huh, Jimmy?"

"Yeah, well, a couple of weeks, I guess."

"You go back later than we do."

"Yes, but our vacation begins a lot later too."

"That sounds like a good system."

"In a way. It depends."

Ever since he had discouraged their fog and accent jokes about England they had discussed it with this elaborate carefulness. They must have very interesting customs over there. Yes, indeed. Many in-teresting customs. Kids had changed since he left. He didn't remember all this politeness.

So they greeted and parted as swiftly as protocol allowed, and Jimmy wandered off with his books—*I, Claudius* this week: Carol would see from the title that he wasn't all idiot. He didn't like to ask Forrest about Carol in front of the others, and Forrest seemed to be cemented to his group, forever walking to and from the ocean with flippers or small surfboards, so Jimmy wouldn't get at him.

Jimmy had just about given up: in fact, he was embarrassed even to dream about Carol now, things had gotten so hopeless. He was rocking morosely next to Mrs. Fletcher one afternoon, thinking *this has got to stop*—Carol hadn't come out, so that Jimmy was feeling more than ordinarily futile: to go to all this trouble just to rock next to Mrs. Fletcher. He was startled by a friendly voice.

"What is that book you're reading, young man?"

He held it up. "A book," he said.

Mrs. Fletcher peered more closely. "Aren't you rather young to be reading *that* book?"

He shrugged.

"Well, you children seem to mature faster than we did." Her voice was much pleasanter than her face. "My daughter is so serious it almost frightens me."

"That so?"

"Yes. I often wish she was a little more playful. I'm always telling her that she should spend more time with people her own age." Mrs. Fletcher fanned herself with a trace of slyness. Jimmy had a feeling that she wasn't quite telling the truth. But maybe she was just intelligent. His father's friends said everything straight, without spin or guile. Mrs. Fletcher, he could see, might throw you a few knuckleballs.

"I've seen you sitting on the porch and I've suggested to Carol that you might be someone nice to talk to, but she just shrugs. She's a great shrugger, you know." Mrs. Fletcher sighed, but not as if she didn't understand: she understood all too well. "And what's your name, young man?"

"Bannister," he said, from English habit. "I mean Jim, James, Jim."

"My name is Lucy Fletcher. And my daughter's name is Carol." She smiled, as if to say—I expect you knew that? For a moment Jimmy wondered whether he really wanted to get in with these people: whether stupid friends weren't best of all. But just then Carol came through the screen door: the girl of a hundred goofy dreams, and it was too late to do anything but plunge in further.

She really didn't look so great from close up. But that was beside the point. Jimmy smiled uncontrollably.

"I see you've found a friend, Mother," said Carol.

"Yes. This is Jim Bannister."

"That's nice."

She looked at Jimmy without too much interest. His waves of devotion weren't getting through to her. "I think I'll go and play tennis in that case," she said.

Carol went back into the Club, clashing the screen door behind her. And Mrs. Fletcher said, "Which do you really prefer to be called, Jim or Jimmy or James?"

"It doesn't matter."

Fifteen minutes later Carol came out in tennis clothes, followed by Forrest and another couple. "Have a nice time, dear," said Mrs. Fletcher. "I will," said Carol. Jimmy watched the back of her legs as she walked down the road to the tennis courts. "I'm glad

she's playing tennis again," said Mrs. Fletcher. "It's a
very good game for the muscle tone. I'm sure that
boy Forrest will make a very good structural engi-
neer, or something, one of these days." She picked up
her knitting and stared at it. "A witless occupation,
knitting," she said. "I don't even know what this is
going to be. Well, one can always call it a rug, I suppose. I was going to ask, do you knit? How silly of
me."

Jimmy didn't know whether to wait for Carol to
come back. Having got so close, it seemed a shame to
give up. So he sat with Mrs. Fletcher, giving her half
an ear, while he scanned the horizon for tennis players. At first he felt nervous that anyone should be so
absolutely non-stop clever as Mrs. Fletcher, but after
a while he stopped noticing it. He tried being clever
himself and she was very nice about it, but that
wasn't getting Carol back, so his conversation became
vague, and finally so did Mrs. Fletcher's.

After three hours or so he gave up altogether. His
neck hurt from nodding and chuckling and rocking
and he had to go to the bathroom. When he got inside the Club the first thing he saw was Carol, playing cards with Forrest and the other two. She must
have sneaked round the back, by way of the beach.

"Did you leave Mother out there?" she asked him.
He was grinning uncontrollably again. The unex-
pected result of dreaming about her so often. It was
all he could do not to seize her arm and make off
with her.

"I'd better go out," she said. "Here, do you want to
play my hand?" She thrust the cards at Jimmy, who
looked at them uncomprehendingly. They were canasta cards, Forrest explained, and Jimmy had to explain in turn that he had never heard of canasta.

Carol was out on the porch in six (counted) strides and he had missed his connection again. He sat down glumly to learn this labyrinthine new game.

Once his disappointment had been properly digested, Jimmy saw that he had in fact made progress. He had insinuated himself into the circle. Tomorrow he would try harder. The canasta game lasted till suppertime, by which time the Fletchers had left the porch for good. His father suggested a movie after supper. So that was it for the day. His father and Lorraine snuggled squelchingly in the balcony and Jimmy slumped next to them with his knees skewing out into the aisle, and felt once again the strangeness of being here at all: a smell of sea air had seeped into the movie house, where it mingled with the smell of popcorn and the smell of people who had been swimming all summer—well, it was pretty hard to sort out, but he could see that smells were what dislocated you more than anything. He tried not to watch his father. His cuddling was of the demurest, but Mr. Bannister looked so fat in that whole connection. Carol came to mind again, but he dismissed her sternly. The dreaming phase was behind him now.

The next day he hit the porch early, armed with his book. Still *I, Claudius*—weird afternoons with Tiberius on the isle of Capri, unforgettable nights with the Empress Julia. . . . The Fletchers didn't show up, so he made some feverish headway with the book. He was expecting some hearty man to ask him if he was glued to the porch, Sonny, but he got off unpestered and passed a lubricious morning with Claudius and his friends.

After lunch he was back at his post, and this time Mrs. Fletcher was waiting for him. "I think I'll call it a shroud," she said, holding up her knitting. Carol hadn't come out yet, and Jimmy was suddenly struck with a terrible foreboding. He started to rise and Mrs. Fletcher draped a light hand on his wrist. "A woolen shroud would be so much comfier, don't you think? than one of those starchy ones. So much more practical in a climate like ours."

He sank back, and the foreboding struck in all the way. Sure enough, Carol came out a few minutes later carrying her damn tennis racquet again. And behind her came that famous tennis player, Forrest Tuckermen.

"I saw you had company," said Carol. "So I thought I'd play tennis again."

"Yes, yes, I'm in good hands," said Mrs. Fletcher.

Carol waved goodbye and Jimmy watched her legs dwindling away next to Forrest's long, stupid ones—when did *he* become such a great tennis player? It was truly aggravating and Jimmy's first impulse was just to leave. But there seemed to be a rule that *somebody* had to sit with Mrs. Fletcher at all times. Otherwise she would capsize or catch fire. He hunched back in the rocking chair, almost too frustrated to speak.

It was a long afternoon. Mrs. Fletcher's chair made a clicking noise on the wooden floor which got on his nerves. The knitting needles sounded like castanets. This was not how he had planned to spend the summer.

At intervals he poked his head into the Club lounge to see if Coarol had doubled back again the way she had yesterday. (If she had, maybe he could ask Forrest to sit with Mrs. Fletcher for a spell.) But the place was empty except for a waiter polishing glasses. It was one of those afternoons when everybody has a mission. You watch them leaving one by one, making plans, checking their lists and tickets, until there is nothing but you and your personal Mrs. Fletcher.

Mrs. Fletcher rocked mechanically like a blind woman, talking, talking, talking. Jimmy fantasized to kill the time. The waiter inside was a zombie, in the pay of Mrs. Fletcher: he would never hear a cry for help. Late at night he usually buried Mrs. Fletcher's victims in a bunker on the golf course. Rock, click, talk. Talked to death, poor devils. The noise was simply deafening. He still guessed that Mrs. Fletcher was O.K. but he didn't like this feeling that he couldn't leave her. He had an unfortunate side view of her face. There was something funny about it and he felt that if he walked away she might begin to scream.

No, not really. He could go away if he wanted to. There just wasn't any place to go. He picked up his book and Mrs. Fletcher politely stopped talking, but he couldn't concentrate. He stared at the book anyway, for a few minute's peace. He found himself thinking about last summer when Gloria was here instead of Lorraine. What a step down in class *that* was, and he thought if all women were like Gloria there wouldn't be afternoons like this. Gloria was the type who didn't want to be appreciated, so he hadn't appreciated her, but she had made last summer better than he had realized at the time, most of the bright memories he had taken to school with him were Gloria's doing. A fat lot he'd take back from *this* summer. This summer that was already slipping away like an ice cube. He couldn't sit here another minute, he decided frantically, he couldn't spend the winter dreaming about Mrs. Fletcher.

But he did sit there, the balance of the lank afternoon, until Carol and Forrest came back nibbling intimately on ice-cream cones. He felt like some sort of defective, obliged to sit with old ladies while the young people played tennis. He hoped that Carol would at least join them for a few minutes, but she went on in with Mrs. Fletcher, and the next thing he knew it was dinner and another day was gone.

By the next afternoon he realized that he was *expected* to sit with Mrs. Fletcher now. Carol had come to lunch in her tennis clothes and afterward stood with Forrest in the lounge. She looked at Jimmy hopefully as he came out of the dining room. If he didn't volunteer, she would have to call off the tennis. He would be the villain.

"Look, Forrest," he wanted to say, "you don't even think she's good-looking, right? Let *me* play with her." Forrest was looking at him blankly, patting his racquet against his hand. No one could beat old Forrest at looking blank. "Look, Forrest. You'll enjoy Mrs. Fletcher. She's a fine woman. You'll learn something. Ah, forget it." He didn't say any of it, but trudged stoically out to the porch. Since it had never been officially stated that Mrs. Fletcher *needed* anyone to sit with her, he couldn't very well call for someone else to do it. A delicate situation.

This time at least Carol favored him with a small grateful smile, a smile that bothered him the more he thought about it. She had doubtless been waiting all summer for someone to spring her from her mother's company; waiting, who knows, to get her hands on Forrest, who was waiting, who knows, to get his hands on her. This kind of thing happened every summer, to some poor mutt—a wild miscalculation of some girl—and it wouldn't really matter if this summer wasn't so short and empty. It wouldn't matter at all.

Meanwhile he had Mrs. Fletcher as consolation prize. He could always make a hit with Mrs. Fletcher. Yesterday she had seemed like a criminal lunatic to whom he was chained. But today the roles were switched. She was chained to him, because somebody had to sit with Jim *Bannister* and she had been too slow to get away. What bothered him during the dusty vacant moments that followed was a feeling that he hadn't even had a chance with Carol, hadn't even been a contender. Last year he would have been a contender.

"The last time I was in England was in 1938," said Mrs. Fletcher after a while. "A funny sort of year, with the war about to start, like the last night of a play, if you'll excuse the trite expression. You might try talking to Carol about England, although I don't suppose she remembers much about it."

"Were you in England? No kidding." He was pleased to hear that *somebody* else had been in England, that there was such a place—even if it was, of course, someone like Mrs. Fletcher. "What was it like when you were there? Did they always eat powdered eggs?"

"Gracious, no. They used to eat very well, of course they never knew how to cook, it's against their religion, I believe. Being uncomfortable is about all that's left of that."

She might look funny, but she was all right. Jimmy suddenly had a warm feeling about Mrs. Fletcher. "They certainly are uncomfortable," he said. "You should spend a night in our dormitory some time."

She laughed at that possibility ("I doubt if I shall, though") and went on to talk about lumbago and plumbing and the prevalence of rhubarb. Jimmy couldn't have enough of her now. "They have this vegetable called 'greens,'" he said. "That's all, just 'greens.' Well, what else could you call it? They have it at every meal."

"And don't forget kippers," she said. "Who but the English would eat kippers? Would even conceive kippers?"

"And jam. They're absolutely nuts about jam."

"Cold toast for breakfast," she said. She was getting excited too at this catalogue. "Cold toast for tea. I wonder how they *discovered* it?"

"And what gets me . . ." Jimmy wondered why nobody else wanted to talk to this fine woman. It must be some sort of curse that England put on you. She did have those funny eyes, of course—a little walleyed. That was why he had always thought she was watching him. It made her look a little crazy. But the real reason she looked funny was that she looked English. He saw that now.

His father came on the porch for a surprise visit. "I see you've found a friend, Jimmy."

"Yes. This is Mrs. Fletcher."

"Hello, Mrs. Fletcher."

Mr. Bannister sat down in Carol's rocking chair.

"Jimmy and I have been talking about England. I was condoling with him about the English diet."

"I guess it is pretty dull."

"We were waxing lyrical about kippers and marmalade."

"Is that so?"

Jimmy felt embarrassed. This was supposed to be funny talk, but Mr. Bannister wasn't getting it.

"Porridge and a really good cup of *tea*," she said.

"I guess things have been tough since the war."

Lorraine joined him and was introduced. She certainly wouldn't get it. Not with her own accent to worry about. Jimmy got up and went inside. He could hear Mrs. Fletcher through the window: *"Long before the war, back at least as far as King Alfred"* . . . He could suddenly see she was one of those silly people who couldn't change her way of talking to suit the company. She was a nut, after all. He was embarrassed for all three of them.

She was—the embarrassment deepened and shot out roots—worse than a nut: she was a freak, like him. His first impression was right. He went to the bathroom although he didn't need to, and decided then and there (a) that he didn't much like Carol anyway; she had a nasty expression; and (b) that he couldn't wait to get back to England.

seven

After Labor Day the Country Club broke up and trooped back to the city. The roar of surf was switched off. Jimmy still had two and a half weeks to kill, and he decided to kill as much of them as possible at the movies. He didn't bother to look up any more old friends. Forrest Tuckerman had taught him what vicious changes summer made in people over here. Faces, interests were washed away, replaced: a sea change. And now they would be all pointed toward school and would have less than ever to say to him. The sight of boys lobbing a football in the park was a melancholy exit cue.

His father was back at work in the daytimes, and in

the evenings Lorraine came over and the hum of
business was resumed. Jimmy felt that Lorraine had
given up on him—at least she seemed to find him un-
suitable for her niece, who was never mentioned any
more. O.K. with him. He didn't want to meet her
lousy niece. Lorraine had been the worst possible
thing that could have happened this summer. Jim
blamed her for everything now—even, improbably, for
the extra two weeks at Sopworth. He devoutly hoped
his father would have found something better by
Christmas, something that would divert him from
mortgages and wealthy families. He didn't like to
keep bringing up Gloria—he hadn't liked her that
much—but she used to steer Mr. Bannister away from
all those dull snobs at the Club. Come to think of it,
he remembered some muffled arguments on the point.
Meanwhile Jim himself was already deep in thoughts
of England, those wonderful country scenes, swinging
tavern signs, tea with friends—perhaps even tea with
Dr. Rabelais now that they knew each other better. A
lot of bad things—the shout scenes in class, the chronic
discomfort—had been magically alchemized into pleasant memories. And Carol had been phased out and replaced by a totally faceless companion, who wore the
same clothes but was a much better sport.

As the time drew to a close, he sensed that his father wanted a talk—a big talk to wrap up the summer.
As soon as Jimmy felt this coming on, he found himself instinctively changing the subject. His father mis-
understood the points at issue. He would say something unfortunate. About England, about the future.
About himself and Lorraine. Several evenings were
finessed successfully, and Jimmy began to feel that he
might escape without a big talk at all. But his father
caught up with him after supper, two nights before

he was due to leave: there was a brief dispirited tus-
sle—neither of them really wanted the damn talk.
Jimmy looked pointedly at the TV and radio listings;
his father gazed wistfully at the door. And they
talked.

"Would you say that it's been a good summer,
Jimmy?"

"Yes, definitely." They were sitting on the sofa facing the TV set so that they were talking to each other
sideways, like people in a Catholic confessional. "Yes,
I would."

"That's good. I've worried about it a little. You know
—a boy of your age . . ."

"I know."

"I haven't seen as much of you as I hoped. We
never did get to go fishing, did we?"

"That's all right."

"Well, a boy your age doesn't want to hang around
with his father all the time, I guess."

Jimmy made a sound that could have meant yes, he
does, or no, he doesn't, or the best elements of both.
He didn't want his father to feel bad about this. He
had had a good summer, in a screwy kind of way.

"How do you feel about going back to England?"

"I feel pretty good about it."

"You do?"

"Yes. I'm looking forward to it."

His father looked at him doubtfully. Lorraine
wasn't here tonight, and he looked thinner and more
reflective. It occurred to Jimmy that he might be
quite a shrewd man, when he wasn't fraternizing with
his truck-driver friends (Gloria's phrase for them). It
was funny the way Mr. Bannister went up and down,
in and out.

"I sometimes wonder if I've done the right thing

with you, Jimmy. I know it's a wonderful education over there, a wonderful opportunity." He rehearsed his old lines in a dry voice. "Socially, you may find it helpful—though that isn't the main reason, of course. But bouncing you around like this, I don't know. Are you sure you don't mind?"

"No, I don't mind."

"I don't know if I would have been so self-reliant. When I was your age, I went to prep school and I remember I was pretty homesick. And that was in *this* country. Maybe I should have settled for that in your case, do you think? A prep school in this country? What do you think, Jimmy?"

"If you're away from home, it doesn't matter how far you're away," said Jimmy untruthfully. "Away is away."

"Well, that's what *I* figured. Of course, your mother was very critical when she heard about it, but your mother is in no position . . . well, we make these decisions, and then we hope we've done the right thing. I'm glad you're happy there."

"Definitely."

"I couldn't always tell from your letters. I worried about them."

"I guess there were some rough moments." Jimmy could hardly recall.

"Yes, of course." His father lowered his voice for a moment, to put a delicate question. "Were there any, you know, cruelties?"

Jimmy said no. This was one of those misunderstandings he had feared.

"It'll be even better next year," he added quickly.

Mr. Bannister rubbed the bridge of his nose for guidance. "It's funny the twists a man's life takes. A few years ago I could never have foreseen any of this.

You don't mind my talking to you about it, Jimmy, you're old enough?" It was a genuine question, he really didn't know if Jimmy was old enough. Jimmy didn't know either, but nodded yes. "I haven't talked to you much about your mother, and I don't know how much you've guessed about her. She simply isn't capable of looking after you any more. Well, I'm sure you'd guessed that much."

Jimmy hadn't. He had guessed nothing. But he nodded again.

"Well, there it is. I don't know what *I'm* supposed to do. I don't know how *much* I'm supposed to do. There is such a thing as being too protective, too much of a father, don't you think?" He looked really troubled: how old is fifteen these days? He wouldn't be seeing his son for a while. Anything that didn't get said tonight might have to wait a long time. "Do you understand what I'm saying?"

Jimmy nodded once more. He had no idea what his father was saying.

"I want you to have the very best education going —that much I can see to. Beyond that I just don't know." He was making some kind of final appeal. Let me off the hook, he seemed to be saying. Confess that a good education is all you want or expect of me. He began talking quite incongruously about his damn business and the postwar boom. Jimmy was puzzled, couldn't quite grasp the point. "It's all right," he said. It wasn't the talk he'd expected at all.

Two days later they drove out to Idlewild with Lorraine sitting quietly between them. They shook hands—again that strange pulpy feeling—and parted. His father still wore a slightly petitionary expression. You're old enough, aren't you? I don't know what to do with a boy your age. As Jimmy boarded the plane, he felt more than old enough; he felt like one of the businessmen with the briefcases who lumbered up the gangway in front of him. After all, this was his third crossing. He waved encouragingly to his father, who waved back almost shyly. At his side Lorraine wig-wagged with vigor. She had white gloves on, he remembered.

The woman in the next seat was alternately thrilled and nauseated with this, her first flight. Jimmy found her amusing. Down below, Mrs. Fletcher and Carol and Forrest Tuckerman whirled away. The summer dwindled, vanished. Long Island became the size of a service-station map, and the motors roared toward the future. His face looked older in the washroom mirror. Surely he needed a shave now?

Mr. Soames, the ghostly ferryman, met him at the airport, and they went through the same process in reverse. There was something rather sad about Soames—he wasn't quite an American any more. Not one of the new models anyway. "You got your accent back," Soames said almost wistfully.

Jim spent what was left of this endless night at the neutral zone occupied by the Soameses. After a short day flying against the sun, and the long comfortable evening, he felt alert and on top of things. Traveling east was much better than traveling west.

The railway station, the next day, had that pleasant rusty smell. Jimmy also approved of the chunks of soot on the glass roof and the empty slot machines. Clusters of boys with school caps or blazers, red, green, brown, sat on their suitcases and looked wretched, or stood up to greet each other, or wandered the lobby searching for errant suitcases. Jimmy sought for traces of Sopworth, and finally found some fellows he didn't recognize, wearing the Sopworth cap.

"Hi," he said.

"Hello."

"Are you going to Sopworth?"

"Yes."

"So am I."

These must be new boys, just up from prep school. They were probably nervous about going to the Big Place. He understood too well. He dawdled with them a moment—an understanding older boy would have been a king-size help to him last year. But he only seemed to make them more uncomfortable. They stopped talking except to say, "I've finished my chocolate. None of the machines seem to work." "I've added three pounds since July, and I'm going to meet a dark stranger." "Ask it if it's got a friend," said Jimmy, but they didn't seem to see the point of this.

Mr. Soames had bought the train ticket and was looking around for him. A tragic, bewildered figure in his American topcoat. Jimmy strolled over to him, took the ticket, said goodbye. Soames wanted to see him right onto the train, but Jimmy didn't want to stand around with Soames. He wanted to look for friends. There was nothing he could do for Soames. The bags with the showy transatlantic labels had been mounted in the baggage car and there was nothing for it now but to wait.

So Mr. Soames left him, and he went on a buoyant prowl. He saw some more Sopworth boys at the newspaper stand, a little older than himself this time. He recognized them as belonging to Cornwallis house. He said hello, and they looked at him queerly. "I'm Bannister," he said. "Are you indeed?" said one of the boys. "He's Bannister," explained another suddenly. "Ah yes, of course he is," they all five nodded. "Bannister, yes, yes. Bannister, upon my soul."

He couldn't think of any way to join in their fun. He thought of dancing around, shouting, "Yes, yes, it's Bannister. Bannister is here." But that didn't seem quite to match. He decided to look for someone he knew. The Cornwallis crowd slightly jarred him. They had knocked a small chip off his confidence and he didn't want to lose any more. The sun, such as it was, had gone in, behind the dusky roof, and the station was becoming huge, noisy and dark. He made another slow circuit, but came up empty. He was half sorry to have released Mr. Soames. A companion gave you a look of purpose. He noticed that a line was beginning to form in front of his platform, so he joined it.

Schoolboys of all ages and sizes—he had never seen or imagined so many schoolboys—jostled and flapped around him. The train would take them en masse to some junction in the Midlands from which they would shoot out like spokes all over the country. Where, then, were Ryan and Samuelson and Philpott? Everyone else was grouped in by now. Jimmy should have made plans to meet his friends.

His ticket was clipped by a man with a white mustache, and Jim boarded the train. Ryan and Philpott were not in the first compartment or the second or the third. He began to walk rapidly along the corridor, banging into people who were, mysteriously, already coming the other way. Everywhere he turned there were red-faced boys, chuffing along the aisle, or chaffering behind the compartment windows. He suddenly saw how strange they looked. Their features, the way their mouths worked. Their cheeks were as red as cricket balls after outdoorsy summers. No doubt about it, people did look different over here.

He gave up at last and came to roost in a compartment up near the engine. He had noticed people charging along the platform, and the train had filled up at blinding speed. Although he was one of the earlier arrivals, he was lucky to get a seat at all, crunched among four boys in yellow and blue caps, an Air Force officer, and two large school-girls, in a space designed presumably for six.

For sheer slowness and longness the journey set some sort of record. The boys struck up a conversation rather bravely with the Air Force man. He told them that he was stationed in Shropshire but had been stationed in Dorset up till a few weeks ago. One of the boys had, it seemed, spent the holidays in Dorset. What part? Do you know a town named Wobbles, it sounded like? Do I know a town called Wobbles? About ten miles outside Ketherington, isn't it? That's the place. On the A-something road. Oh yes, I know Wobbles all right.

Jimmy listened to the train for a while. When he tuned in again, one of the boys was asking if the Air Force man knew a town called Bumby, just outside Witchester. Is that anywhere near Flooding? Yes, just three villages away, actually. Humpletrimmer, humpletrimmer was the word from the train. It was carrying him farther into this alien countryside: where, if you didn't know Wobbles, couldn't even make a decent guess at Bumby, you were like a blind man. But at the other end of the tunnel lay Sopworth, and he knew all about Sopworth.

A porter looked in and told them that tea was served. They all stood up, after a round of "coming? coming? coming?" Jimmy decided to stay where he was. They would all be sitting in their groups, and he would have to find a vacant chair at someone else's table. Besides he remembered the terrible stuff they put in the cakes over here.

The Air Force man had left a small magazine to mark his seat. Jimmy crouched over it, and had a look. There was a picture in the center spread of a girl with naked breasts. Nothing new about that, of course—but he was suddenly scorched with lust. He couldn't take his eyes off the huge charcoal-gray nipples. He shut the magazine, and opened it again quickly. He wanted to bury his head in those paper breasts and leave it there. What *had* become of Mrs. Bannister anyway? He thought he could see for an instant two waxen breasts hanging dementedly out of a gold dressing gown . . . but that was impossible. His mother's dressing gown was royal blue.

After about ten minutes he decided he had better put down the magazine and creep back to his place. He didn't want them all to troop back in and find him staring at the magazine: with red-eared ardor.

This freakish burst of excitement left him suddenly drained and weak. He could hardly face them when they got back from tea. The Air Force man picked up the magazine and glanced at it for a moment, as if checking for fingerprints, and then stuffed it casually into his pocket. He knows I've been reading it. It's written all over the cover. The signs of Jimmy's own helpless dwindling desire must be apparent to everyone—only it isn't desire, he wanted to explain. It's loneliness. The girl in the magazine looked a little like Gloria, he decided, his father's companion of last summer. And a little like who knows who else? Some valuable cockiness had seeped out, spent on that stupid picture.

They got to their junction, and had to stand about on another platform for half an hour. Jimmy couldn't wait to get to Sopworth now, to see some friendly faces. He strolled along the platform to set the blood flowing again: looked at the big hoardings advertising oxo, whatever that was. Bovril, Cadbury's chocolate: this wasn't the England he remembered. There were so many small things he hadn't accounted for. He read a playbill which announced the arrival of someone called Nervo and Knox for a limited engagement at the local Palladium, to be followed by Evelyn Laye in *Babes in the Wood*, our ever popular Christmas Pantomime. He turned away. What he wanted was one token, one small sign that he was on the same globe he had been on yesterday.

There were certainly many more people with sandy hair than he remembered. The smell of the train conductors was a new development. The girls' legs were redder. More mustaches, hair in buns; bad teeth and tin spectacles. The people came in funny shapes too: high shoulders and short necks, round shoulders and furry ears; also faces like pug dogs, beetles, eagles, flamingos, weasels—and one actual pig, walking toward him now down the platform with a snout and a rolling gait. Stopping at the chocolate machine and jiggling the handle. Some crazy natural disaster had occurred during the summer, causing a biological jumble. He tried to think of it as funny, all these marvelous English characters, etc., but the effort made his throat dry. The odd thing was that he couldn't remember any of this from the last time.

He considered having some tea in the station tearoom, but it looked so dreary in there. A long line of schoolboys and adults in raincoats shuffled past a fat girl in a stained white uniform. They carried their cups to marble tables and lowered their faces into the tea. You would die of despair in there. Confidence, he was beginning to see, required a certain amount of strategy.

His heart lifted as his own train pulled in. Once he was at Sopworth, he would know where he was. A number of Sopworth boys had converged on this train, and while he still didn't know any of them too well, they made a more familiar sound.

Traveling to Sopworth was like traveling to a warm spot—bosom was one word that came to mind. This wasn't just England any more, not just unadulterated foreignness, but something he could cope with. There were two other Sopworth boys in the compartment, and he could almost have hugged them. (Perhaps sensing this, they avoided his eye.)

The train arrived in chilly twilight. The station was the size of a postage stamp, good for maybe two trains a term. The Sopworth boys got off in a tumbling stream, and Jimmy was surprised, now that he saw them all together, at how few boys he knew to speak to. Ryan, Philpott, Samuelson, were definitely among the missing. He nodded at Peters and Featherstone, who nodded back. And that was about it.

The school had provided buses, and everyone went pounding toward those. This must be the runningest country in the world. He supposed he ought to look for his bags, but he couldn't find the baggage car; and finally someone told him—in a voice implying that he should have known this—that the baggage car had gone on to the depot at Greater Sopworth, where it would be unloaded in God's good time. The three minutes wasted on this quest deprived him of a seat on the bus, and he was obliged to stand jiggling in the aisle crisscrossed by four conversations, none of which made any sense. Words like devizes and assizes and scrum-half put him off the scent every time. There were no lights, and nothing much to look at except the backs of heads; but if he crouched low he could see the last shoals of bicycles lit like glow-worms, passing through Sopworth's shopping center on the way home, and after that the darkening hedges and fields that he remembered so well—a little past their friendly best at this hour, but still reassuring.

Ryan, Philpott, Samuelson, where are you? It was cold and dark, and the voices wouldn't stop their bird song: that bloody man Prothero called "leg-up" five minutes from time. Honestly, I could have scragged him . . . (Shyly) No, *I* shall be hooker, and *you* shall be prop. He remembered no such sounds as these. But Ryan, Philpott and Samuelson would speak properly and understandably. It was a rich diet of change that he'd been on today: but familiarity lay just ahead now.

Twilight had very nearly given in to night. (It certainly took its sweet time about it over here.) The bus pulled up at the school gates and the driver climbed irritably from his perch to open them. He reascended and the bus started chuffing up the dark drive. Without warning Jimmy's pulse began to race wantonly. Just a few yards to Philpott and company. The great black buildings (he swore they'd grown during the summer) came swinging round a bend in the drive. Grotesquely, feverishly desirable. Boys began to clamber from their seats, like animals from cages, trying to squeeze past Jimmy or push him out in front of them. Other buses had come up behind, teeming, suppurating with boys. Jimmy felt, incongruously, a little bus-sick. "Excuse me," he said, but found himself tottering down the steps under an implacable pressure of boys.

Nothing rude, nothing personal. One always gets off buses like that. They danced past him and ran toward the school. He began to run too. Eagerly. As toward home.

eight

Down the long main corridor they poured, wildly, as if someone had started a panic or, more likely, as if this part of term must be got through quickly—the settling in, the forgetting about home, all done on the double.

They swarmed at the bulletin boards, where their classrooms, sleeping quarters, rugby and soccer games (Sopworth was one of those rare schools that supported both sports—indifferently to be sure) were allotted. Cries of "blast" and "wizard" rent the air. "I've got the Foghorn again." "Oh, good—Mr. Moore," and a groundswell of damns and bloodies.

Jimmy craned. Sopworth boys were slightly taller

than the national average, and much ruder, but he managed to make out that he was back in the Frisby dormitory again. that was rather a blow. He had looked forward to a private room. He peered at the other names—Ryan and Samuelson had disappeared altogether. Dispositions made by stealth during the summer. He would have to make do with Philpott: the other boys on the dormitory roster were new to him.

He didn't really want to know what classes he was in but found himself shoved in that direction anyway. Here again he found that everyone had moved on except Bannister. Bannister was some sad relic, lost in the examination shuffle. More Foghorn, more Smiles. For a whole year. Ryan and Samuelson had presumably got their school certificates and had passed into the upper atmosphere where you specialized and the masters treated you like human beings. Philpott had been kept behind for general childishness, his character left to ripen in the Frisby dormitory. But even he had left Jimmy in the dust scholastically.

Jimmy had been pushed to the very end of the bulletin board by now, and it seemed to be time to resume running. The footsteps led now to the school dining room, where some kind of snack was in the works. Here surely he would find Ryan—the most food-minded man of his acquaintance: talking no doubt of lovely horsemeat from County Kildare, lovely toad-in-the-hole from County Mayo, ravishing bubble and squeak: "And now back to *this* muck." (Confirming belch from Samuelson.)

But again he was disappointed. None of his friends had arrived yet. The long Frisby table was runged with place cards, and he went on a reconnoiter. Samuelson had advanced a good twenty places during the summer: even the lowly Philpott had moved up about twelve. But Bannister was exactly where he had been. Surrounded by new names, just up from the junior school, presumably. Bannister, you're in the dustbin of history—a phrase from his summer reading. The school certificate seemed to be the great watershed.

He sat down at the place marked Bannister. A plate of jam sandwiches was being scrambled for in front of him and he plunged his hand into the scrum. Jam sandwiches. "Plums from fair South Africa. Whackol" said a dismal twit. A too familiar brown teapot also was shimmying down the line, and he extracted some stewed tea from it. Bit into a jam sandwich, listened to the chatter of the boys around him—arrogant chatter of strangers, chatter he would be hearing all year, over his jam sandwiches and tea.

So far he had observed everything through a glaze of excitement and objectivity. There was this and then there was that. Movement and noise. All quite amusing and interesting. But now, as he sat still, a feeling that was not so good began very lightly to assert itself. Not so good at all. The roar of the dining room, the taste of the jam. Everyone was racing and shouting to avert some great tragedy.

He wolfed his sandwich and stood up. It was important for him to get moving again. He ran now, almost blindly, back along the main corridor. He had looked forward to finding his friends. He must find them now.

They were not in the Frisby recreation room. Some fellows that he knew only slightly were playing ping-pong. A couple of others were reading newspapers, like old men in a club, left over from the spring. They didn't look round as he burst upon them. There were no glad cries of "Bannister."

"Have you seen Ryan or Samuelson?" he said.

"What? (thunk) Ryan, you say? (thunk) I don't think he's here (thunk) any more." The ball scudded into the net. "No, I'm pretty sure he's somewhere else by now."

"That's not possible. I didn't hear anything."

"Oh well—if it's not possible, that's all right then. Whose serve is it?"

"It should be mine, actually. But since you've taken the last eight in a row, perhaps you'd care to continue . . ."

"Oh, sorry."

Their voices dimmed. "I mean to say some people *like* serving . . . like it very much indeed."

Jimmy went careening out again. If he stopped moving, his lungs would congest. Where were his darn friends? Well, there was always Philpott. Philpott at least would be up in the dormitory, unpacking his tooth mug, pinching things from other people's bags. Philpott would do for openers.

He felt himself running desperately like a man in a dream. All the other characters seemed to be going the other way. Some of them had no faces, others had too much. Jimmy was tireder than he thought and not too far from hysteria. This wasn't the place he remembered at all. He had never been here in his life. The geniality of last summer had been locked away. The prefects were already stiff and beady-eyed. The very walls and floors had hardened. And there was to be a whole year of this. A whole year.

He whizzed up the stairs. Philpott had better be in that dormitory. There must be some satisfaction in the here and now. Last year he had kept in shape by dreaming about America; then he had dreamed about England; but now there was nothing left to dream about. Reality must deliver the goods.

To his amazement, Philpott was indeed in the dormitory, unpacking rather quietly and solemnly: folding things carefully and putting them in his cubicle.

"Hey, Philpott!" It was wildly elating to come across Philpott, at this juncture. "Man, it's good to see you."

Philpott looked up uncertainly. "Hello, Bannister." He was smaller than Jim remembered, and his features less pronounced; he was, as far as his face went, just a little boy. "What sort of holiday did you have, Bannister?" he asked solemnly.

"It was all right. How about yours?"

"We went to Brighton, actually," said Philpott. It was almost an apology. They sat silently. Jimmy had assumed they would just fall into conversation. "Do you always go to Brighton?" he gave a desperate prod.

"No. Sometimes we go to Keswick."

Sometimes to Keswick, indeed. He was worse than small. He was unformed. He also gave the impression that one mustn't get him too excited. He had turned pale at Jimmy's whooping introduction and remained slightly under-par.

"Where are the others?" Jim asked. "Where's Samuelson?"

"We won't be seeing much of Samuelson, I fear," said Philpott. "He's been given a room to himself in Dr. Rabelais' house."

"How'd he rate that?"

"He got seven distinctions in the school cert. They're hoping he'll get a scholarship."

Somebody else in the headmaster's house. He didn't want to hear about that. He didn't especially want to be told about Ryan either, but it was between that or asking, how was Brighton?

"Yes, it's true, he's been taken at Sandhurst."

Jimmy started to say something, but he noticed that Philpott's lips were trembling. He was the kind of boy who probably cried at the beginning of every term; he had come up here by himself to be ready for the first sad thought to strike.

The logical thing was to leave him alone. But he was the only friend Jimmy had left. So Jim sat awkwardly on Philpott's bed watching him cry, and then looking away, off down the dormitory, hoping he would stop soon. But Philpott wept on, quietly but insistently, in line with the Sopworth rubrics. At the far end of the room, another boy sat hunched over his locker, presumably sharing Philpott's unpretentious agony. By midnight this place would be a bawling, sniffing chaos.

Jimmy sat for several minutes, expecting Philpott to pull himself together for very pride. But Philpott treated his tears as if they were some simple allergy, to be endured patiently and without embarrassment.

His composure began to make Jimmy fidgety. He refused either to break down or to pull himself together, but paddled along in the middle. Finally the little fellow wiped his eyes in a business-like way, excused himself politely and wandered to the bathroom. There goes my last friend. There isn't much to him, is there? No, not too much.

Jimmy shut his eyes. Philpott gave the toilet the first of several flushings as if each tear must be cleared away scrupulously to make room for the next. The humorous side of Philpott was simply an invention of Ryan's, and now Ryan was gone; leaving not one but two gaps, and possibly three, if you counted Samuelson.

If I gave in to my feelings, it wouldn't help me to cry, thought Jimmy. That was last year. His problem would not be solved by a trivial sprinkle now. He didn't know exactly what his problem was, but he pictured it as more a deep cracking kind of thing—much too dry to be helped by tears. A Mohave Desert jeweled with cactus plants. If he masturbated tonight, disturbing the neighbors, it would be no more than the dry heaves: perhaps a little sand and sawdust. Masturbation was out. Crying was out. But what was his problem?

He went to his own bed and lay down. His mind went back to the picture in the magazine, but this did not produce the desired effect. There was no warming spring in his loins. What had become of Mrs. Bannister anyway? For all those years he had honestly not thought about it. He had, just three days ago, evaded his father's hints very dexterously; but of course he knew. He knew very well. Her last few months at home had been clear enough. "Wise up, Bannister. You know she's crazy," he said out loud, and he couldn't tell whether the voice that said it was American or English.

This frightened and sobered him. These last two days had been more confusing than he realized. His heart still beat to American time, his nervous system had gotten stuck somewhere over the Atlantic. To call him American, or fifteen years old, or anything else, was quite meaningless. For a moment he frankly hadn't known who he was.

He sat up and looked around. This was his home now, even if it didn't look like it. The sound of Philpott sobbing and flushing had a homey ring to it anyhow.

The new boys began to trickle in and get ready for bed. And Jimmy had to endure again the sight of the rolled trouser leg and the foot dipped modestly in the basin. He would never know why that set his teeth on edge so. The new boys in the dormitory were subdued by now, caught up in the place's black spirit. Philpott had timed his collapse with some skill and left the bathroom, fully composed, even bored, just as the others were entering. He said good night to Jimmy in a rather stiff way: and Jimmy realized that he had minded very much about being watched at his evening tears.

Jimmy was terribly tired and thought he could escape into sleep without further fret. His fears of a wailing dormitory were not realized: outside of an occasional mutter that might have been protest, or sheer disbelief, and the usual grind of breathing and scratching and turning over, the place was practically silent.

After a few minutes a slight burbling hum asserted itself. Well, to be exact, one boy was burbling and another two were humming. A new group was forming at the far end of the dormitory, similar to his own group last summer. A Bannister-less group. They were quickly shushed by the new prefect, a fellow called Fingal: but the sound lingered sweetly on the air. When he shut his eyes he saw that things were still quite bad, very bad in fact. Luckily he knew how to handle such things now. It would not be like last term. He could not bear to go back to that. But there was no denying things were bad. Who was he kidding about this place being home? What kind of joke was that . . . ? Interesting, isn't it, that Mother op-posed the whole thing? You bet she did. Poor old crazy Mother.

Battered all day by sights and sounds, he was now kept awake by this seeping rivulet of reflections. In a normal room he would have snapped on the light to chase the spooks, but here that would have caused a sensation. In the dark, he was stuck with his thoughts. He slipped a quarter-inch further into unconsciousness and found himself barreling along a gallery of some kind while his mother, hair flying out over her gold dressing gown, pleaded with Mr. Bannister not to send Jim to England. The combined noise of the roller skates was deafening. Finally Mr. Bannister scraped her off his legs, where she had flung herself, and left her face down on the floor. (That was a dream—no, it wasn't. That was the truth. That was exactly how it happened.)

He shook himself awake. It *was* a dream, or the grubby outskirts of one. He still had the taste of it in his mouth. The dry taste of fear. "*Could* you be quiet," mumbled someone from the next bed. "*Is* it asking too much?" You know, going crazy wasn't too impossible. A few dreams like that would get you there in no time. Having a mother like that helped show you the way.

For heaven's sake, Bannister, what a silly thing to say, in any accent. Going crazy probably takes years of preparation. The summer had been altogether mild and sane. He was miles away from insanity.

Again he addressed himself to sleep. But he now felt that in order to get there he must first say something—*anything*—out loud. It was a strange requirement, but absolutely inflexible. And if he met it, he would arouse the whole dormitory, and bring them, like the night animals in *Snow White*, blinking around his bed.

A dormitory would certainly be a heck of a place to go crazy in. You would have to do it without disturbing anybody. He lay with his eyes very wide open, wondering if he could somehow leap across the moat of viper-like dreams that surrounded real sleep. He tried various word and number games, but found he had to play them with his eyes open. The moment his eyes were shut, pictures of America began to form behind the lids, and he knew now that they were lies. Those sailboats, Huckleberry Bannister's raft, lazing away the summer with his friends—all terrible, terrible lies. If he gave in to them now, his whole mind would be a lie.

But the only alternative was to attend to the dormitory, with its callous night sounds. The snorers and scratchers knew, at worst, that they were snoring and scratching in their own country, so that their homesickness was superficial, verging on the smug. And closer to hand there were the rock-hard sheets, insufficiently pulped, the better to build character. In his present fever, there was something really tragic about these sheets. If he cried over anything, it would be over that.

And if not the dormitory, the Bovril signs and the oxo signs. And if not the Bovril signs, the R.A.F. man talking about his billet in Nether Wobbles, or the stand-off half comparing notes with the wing three-quarters. And if none of these, the girl in the magazine, and, mysteriously, Mrs. Bannister in her imaginary gold dressing gown.

Why did his mother have to pick tonight? And why did his head have to form pictures at all? He tried blanking out, and that brought him full circle to a total quivering consciousness of his sheets. It was as if the nation had lost all its good sheets in the war. The most daring part of Goering's plan. "Destroy a nation's sheets and you have *achtung schicklgruber sweinhund*" . . . He resented the way these ones touched him too firmly in places, missed him altogether in others. The stiffness formed tunnels along which the draft could winnow; so that, bad as the sheets were, he tried to wrap them tighter, stuffing them under his belly and pinning the harsh substance there.

He wished the American scenes were not lies. They had a kind of sickening attractiveness. He knew that he absolutely must not give in to them even for a second, but this made them all the more tempting. They promised, beyond everything else, sleep.

Very well—he would lie awake all night. Not so fatal. He would try to relax. . . . But even this was not vouchsafed him right away, for he kept slipping into the moat of waking dreams. Or getting locked in hopeless debate with his fluctuating consciousness.

You know that in real life there is no raft and no Huckleberry Bannister. The yachts in the Sound are manned by fat businessmen with big mouths and soft white arms. Fishing is what your father thinks he likes. To wish for these things is to wish for nothing.

Yes, yes, I know. But here comes the raft now. And who is yon gawky teenager playing the banjo? Why it's——. He turned over, dislodging the top sheet again. His skin would be covered in fever blisters by morning, and he would have a cold. Fine way to face the Foghorn. Well, forget *that*. Jim thought instead about baggage labels. No one else in the school could match his collection, except maybe that quiet boy from British Guiana, if he was back. And that was *all* he had, just baggage labels . . . poor devil. Which gave Jimmy a funny idea about traveling: namely that bits of you came off in various places and took time to reassemble. The boy from Guiana left his tongue at home. And parts of Jim Bannister still haunted his father's hotel room, reveling in the soft sheets and the air conditioning. A whole different Bannister, left handing in the air.

Not only soft sheets, but no school tomorrow. The other Bannister had it made. Jimmy watched enviously as his transatlantic self dug his head into the pillow. A nice pillow without a single brick in it. Tomorrow this bum would start the day with ham and eggs and delicious box scores.

. . . Another myth, Bannister. Breakfast was never that good. The days that followed breakfast were usually long and boring. Admit it, Bannister. All right, I'll admit it. I won't think about the breakfasts. Or about lying in bed? That was pretty boring too, wasn't it? O.K. Or about lying in bed. Just let me sleep *now*.

Tomorrow's classrooms were beginning to weigh on his mind also. He knew from today's experience that anything pleasant he remembered about them would be missing tomorrow. It was a feature of reality to be unexpectedly lousy. He saw himself, too sleepy to think, being roasted alive by the Foghorn, and then on to another classroom to have his geography mocked by Mr. Smiles. (And *your* country, Bannister. Which direction is *that* in?) And then the *dernier* straw—M. Necker's gentle disappointment over his French.

He would want to go somewhere to rest up. But that was impossible. The day was a seamless nightmare. The din in the corridors unceasing, the legs churning, the feet how they pound; and in the afternoon, dropping with fatigue, he would be introduced to a new game. He supposed that all the talk about hookers and fly-halfs referred to that. A roaring, hostile game, with Bannister caught in the middle, being hooked and having his legs torn off like fly wings.

It didn't matter, he could take it. So long as he was *wide* awake, none of these thoughts were very terrible. No game could be as bad as that, they wouldn't allow it. Some society would step in. In general, things would not be half as bad as last term. He knew so much more. He was older, had two solo flights to his credit, had flashed a passport around.

—But I don't *know* any French. Whatever I learned last year is gone. Don't be disappointed, sir, please don't. Oh, my God, he's crying. Don't cry, sir. For pity's sake.

The picture in the magazine came round in its turn, as if his fantasies were on a revolving band. He flung himself between the breasts once more, almost breaking his pillow in half, trying to get there before it turned into Mrs. Bannister again. But it wasn't Mrs. Bannister at all, it was Carol Fletcher. No need to hurry. His heart rose for a moment. But she carefully picked him off her left breast and deposited him on the rug. She walked slowly away, swaying her hips about twenty feet to either side.

. . . It wasn't much of a dream, but he clung to it now, prostrate on the marble floor, trying to grip the smooth slabs. This was the closest he had gotten to sleep so far. He mustn't let it get away.

But he slipped back inexorably the other way. A dog was barking nearby, ordering him to his feet. Carol disappeared with a snap, like a cud of bubble gum, and there he was, face down on his pillow, which was hard as any marble. The boy in the next bed had pushed back his own crusty sheets and was having a coughing fit. Why, why did he have to pick that moment to cough? Another few seconds and Jimmy would have been out of reach.

"*Can't* you wrap up?" said a voice in the dark. "*Is* it asking too much?"

"Sorry, I've got a tickle."

Oh, well, it didn't matter. Jimmy forced himself all the way awake, to resume his hold on things. He was, bear this in mind, older than last term, and more experienced. The masters would look smaller, if nothing else. He could give Smiles a thrashing, if worst came to worst.

Tomorrow, after lunch, he would sneak up here for a few minutes and have a nap. When he woke from that, he would be acclimatized. Two sleeping sessions was all it took. He knew how these things worked now. He had the strategies down cold.

. . . A nap in this place might be hard to come by, though. With no shades on the windows. And your head on a pillow that you're already sick of. You'll have a cauliflower ear, you'll have scars on your face . . . honestly, you ought to be here in this hotel room. The thing is, it's private. You know what will happen when you try resting in the dormitory, Banister, don't you? Some darn fool will come in who can't find his hockey stick. He wonders if he might possibly have left it under your bed. There is no more depressing sound in the world than a man looking for his hockey stick under your bed.

Why were there no shades on the windows? He saw himself lying in streaming daylight, itching to yank at nonexistent shades. Pulling them down over his head finally, and sitting on the floor wrapped in brown paper . . . it didn't have to be someone looking for his hockey stick. It might be someone on the prowl for Brasso to clean his Army boots with or the button on his hat; or just the threat of someone coming to look for those things. Or just the big empty space—bedrooms are meant to be enclosed. That's nature's way, Bannister.

I suppose I shall skip Army drill again this year. That is not for the reason you think. It is not because I am an American, but because I have some hidden defect. I would crack in the jungle, for one thing. My pimples would give me away. Glowing like lightbulbs. Give the whole platoon away, in fact . . .

He tried quickly to make a dream of this, but it was just another waking-sleeping reverie. Perhaps he was really afraid to go to sleep. Perhaps it didn't take months to go crazy either, but could happen overnight, if you went to sleep with your head in the wrong position. Three hundred bad dreams in a row could splinter the strongest intelligence. And let us face it, Bannister, yours is not the strongest intelligence.

Several voices seemed to be at work in his skull now, old men and boys taking turns, Englishmen and Americans. Which one would win? Which would own the title to the Bannister estate? He wondered what time it was. He had no watch, and the chapel bells were dim and jumbled up. He could have been here for hours, or just minutes; he couldn't say for sure whether he had slept yet or not. Perhaps the summer had not been mild and sane at all, but a perfect preparation for the funny farm.

How had his mother known that *she* was going crazy? And how had she taken the news? There was a moment of heavy stillness in his mind, as if before a

thunderstorm; he pictured his mother moving slowly
around the kitchen, preparing a calming cup of tea.
His father sat discreetly in the next room. It was very
bad taste to mention her craziness at this particular
point.

And then suddenly she began to scream like a
frightened animal. His skull split with the noise. The
only other sound was the front door banging, meaning his father had probably gone out. Without thinking, Jimmy sat up and reached for his slippers. He
was going out too. He was halfway down the dormitory before he woke up fully. He had better talk to
someone right away.

"Fingal, Fingal." He shook the prefect's thickly pa-
jamaed shoulder.

"Who the devil are you, devil do you want?" Fingal, what could be seen of him, was a muffled ball of
fear and rage.

"I had a bad dream," said Jim lamely.

"What? What dream?" Fingal was still asleep himself. That was what was so strange about him.

"I forget. I wanted to talk to someone. I think I'm
going crazy."

"Who are you, anyway? What's your *name?*"

"Bannister, sir."

"And you think what?"

"That I'm going crazy."

Fingal grunted and turned onto his stomach. "You
probably are," he said slyly. "You seem like that sort
of boy." He lay like a beached whale; nothing would
rouse him, now that he was warned. Jimmy wandered
back toward his bed. He didn't really think he was
going crazy—it was just that you needed a pretty
good excuse to start a conversation at that time of

night. Someone returning from the bathroom slipped by like a ghost ship, trying not to wake himself up.

He, James Bannister III, could not face another dream like that last one, not for a while. It had shaken him, dislodged his insides, splintered the walls of his skull: like the caving in of some mineshaft. And yet he had spoken truth to Fingal. He could not remember anything about it.

Eventually the bell in the distance gave three distinct chimes. Three in the morning. He had just two things left up his sleeve to see him through the night. One was too fragile to contemplate—that was the thought of seeing Rabelais tomorrow. He sensed that it would be bad luck to invoke that right now; also it was too sweetly painful, like some oozing of bone marrow. Instead, there was this other thing. Simple damnation, you might call it.

Well, just this once, he whispered out loud to himself, just until he got acclimatized: he opened, slyly, lasciviously, his treasure chest of lies. The American slides, rivers, boardwalks, penthouses, the jabbering gaudy crew: picked out a Technicolor riverboat and lay himself sensuously down beside it, next to a phantom girl, both warmed, caressed by lies: a stiff, ruinous price to pay for sleep, and for avoiding nameless, faceless dreams. But a price that simply had to be paid.

nine

The next morning Rabelais addressed the whole school. It was a cold sharp morning. Mrs. Fletcher would have been amused by the breakfast. Wooden oatmeal, flannel toast. Everyone into the gym for a talk. Jimmy was so tired he hardly knew what he was doing. Great scrapings of sand in his eyes and temples lined with frost. He stumbled drunkenly behind the others. They shoved and gouged because they were too shy to express themselves any other way. They were really very decent chaps, guys, whatever.

The boys dragged their folded wooden chairs across the floor and banged them into place. Jimmy found himself sitting underneath the parallel bars.

There was some mysterious gray padding on the wall behind him; Something that lunatics might fling themselves against. Three small boys, jabbering like monkeys, squeezed in behind him. Crazy as jaybirds. Rabelais would come in soon with a fireman's hose and quiet them.

Jim was waiting for Rabelais with a furious excitement. He wiped his mouth with the back of his hand. He had been banished from his own country, from his father's house, but this vague spindly man had taken him in and given him a home of sorts. Rabelais would take care of things from here on in.

The headmaster was several minutes late, and a few venturesome souls began to stamp their feet: to be shushed furiously by the local prefect. Jimmy's eyes had gone stiff from weariness and were fixed in a stare. Rabelais would come through that door on the upper left. He would wander toward the lectern, rubbing his thin, kind hands. He would trip on the raised step, spread-eagling across the platform like a wounded bird.

The dear old man entered at last and did more or less as he was supposed to, although he didn't quite go down when he tripped on the step, and, grasping the frayed lapels of his great black gown, he began to talk. He welcomed them back, with a nasty cough. He told them they must all have haircuts within the next three days, or risk the usual caning. Something was a positive disgrace, Jimmy didn't catch what it was. At any rate, one hoped that the baggage would all be collected by this evening. Positive disgrace. The back of the gym was already lined with trunks and suitcases relayed from Greater Sopworth. The thought that the bags hadn't even been *opened* yet was a sad one. A very sad one indeed.

A special word for the new boys. Expect take time grow accustomed to ways. Stop. Any difficulty come me. Stop. Jimmy yawned and looked around. All those faces. Just the noses alone. You will find your classrooms on the bulletin board, you will find the bulletin board . . . Rabelais looked so nice and friendly after all those others: once we've shaken hands with him, it will be all right.

Meanwhile he examined his conscience about last night, most specifically the wheatfield. The wheatfield had come with first light, a sheet of gold. Huge, far as the eye could see, none of your back-to-back houses and Bovril signs. Just a plain wheatfield. You didn't have to draw any conclusions about that. All you had to do was look at it. Gold. Blue. Uniform breeze combing it all back. No lie in that that he could see.

Will now read to you from this little blue book. School regulations, chapter 1, section I. What would be wrong, because untruthful, would be to imagine, say, a farmer in blue dungarees. At prayer with his wife. One must draw the line at that. Nothing wrong with plain scene. But no conclusions.

Walking on the grass. Expressly forbidden . . . playing gramophones after supper, going out after dark . . . *expressly* forbidden. An old-fashioned schoolhouse would also be a mistake at this point . . . A flag on the blackboard. A teacher in a mother hub-bard. There must be definite rules about that sort of thing.

The tone of the headmaster's speech had gotten spliced on somewhere. We will allow absolutely no freckle-faced kids into our schoolroom. We do not especially *like* freckle-faced kids, do we? Fishing is prohibited until further notice. You may sit quietly by the side of the stream, but that is all . . . Rabelais seemed slightly out of sorts, but that did not hide the fact that he was a thoroughly decent man. You could see the kindness in his eyes.

The headmaster came to a pause eventually and asked if there were any questions. A large earnest boy got up and asked for further refinements of regulation. Was one permitted, say, to keep one's bicycle in the Bywater area *after dark?* It was rather a fine point: Rabelais scratched his nose and said he had never considered it before. In a few days he would pin a ruling to the notice board.

Another question, then. Did the ukase pertaining to school lockers also apply to *desk drawers?* Jimmy's mind went spinning off again, into his own rule book. Military parades, for instance. What did they come under? Holidays, special events. See *firecrackers.* (Breasts? See under *dressing gown.*)

He had a notion that these were not the questions that Rabelais really wanted. The dry tonelessness of his answers could only mean profound disappointment. These people were not making contact with the real Dr. Rabelais at all.

Without any exact plan, Jimmy stood up himself and raised his hand. For a moment nobody noticed him and he reveled in the sense of standing up unseen. Then Rabelais caught his eye and said, "Yes, what is it?" Jim had no definite question in mind. He wanted to say, "Hello, sir. I got here all right. We're all very glad to see you." Things that needed saying. He looked at Rabelais with warmth and encouragement—somebody should say these things at the start of a school year.

"What is it, what do you want?" The glasses glinted like ice cubes. Contact had not been made yet. Perhaps Rabelais' eyesight was not too good. Incredibly, he didn't even seem to recognize Jimmy.

"It's me. I'm here." This place could still be saved by a simple gesture. He decided he had better get closer. He began to forge forward and politely a path was cleared for him. His eyes were fixed on Rabelais', waiting for the moment of recognition. The shy smile that could hardly be refused him. He felt that he was moving gracefully, not bumping into things.

Nobody interfered as he climbed the platform. They would give him a hearing. It was the English way. He was grinning uncontrollably at Rabelais as he had at Carol Fletcher. He even put out his hand—nothing could be fairer than that.

"What is it? What do you want? What are you doing up here?" It was almost a scream.

The scene froze. High on a lecture platform. Jimmy with his hand out. Rabelais' glasses glinting now like haw frost, concealing the great kindness of the man; the audience polite, curious.

Then everyone started to roar and bang their chairs. And the tension that had held him erect worked the other way and he pitched forward slightly into the great black arms of the headmaster, just too tired to stand. He said something but it was lost in the thick coarse folds. He was rather afraid he had made a fool of himself.

He heard a lot of quite distinct voices saying quite intelligent things. The one he liked best belonged to someone he took to be a very old, very fragile man, although he had noticed none such in the gym.

"This boy needs attention," the voice fluted. Jimmy tracked it down eventually to Rabelais himself and felt that although James Bannister III might have made a mistake in his approach to the headmaster, he

had Rabelais on his side now. It was worth coming
from America for that.

He turned to the crowd with a half smile. And he
saw that what they were doing actually was laughing.
The long strange faces were twisted. The big teeth
stuck out viciously. The sound was like the shrieking
in a stockyard.

The English way, indeed. He realized that he was
clutching the headmaster's lapels—well, it wasn't that
funny. And was it his imagination, or was the headmaster laughing too? Smirking anyway.

He often wondered what happened next. Did he, as
he fully intended to, hit the headmaster in the face?
Did he grab the icy spectacles and twist them across
the man's nose, and did he then volley his few ob-
scenities into the crowd? Or did he do nothing but
simply dream those things? For very shame, he could
never remember what happened between that moment and his return to the United States, ticketed for
a regular American prep school, a couple of weeks
later.